Raining Down Release

BK Rivers

Raining Down Release

Limitless Publishing, LLC
Kailua, HI 96734
www.limitlesspublishing.com

Formatting: Limitless Publishing

ISBN-13: 978-1-64034-044-2
ISBN-10: 1-64034-044-0

Dedication

To my Grandpa Dave, the brownie guru, who taught me that brownies made from scratch and with a wooden spoon are sooo much better.

Chapter 1

July

Stacey

It's hot as hell and I'm sweating in places I never knew could sweat until moving here when I was twelve. Whoever decided to settle in Phoenix back in the day was a complete and utter lunatic. A hundred and thirteen degrees and we still haven't hit our summer peak.

I hate the summers here.

I especially hate the fact that the apartment complex I live in doesn't have a pool. You know what else I hate? My apartment and the neighbors who smoke more weed than is medically necessary, if you know what I mean. To top it off, the vents in my place are somehow directly linked to their pot-filled living room and I'm pretty sure I go to work every day partially stoned.

Which is altogether strange, because the few

times I actually smoked pot in high school, it made me feel like I loved everyone. Can you develop an allergy to weed? One that comes with bitter rage that strikes at any hour of the day, especially when you least expect it?

Like today.

In front of my boss.

That was fun.

My neighbors' pot addiction better not get me fired from my job. Speaking of weed, an actual plume of smoke just wafted through the stinking vent over my head. What the heck? This has got to stop before I have a freaking meltdown. Remote in hand, I press pause on *The Walking Dead*, jump to my feet, and climb on top of the back of my brown chenille couch and peer through the vent. I can seriously see right into their living room.

"Hey!" I shout, pounding on the dusty metal vent. Three sets of heads glance around the room trying to find the source of my voice. "Up here, jackasses." One of them stands, turns, and meets me at the wall. Swallowing back a little bit of fear when I catch a slight glimpse of his tatted up face, I say, "You guys are smoking me out over here. Could you please move to another room to get high?"

The guy laughs, turning his head toward his buddies, who also burst into laughter. "Dude, give me the reefer," scary tattooed guy says. He turns back to me, joint in hand, and brings it to his mouth. Before I have time to back away or process what he's doing, he blows a long puff of smoke through the vent. It hits me square in the face, making my eyes tear up and my lungs constrict, sending me into a coughing fit.

The guy and his friends' laughter sends chills down my spine as I recover. My head spins a little, so I sit back on the couch and press *play* on the remote. I have got to find a way out of this lease. On the plus side, the zombies on *The Walking Dead* are starting to look hot. So maybe I'm not allergic to weed after all.

Thank goodness I leave tomorrow. When I return from my trip to attend Reggie's wedding, I will figure out how to move out of this hole. I can't stay here much longer.

When I wake up the next morning, my head is foggy from the weed blown in my face. But remembering what day it is, I squeal and kick my legs under the sheet on my bed because in a few hours I'll see my best friend and I can't wait. Everything is packed and loaded into my car, and when I lock the front door, I can hardly contain my excitement. At the airport, the lines to pass through security are a joke. I barely have time to board the plane before they close the gate.

The airplane smells like sweat and dirty carpet, not great scents to have to deal with for the next two and a half hours. Though in some respects, it's better than the weed from next door. I am definitely not going to miss that over the next ten days.

My BFF, Reggie, is getting hitched, and since I'm the maid of honor, I plan on living it up with her during her last days as a single lady. According to her, a group of us will be going dancing tonight, which loosely translates to couples plus Stacey. This should be interesting.

I mean fun. Tonight will be fun.

Staring out at the tarmac, my elbow is suddenly knocked from the armrest, making me toss my phone to the floor. "Shit," I say, trying to lean forward in the cramped space to find it. Stretching awkwardly between the wall of the plane and the seat in front of me, my fingers finally wrap around my cell. Sitting up quickly, the back of my head smacks into something hard. Rubbing the sore spot with my free hand, I turn to the person trying to kill me.

"Sorry," he says, slowly reaching his fingers toward my head. Um, hello, tall, not so dark, and handsome. The guy is wearing a pair of trendy jean shorts and a thick white t-shirt which shows off his muscular, corded arms and the intricate tattoo on his left bicep that stops right above his elbow. His icy blue eyes search mine and my mouth goes dry. His dark blond hair is longer on top and shaved close to his scalp on the sides. A thick, neatly trimmed beard lines his face.

"You okay?" he asks, leaning closer, allowing me to catch his scent of citrus, rosemary, and musk.

Pasting on a smile, because ouch, but *hello, gorgeous*, I say, "I'm good. How's your elbow?"

Man Candy grins, though it fades quickly and never meets his eyes. There's a depth to them, unlike anything I've ever seen. He carries something inside, tucked deep down, but that kind of sadness still seeps through eyes like his, like pale blue glass.

"Elbow's good," he answers, sitting in the seat next to me. This plane isn't big, it has three seats on one side and two seats on the other, and when I booked the flight his seat was empty. Now he fills it—completely. His long legs barely fit in front of him, so his knees are bent, hips open wide, making it impossible for any personal space. My eyes travel down the length of his body and stop on his tanned and toned legs with a dusting of dark blond hairs. I'm wearing jeans, but I can still feel the heat of his skin through the dark denim and it rushes through me like a gust of wind racing through my veins.

"This okay? My leg here?" he asks, forcing my gaze back to his eyes. I flash a tight grin and nod my head. Rather enthusiastically, unfortunately. "I'm Ace." His hand crosses the armchair, reaching for mine. Shaking hands is a dying art, and when done in the small confines of an airplane, it's awkward. But I'm not one to deny myself the pleasures of a touch from a good-looking man. My hand reaches his and it dwarfs mine. Ace's grip is firm, warm, and when he doesn't release his grasp, I start to pull away but stop when his thumb moves over the back of my hand.

When the skin of his knee touches my jeans, it sends a pulse of heat zipping through me. And the graze of his thumb on my skin is like multiple lightning strikes. My entire body is on fire.

"Stacey," I say, clearing my throat, trying to fight the heat rising to my cheeks. I'm a redhead, so when I blush, I blush everywhere.

Ace slides his hand from mine, pulls out his phone, and unlocks it. Just when I think he's going to ask for my number—which I wouldn't have given him...*probably*—he switches it to airplane mode.

"Nice to meet you, Stacey."

"Yeah, you too." For the next two and a half hours we banter back and forth until the plane lands in Warner, Washington. I'm eager to meet up with Reggie and give her one heck of a hug since it feels like we haven't seen each other in years. In reality, it's only been a little over a month since I watched her, Jordan, and their son, Micah, drive away. I cried. A lot.

As Ace and I walk up the jetway, it occurs to me that since he lives here, maybe he'd like to meet up later and go dancing. I've enjoyed his company and I could use the moral support since I'm the only single one going out tonight.

"Hey," I say, stopping in the middle of the tunnel. "A group of us are going dancing later at some place called Club Beach. You wanna meet up?"

Ace's lips part and then quirk to one side. His icy blue eyes drill into me, making my body flush with heat. I left the scorching temperatures in Phoenix only to come to Warner and practically get heat rash from this guy. We separate, letting other passengers through the jetway.

"Wouldn't that be weird?" he asks, pulling his phone from the shorts pocket over his thigh.

"Um, no." I laugh awkwardly, feeling the heat climbing up my neck. *Calm the spaz, Stace.* "The only weird thing about tonight is the fact that I'm going out with my best friend, her fiancé, and another couple. I'm the single one...hello, awkward."

6

"So, it's a couples thing?"

I shrug, letting a few more people by, and then start walking toward the gate. It was just a thought; maybe it would have saved me from feeling like the third wheel. Scratch that—fifth wheel. But he's not into it, no biggie.

"Hey, wait up," he says, wrapping his large hand around my elbow, turning me to face him. "I didn't say no."

"You didn't say yes either." Gently, I pull my arm from his grasp and plaster on a fake smile. "It was nice to meet you, Ace." My purse slips down over my shoulder, so I return the strap and then rush out of the jetway into the terminal gate. Finding the signs for baggage claim, I make my way through the airport but stop at the restroom first. On my way out of the bathroom, I run—forehead first—into a firm chest covered in a thick white t-shirt that smells like citrus, rosemary, and musk.

Ace's hands grip my arms to steady me, but really all they do is make my knees weak from the way my body reacts to his touch. What the freak?

"What time do I need to show up tonight?" he asks, running his gaze over my face, pausing at my lips before quickly returning to my eyes.

"I'm not desperate." I shake out of his grasp and step back. "Don't feel like you *need* to show up to put me out of my misery. I don't *need* you to go."

"Okay, let me rephrase that." A muscle in his jaw ticks before he continues. "I would love to meet up later. What time and where can I pick you up?"

"It's not a date," I say, smiling and ducking my chin toward my chest.

7

"Are you going to let me take you out or not?" he asks, laughing and closing the small distance between us. His head drops level with mine, and his eyes drill into me. Ace brings his hand to my wrist and settles his fingers over my racing pulse.

I inhale sharply at how this touch feels so intimate, how it takes my wildly beating heart and makes the blood rocket through my veins. I seriously need to rein in these crazy hormones. Because that's all this is—over-reactive, lust-filled hormones that will only end in disappointment.

"We're all staying the night at the Parkview Inn. Do you know where that is?" I ask, unable to stop the heat creeping up my neck. He nods, offering me another grin that doesn't reach his eyes. "Pick me up at eight?"

"Eight, got it," he says, unlocking his phone. "What's your number?"

I shake my head. "I'll just meet you in the lobby."

"All right." Ace drops my wrist, winks, and walks away. This should be interesting telling Reggie I've got a date.

Once I pass by security, I see Reggie and Micah waiting for me and my heart swells. Space is what I wanted when I moved out of the apartment we'd shared for nine years, and space is what I got. Never would have guessed it would be a distance of fifteen hundred miles, though.

Micah runs to me, wraps his arms around my waist, and squeezes me tight. Reggie joins our hug and relief washes over me that I'm finally here. My best friend is getting married and I couldn't be happier for her.

Chapter 2

Ace

"You're doing what now?" Ethan asks incredulously from the doorway of my room. His shaggy brown hair hangs over his brows, which are raised high like he's pulling his skin back too tightly. It's a valid question, one I'm sure he's dying to know the answer to. But the truth is I have no idea what I'm doing. The last thing I expected upon returning home from the National Sherriff's Conference in Phoenix was to wind up with a date when I stepped off the plane. Especially with a girl from Arizona who is only here for a friend's wedding.

"I think I'm going crazy," I answer honestly.

"Nah," Ethan says, petting Duke, my German Shepherd police dog, who still appears mad at me for leaving him for five days. "I think Mr. Willy finally got fed up with Mr. Lefty."

"First of all, I'm right-handed, and second, seriously?" I glance up at him from the edge of the bed where I'm lacing up a pair of saddle brown oxfords. "Here." Duke's ears perk up and he leaves Ethan's side to sit next to me. So maybe I was a little jealous my dog has hardly given me much thought since I stepped through the front door two hours ago.

"He pouted for three days," Ethan says, chuckling. "I think he thought you died or something. It wasn't until I bribed him with some of those dog treats you keep in your bag that he finally stopped sleeping by the door."

My jaw clenches while I take a few calming breaths and work through my irritation. "I've told you before those treats aren't to give him freely. They're for work and he knows it."

Ethan rolls his eyes, shaking his head. "Lighten up, they're just treats. Besides, Duke really likes me now."

"He liked you just fine before."

"True." He shrugs, smiling wide. "So you're really going to go out on this date?"

"Bed," I say, ordering Duke to his kennel. His brown eyes gaze up at me with longing. Actually, looking at him, I'd almost say he's pouting. "Bed," I say again with a huff. Duke turns and trots off to his kennel.

"You didn't make him sleep in there while I was gone, did you?" I ask, already knowing the answer.

Ethan's smile grows wider before he turns away from the doorway and I follow him as he pads barefoot down the hall.

This is what I get for living with a child—a twenty-eight-year-old child.

"Tell me about this girl who managed to snag a date with the non-dating Ace. She pretty?" Ethan pulls a beer from the fridge, pops the tab, and downs it in one long drink. "You want one?"

"You do know I'm a police officer, right?" I ask, shaking my head. Ethan shrugs, pulls out another beer, and drains that one just as fast. "You on a mission to get wasted tonight?" He doesn't typically drink like this, at least not since the night Marley died. But I can't think of that right now, not when I'm taking some other girl out. Even though I really have no idea why I agreed to do it.

"It's been a rough couple days at the hospital," Ethan says as he strides across the kitchen, heading for the couch in the living room. "And don't think I didn't catch the fact you didn't answer me."

"Answer what?"

"Is the chick hot?" The television clicks on to the Adult Swim channel, yet another tell that something's bothering him.

"Hillary riding you again about your survey results?"

"I'll have you know that ever since that crazy lady's survey I haven't had anything but positive reviews. All my patients leave thoroughly satisfied with my care." Ethan chuckles from the couch.

"Why was it again that woman rated you so poorly?" I love giving him a hard time about being a nurse.

"Asshole," he grumbles. He hates it when people make fun of him for being a male nurse. "You're still avoiding my question. She must be really hot."

Stacey's nice to look at with her fiery red hair,

fair skin, and sprinkling of freckles across her cheeks. Her eyes are almost milk chocolate in color, yet they have specks of gold dotted around her pupils. And she smelled incredible—peaches and lilies. She was wearing a simple pair of worn jeans with holes in the thighs, revealing her creamy white skin, and a white, relaxed peasant top almost made it appear like we were traveling together. Like we coordinated our jeans and white shirts.

"Okay, yeah."

"Yeah, what?"

I'm going to kill him. "Yes. She's hot. Happy?"

Ethan's lips curve into a smug smile. "Happy? Nah. I'm ecstatic that you're going out. It's about damn time."

"Well, don't get ahead of yourself, she's from Phoenix and it's not a date."

"Are you picking her up?" he asks. I have no other choice but to nod. "You planning on buying her drinks or dinner?"

"Naturally. It's the right thing to do." *Shit.* It's a freaking date.

"Then it's a date."

"But she said it wasn't a date."

"It's a date. Get over it and get out of here."

Right about now I'm wishing I would have pushed her a little harder for her number—at least then I could have called and cancelled. Or even texted. Now I have two choices, stand her up or suck it up and go on the date that's not supposed to be a date. Going out with a girl shouldn't be difficult, it shouldn't make my pulse race or my palms sweat. A decision like this would have been

13

easier several years ago. But circumstances as they are have made me lose all interest in dating.

Glancing at my watch, I realize if I don't leave now, I'll be late. I'd like to think I'm a stand-up guy, so pushing away the nerves, I grab my keys, mumble a goodbye to Ethan, and head out the door. Stacey had better be okay with a motorcycle, because when I'm not on duty, that's what I drive.

Twenty minutes later, I park and make my way into the lobby of the Parkview Inn. The double doors slide automatically and open to a grand lobby decorated in creams and golds with light aqua accents. Fresh floral arrangements adorn each flat surface and a massive river rock fireplace sits on the back wall.

A group of five people sit on the couches laughing and talking, making my chest constrict. Stacey's red hair stands out above them all and in the light of the lobby, it nearly glows a coppery color. Heads glance up as I approach, and when Stacey turns, her lips turn up in a warm smile. She's put on a little more makeup, especially around her eyes. She looks gorgeous, and the shimmery gold top she's wearing hangs off her right shoulder, making me suddenly hungry to nibble on her soft skin.

"Ace?" says a guy I recognize.

"Vic, been a long time, man," I say. He stands, meeting me to shake hands. I glance down at his wife still sitting on the couch and tip my head. "Jemma. I didn't know you'd be here." Here in Warner, the police and fire stations are a tight-knit community—we all know each other.

"What are you doing here?" Vic asks, releasing my hand.

"He's with me," Stacey says, coming to stand next to me.

My arm moves to pull her to my side, a familiar but misplaced gesture. I stop myself before touching her and smile tightly.

"How do you guys know each other?" Stacey asks, glancing between us.

"Ace and I work together. Indirectly, I guess. He's a police officer." Vic helps Jemma to her feet and twines his fingers through hers. Stacey glances up at me, smiles brightly, and threads her arm through the crook of my elbow. My heart squeezes in my chest, but I swallow back the urge to squirm away from her touch. It's nearly too much...too soon. Maybe it's too *late*?

The other guy and his girl stand, and I immediately recognize him as well, but do my best to hide my surprise. He reaches his hand to me and we skip right to introductions.

"Jordan Capshaw," he says, smiling as he looks to the girl at his side. "This is Reggie, the future Mrs. Capshaw."

"Good to meet you," I answer, shaking her hand. "When's the wedding?"

"Next Saturday," Reggie says, glancing up at Jordan. I'm sure there's a story there, but now's not the time to get into it. How anyone can tame a rock star is beyond me. Especially one with a background like Jordan's.

"You guys ready?" Stacey asks, pulling me toward the door. "I'm starving and I can't wait to see if this guy knows how to dance."

The six of us leave the lobby and part ways. Guiding Stacey to my motorcycle, I figure she'll be hesitant to climb on behind me, but she turns to me, giving me an appraising smile. She waves me onto the seat and while I pull on my helmet, she grabs the passenger helmet, shoves it over her head, and climbs on behind me. Her black leather pants reflect the lights of the parking lot like a mirror and they show every ounce of uncertainty I'm feeling.

Stacey's arms loop around my waist, her fingers lace together, and she rests her chin on my shoulder. A chill erupts from where her chin touches me and it shimmies through my whole body. I can't shake her off, but the desire is there. Like a lingering shadow of the past, creeping up on you when you least expect it. Except something always reminds me of the past no matter how much I try to push it down. The past is the lingering smoke after you snuff out a candle—no matter how much you wave it away, it still comes back to haunt you. Tonight, for the first time in five years, I wish I could have snuffed that damn candle out with cold water. At least then the smoke would be gone along with the memories.

"Ready when you are," Stacey says, squeezing me around the middle.

I could laugh at that—ready? I hardly think so. But I'm here and agreed to this, so I lean the motorcycle, shove the kickstand back with the heel of my shoe, and start the engine. It revs to life with an ear-splitting growl, Stacey's grip tightens around my waist, and we ride out of the parking lot.

Chapter 3

Stacey

It's hella-cold riding through the streets of Warner on the back of Ace's motorcycle. It's the middle of July—a jacket shouldn't be required. I shouldn't be shivering either. But here I am, arms wrapped tightly around Ace's waist, trying to absorb as much heat as I can. Each time I scoot closer, he inches forward in the seat, like I'm making him uncomfortable. Okay, so inviting a guy I just met to go dancing with me and a group of others maybe wasn't the brightest idea. In fact, Reggie made a point of telling me just that, twice tonight. Our conversations went something like this, "You can't just pick some random guy to take you dancing. You don't even know him. He could be a serial killer for all you know." Her hands flailed a lot like they do when she's stressed out.

But I laughed and said, "No way, you have to see his eyes. They don't look like the eyes of a serial killer. They're more haunted, like he's dealing with something pretty hard."

"Just be careful, and...don't sleep with him."

I guess not being roommates for four months had made her forget the years living with her and my track record. Since high school, it's been pretty clean. "Thanks for the vote of confidence," I said.

Reggie's shoulders fell, her eyes pleading with me, as though she was already asking for forgiveness for what she was about to say.

"You have a really bad habit of helping out complete strangers, and one of these days it's going to come back and hurt you."

Okay, yep. *Ouch*. I'm not sure if I've completely forgiven her yet, even though it's been a couple hours. But I love her like a sister, and even if what she said hurt, I'm here for her while she counts down the days to her wedding.

Ace pulls to a stop, parking his motorcycle alongside the club. Even from this distance, the thumping of the music reaches us. We remove our helmets and I do my best to tame my hair, hoping I don't have helmet head.

"Do you want to wait outside for the others?" he asks, shoving his hands into the pockets of his dark jeans. The sleeves of his navy blue Henley are pushed up to just below his elbow, giving me a glimpse of the corded muscles of his forearms, and I realize I don't know a whole lot about him. Sure, we chatted it up on the airplane, but the topic of what he did for a living never came up. He told me he had been in Phoenix for a convention, but I didn't press for more information than that. I didn't need more. He was just some guy who was nice to talk to, who kept me company for two and a half hours. Now I'm interested and want to know more.

Which sucks because I'm only here for ten days.

"They're probably already inside," I say, remembering how it took him a few minutes to leave the parking lot of the inn. "I'm sure they beat us here."

Ace jerks his head in a swift nod and flashes me a tight smile. "Shall we?" he asks, pulling a hand from his pocket and resting it on my lower back. He guides me through the blacked out door and into the club.

There are tables scattered around the large room for dining and a dance floor off to the right that is already fairly crowded for being early in the evening. I spot Reggie and the others at a circular booth near the back and we work our way through the maze of tables.

"Have you been here a lot?" I ask, speaking loudly to be heard over the music.

"Used to, but it's been a while." Everyone scoots closer, allowing us to slide in the booth.

"Thought maybe you two got lost," Vic says, laughing. I like him, Jemma too. Apparently, Jordan met Jemma a couple years ago and she got him started on his sobriety. Now, he and Reggie live in Jemma's old house in Torrance and they love it. I'll be driving there tomorrow to stay with them to help with the wedding prep.

Deciding to save Ace from whatever held him up at the inn, I jump in and say, "I had to get reacquainted with a motorcycle. Hadn't been on one in a long time."

Reggie glances up from the menu, raising an eyebrow at me.

"What?" I mouth to her, not understanding why she's questioning me.

She shrugs, shakes her head, and returns to the menu. Of all the people to be judging me right now, she shouldn't be one of them. I held my tongue for a long time when she and Jordan got back together, she has no right to assume anything or question my motives.

"Where's the bathroom?" I ask, trying my best to mask my irritation. Jemma and Vic point me in the right direction and Ace stands, letting me slide out from the booth. "I'll be right back." I wind through the tables, find the short hallway, and slip inside the ladies' room. Other than checking my hair, I have no other reason to be in here. Well, that and so I can release the growing frustration I'm feeling toward my best friend.

I know she's stressed—planning a wedding will do that to the best of us. But I didn't fly all the way up here to be lectured or judged for my actions. I just want to spend time with her before I have to go back home and return to the apartment with the weed problem.

Now that I'm sufficiently calmed down, I return to the table to find a lively conversation taking place without me. *Breathe, Stacey...breathe.* Ace stands, letting me slip back into the booth, and then hands me a menu. My fingers graze his as I take it and heat rushes up my arm, making me gasp quietly and Ace's back stiffen. This is crazy, nothing can happen between us because I live two thousand miles away. Tonight was only about having fun dancing with a guy who made me laugh.

"Do you dance?" I ask suddenly, leaning close to him. "I guess I should have asked that before asking you to come out tonight."

Ace folds his menu closed, places it back in the center of the table, and smiles. Like a real live smile that touches his pale blue eyes, warming my insides. He has straight white teeth that would make any dentist envious. Heck, it makes me want to hide mine because I know they're not as white or as straight as his.

"No," he answers, shaking his head.

My jaw drops. "Then why did you agree to go dancing with us?" Now that I've asked, I really want to know. Ace's smile turns into a warm chuckle and now the whole table is looking at us. More specifically, me. Giving up, and growing irritated at Reggie's glaring and Jemma and Vic's googly-eyes, I change the subject. "What's everyone ordering?" I don't even know what I'm going to get, but I'm ready to eat and let loose a bit. And by let loose, I mean have a drink or two. I'll be respectful, though, and do it at the bar and not in front of Jordan. I know he says it doesn't bother him anymore, but I wouldn't want someone drinking in front of me if I were a recovering alcoholic and drug abuser.

After we've all ordered, Reggie and Jemma start talking about the wedding and I have to struggle to hear what they're saying. The guys talk about whatever it is guys talk about, and I get stuck between a fireman, a rock star, and a cop who hasn't relaxed since he showed up to pick me up.

By the time our food arrives, I'm so far removed from any conversation I inhale my food and excuse myself. I push my way through the tables, find a far corner at the bar away from Jordan and Reggie, and order a Fuzzy Navel—something a little sweet and tangy with just enough alcohol to help clear my head from the negativity I'm feeling. The bartender serves me up and in five quick slurps, I guzzle the drink and order another.

"Wanna talk about what's bothering you?" I cringe at the sound of Ace's low voice behind me. He moves around me, sits down, and rests his elbow on the bar top. When the bartender brings me another Fuzzy Navel, Ace orders a water with a lime.

"Nothing's bothering me," I answer, taking a long sip.

Ace's arm snakes behind me, stopping on the barstool. His body angles toward me; his wrist touches my ass and his breath sneaks through the veil of hair at my bare shoulder, reaching my skin.

"That's a lie and you know it. I hardly know you and I can tell something's bugging you." He makes no sign of moving away, and truthfully, I don't mind. I like the heat flowing like waves off his body and crashing into me. It feels good, the proximity of him. But will it feel as good when he pulls away after I unleash the dam of emotions I'm feeling right now? I guess we'll see.

"You really want to know what's bothering me?" Ace nods, a quick jerk of his head with a slight upturned lip. Sitting fully upright, I practically leap off the barstool, wrap my fingers over his elbow, and drag him with me across the floor and out of the club. It's too loud and stifling inside to really talk, yet outside in the evening light, with the sun still on the horizon, the heat is just as bad. At least I won't have to yell.

Still gripping his elbow, I pull him down the sidewalk, passing a stream of large windowed shops that have long since closed for the evening. Cars pass us on the road, not paying us any attention, and when we round a corner, I breathe a sigh of relief to see a darkened alley up ahead.

"You sure you want to go down there, sweetheart?" he asks, slipping from my grasp.

I stop, turn around and fold my arms across my chest. "I'm from Phoenix," I say bitterly. "I hardly think a dark alley in little old Warner, Washington has anything on what's lurking around corners in Phoenix."

"How often do you go out alone at night? Do you carry any protection with you?" Lines of worry etch across Ace's face, making me giggle. "It's not funny. You shouldn't be walking alone at night."

"If I had any question about you being a cop, I sure don't anymore," I say, laughing while Ace's jaw tenses and his head slowly moves side to side.

"I'll let it slide this one time, but we don't like to be called *cops*. It doesn't exactly have the best connotation." His eyes hold an ounce of humor, but his tone suggests he's pretty serious.

"Yes, sir, Mr. Officer," I say with a mock salute. Okay, so maybe the alcohol is starting to kick in. I lean up against the cool bricks of the building, willing the heat in my cheeks to fade. I'm not normally a lightweight.

"So, you gonna tell me what was going on inside?" Ace leans up against the wall opposite me in the alley and now there's a good fifteen feet or more between us. The air is even thicker here and the sharp angles of Ace's jaw and chin are blurred by the shadows crawling over him as the sun continues to set. He really is quite easy on the eyes, and thus far, dang good company.

"You really want to know?" He nods and I unleash it all. And I mean everything. "I hate that I'm here for my best friend's wedding and she doesn't seem to really care. Ever since I told her you were going out with us tonight, she's been giving me the evil eye and lecturing me. Then to top it off, I seriously think I'm going through pot withdrawals because I'm freaking all over the place with my mood. And when I get back to Phoenix, I have to put up with the shit even more and I hate it. I don't want to go back to my apartment."

Gasping for air after I release the rant makes my head spin. Pacing myself has never been a strength of mine.

"You're coming down from a high?" Ace asks incredulously. His eyes are narrowed and his arms are crossed over his chest, showing off those tight muscles of his forearms.

"What? No!" I say at the same time Ace puffs out a sigh. "My stupid neighbors and I share this weird vent in the wall of my apartment and they're always getting high. Last night I yelled at them through the vent and all I got was a face full of smoke and I, uh…yeah, I got a little high."

"Feel better?" he asks. His lips turn up into a smile—the one that lights up his face—and my stomach does a little flip. I nod, push off from the wall, and stand in front of him.

"It's a shame I have to go back to Phoenix after Reggie's wedding," I say, looping my arm through his elbow again. We walk back inside the club and spend the rest of the night dancing and laughing with my friends.

Chapter 4

Ace

"Black tie or navy tie?" Holding both up to my neck so Ethan can help me chose which to wear to Reggie's wedding is humiliating. I never have a problem knowing what to wear. Ethan glances over his shoulder, shrugs, and returns his focus to the morning news. Screw it—I don't need to wear one. I toss both aside, unbutton the two top buttons of the white dress shirt, and leave my suit coat open.

I'm probably an idiot. Scratch that, I know I'm an idiot. When Stacey asked if I wanted to go to Reggie and Jordan's wedding, I had said yes. Why? I have no idea. And since she still didn't want to exchange numbers last week, I have no way to reach her and cancel. Not that I necessarily would, but I'd at least have the option to. Instead, here I sit, lacing up my brown derby shoes and muttering a string of curses under my breath.

The girl is freaking leaving tomorrow and here I am going to a wedding with her. Sure, dancing and hanging out with her last week was fun and I enjoyed her company. She's nice to look at and sexy without even thinking about it.

But she's not Marley.

No one will ever be Marley, and I don't deserve to feel anything close to what I felt for her.

"I won't wait up for you," Ethan teases from the couch.

"Yeah, well, I'm not planning on coming home tonight." Wincing, I pull Ethan's keys from the counter, shove my wallet into the back pocket of my black dress pants, and slap my hands down hard on Ethan's bare shoulders. I didn't want to ride my motorcycle while dressed for a wedding, so he let me borrow his black Audi A4. I'm pretty sure he likes my motorcycle just as much as I do based on his eagerness to offer his keys.

"Jesus, man," he shouts, jerking out from under my hands. "That hurt like hell."

"Just letting you know that nothing's going to happen tonight."

"I wouldn't fault you if it did, dude." Ethan rubs his bright red shoulders and I smirk, noting the handprints forming on his skin. "No one would."

I would. It would gut me—pull me apart— knowing I was betraying her memory. I won't do that to her. "Whatever, man. See you tomorrow."

"Later."

***

I can't say that I've ever been through Torrance before. It's small, like three stoplights small and they aren't timed at all. You go a hundred yards only to be stopped by a red light. Then you repeat the process. It shouldn't take fifteen minutes to drive through a town this size.

The buildings lining the main street are a mix of red brick and stacked beige stone and gothic in architecture. The one grocery store in town is busy, as is the drive-thru coffee hut in the center of downtown. My cell reception has been spotty and I'm hoping the GPS holds out until I reach my destination in…seven point eight miles.

I pass golden fields of wheat slowly waving in the breeze, and as the tops of the hills kiss the cloudless robin's egg blue skies, I can't help but feel a twinge of guilt. I'm still here to enjoy a beautiful day like today and she's not. And there is nothing I can do about it.

A large white sign painted with bold plum-colored letters that reads '*Wedding This Way'* is posted at the beginning of the long driveway leading up to the event. Massive trees line the driveway that seems to go on and on. I park behind a long line of cars already here for the celebration, toss a mint in my mouth, and climb out of Ethan's car. The house is a good hundred feet from where I parked, but I don't mind walking. It is an older, small, two-story farmhouse style with a green shingled roof and good-sized windows all around. I walk up to the front porch, knock on the door, and shove my hands in the pockets of my pants.

A barrage of footsteps sounds from inside and then the door swings open, revealing a toothy little boy with shaggy dark brown hair wearing a tailored suit.

"You here for my mom and dad's wedding?" the boy asks, wearing an ear to ear smile.

"Uh, yeah?" I glance inside quickly and then over my shoulders. I sure as hell hope I have the right wedding. "Is Stacey here?"

The boy nods eagerly, turns, and high-tails it up the stairs, calling for her. I step inside, close the door behind me, and wait in the entryway. Three deep breaths later, and a pair of sculpted, pale legs descend the stairs. Swallowing the lump in my throat, I silently pray she's wearing more than my imagination is dreaming up. Finally...*finally*, the rest of her is revealed, however, she's wearing a short black silk robe tied around her narrow waist.

A wide, genuine smile graces her lips, making my heart stutter in my chest. Her fiery red hair is in a loose braid on one side and trails over her right shoulder in loose waves. The makeup on her face accentuates her golden eyes and highlights the natural pink in her cheeks.

"You look beautiful," I say as she pulls me in for a hug. Her arms wrap around my back under my arms that somehow return the embrace.

"You should see me in my dress," she whispers at my neck.

"I like what I'm seeing here," I say, not recognizing the roughness in my own voice.

Stacey backs away from our hug and searches my face. I know what she's looking for, but it won't be there. Truthfully, it hurts seeing her trying to find it.

"You clean up pretty well too, Mr. Officer." Her

eyes travel over my black suit coat, to the V at my collar, exposing my neck and the top of my chest. Her gaze travels south, stopping briefly near my belt and then she quickly glances back to my face. "I like what I see too," she says.

"What can I do to help, anything?" I can't stand awkward, and right now this entryway is filled with it. I'm a take-charge kind of guy and prefer to be put to work rather than sitting around doing nothing.

"The guys are in the back, you can see if they need any help. I've got to run back upstairs and finish getting dressed." Stacey turns and yeah, I check out her legs and how short the hem of her little black robe really is. Damn. I accept my earlier sentiment: I'm an idiot.

***

The guys and I finished setting up the white wooden chairs as per the sketched diagram Reggie had given Jordan and thankfully there wasn't much left because the music began. Jordan makes his way to the front, standing next to the minister. Standing up there with him is his best friend and old band manager, Jeremy, and Vic. The rest of the band was already seated near the back, which is where I planted my ass as well.

A cute little blond-haired girl in a fluffy white dress walks next to Micah, Reggie and Jordan's son. The little girl tosses white rose petals like she's done this several times. Her smile lights up her squishy face.

Next, Jemma makes her way down the aisle, followed by Stacey, and I nearly choke. She's wearing a dark plum floor-length gown with a sweetheart neckline. Her shoulders and back are bare and the way her hair falls over her shoulder takes my breath away. When her eyes find mine, her lips form a shy smile. The wedding march music begins, and everyone stands and turns to face Reggie as she makes her way down the aisle escorted by her father. While all eyes are on the bride, mine find the redheaded beauty up front standing next to the minister. She's stunning, and just like last week when we went dancing, I find myself curious. What would it be like to let myself feel something for her? For anyone?

The ceremony goes off without a hitch, the happy couple jogs down the aisle and heads toward the side of the house for pictures. What feels like hours later and after the tables have been set up for the reception, a pair of milky white arms snake around me from behind and close me in a warm embrace.

"Thank you so much for coming," Stacey says, releasing me from the hug.

I turn toward her and am struck by the realization that she's leaving for Phoenix tomorrow and it's likely I'll never see her again. It's no use worrying about it, as nothing can come out of this anyway. Instead, we enjoy the reception, eat a great dinner, and watch as Jordan and Reggie take their first dance as husband and wife. After the father-daughter dance, the DJ calls the wedding party out onto the floor. Stacey joins Jeremy, and even though he's married and expecting a baby in a few months, my chest tightens seeing Stacey's arms wrapped around another man's neck.

By the time other couples join the wedding party on the floor, I find myself walking toward the fiery redhead and asking her to dance. I tap the smooth, warm skin of Stacey's shoulder and she pulls away from Jeremy, who tips his head and walks back to his bride.

"My turn," I say, sliding my fingers down her arm and catching her hand in mine before spinning her around to face me. I pull her close, pulling a sharp intake of breath from her painted on lips, and erase the air between us and guide her along the floor.

"You said you couldn't dance," she says rather breathlessly.

My lips turn up in a lopsided smile as I hold her even tighter. "You asked *if* I danced," I whisper above her ear. "I never said I couldn't." And to prove it, I push her away from me, hold onto her left hand, and then spin her around until her back is resting against my chest. Her ass is rubbing against the front of my dress pants as I move us around the dance floor and I'm literally thinking of anything accept how good it feels to have her body so close to mine. Quickly spinning her around to face me, hoping to avoid the growing situation in my pants, I rest my left hand at the base of her neck and my right clasps her hand. Space. My body needs space between us...now. Otherwise I might do something I'm likely going to regret later.

After several dances, we return to our seats to

grab some water. At this point, I'm ready for a long, cold shower for multiple reasons.

"Well, count me impressed, Mr. Officer," Stacey says as she glances at me from beneath her long lashes. Her cheeks are flushed from dancing and I'm wondering if she's feeling any of what I am. It's been...five...long...years since Marley passed away, and I'd be a fool if I didn't recognize the stirrings within myself for what they are. Stacey's a beautiful woman and I'm still a man. And that's all this is—*want*—the desire for a release I won't allow myself to have.

Chapter 5

September

Stacey

My landlord has finally agreed to let me out of my lease, which means I'm scouting grocery stores for boxes to pack up my apartment. I'm twenty-seven and I'm ready to see where life takes me. And right now, the compass is pointing north toward Washington.

If there is one thing I've learned since moving out on my own, it's that I miss my best friend, and living so far away from her really sucks. After her wedding and on the flight home, I cried not because I was sad to go, but because I couldn't tell you the next time I would see her. That right there will always be the death of a friendship, and I'm not willing to bury thirteen years of history.

My parents and my brother, James, will be here in an hour to load up the U-Haul truck I've rented and to help drive my car onto the trailer. James offered to drive up with me, but that would mean he'd have to take time off of work, and he's barely scraping by as it is. So, instead, I've promised to drive at least ten miles under the speed limit and to take frequent breaks. Dad has also asked that I not pull into any parking lot where backing the truck and trailer up is required. He says I don't have enough experience with that sort of thing. Even though I laughed him off, he's right.

A knock on my door signals the arrival of my family and the realization of moving fifteen hundred miles away from them. Don't get me wrong, I'm excited to start fresh, but sad knowing I'll be so far away from them.

James stands with his hands in the pockets of his tan cargo shorts wearing a halfhearted grin on his handsome face. He's two years older than me and an amazing guy, but is somehow still single. Mom and Dad stand behind him wearing similar expressions and it hits me: they're going to miss me just as much as I will them. Mom pushes past James and Dad and wraps her slender arms around me. Her strawberry blond hair tickles my cheeks as she quietly sobs on my shoulder.

"We'll get to work," Dad says, patting my arm as he passes by.

James quirks a brow and follows Dad into my bedroom where I hear the whirring sounds of power tools. I won't even be able to sleep here tonight, which would be upsetting to some. But for me? Not so much. I can tell you I will not be missing the smell of pot wafting through my living room.

By the time all the large furniture is loaded into

the U-Haul, Mom and I have finished packing all the small things into boxes. Truthfully, I don't have much, but what I have I love. Pieces gathered here and there at random thrift stores make up my home and I can't wait to find some place in Washington to make my own.

It's after six when we finish loading up the U-Haul and Dad drives my car onto the car trailer. I've never towed anything behind me—or driven a truck like this before—but I'm doing all I can to act like a twenty-seven-year-old and man up...or woman up in this case. I've given myself several pep talks over the last few days and I think I'm ready for this two-day trip.

"I'll drive the truck over to the house after we've eaten dinner," Dad volunteers.

We all agree and climb inside Mom's SUV and stop at our favorite pizza place. James and I pile out of the backseats. Mom and Dad follow us inside and I'm hit with the warm scents of pizza dough, tomato sauce, and fresh herbs. I love this place and secretly hope I can find a place just as good up in Washington. Once we've taken our seats at a table and ordered our food, the conversation quickly turns to my upcoming drive.

"You have your route all mapped out?" Dad asks over the top of his wire-framed glasses. He's a little old-fashioned and still reverts to paper maps when traveling.

"My phone has GPS, remember?"

Dad harrumphs, removes his glasses, and cleans them with the hem of his t-shirt. "Well, just in case reception is poor, I put a United States map in the glove compartment. I highlighted the most direct route and included the best cities to stop overnight."

Sometimes I don't think my parents realize I'm an adult and have been one for a decade.

"Thank you, Dad."

"Now, honey," Mom starts. "Do you have your phone charger for the car? I'd hate for you to run out of batteries. You know how I'm going to worry."

"Yes, Mom. My car charger is in my purse." Mental note: check for car charger. "Anything you'd like to add, James?"

He smiles, slides his arm over my chair, and pulls me in for a one-armed hug. He and I aren't terribly close, but we're friends and I'm going to miss him. We fought like cats and dogs as teenagers, but after I moved in with Reggie, we started hanging out occasionally.

"Nope, I got nothin'," he says, then proceeds to ruffle my hair with his beastly hands. I swat him away and he continues. "Actually, just make sure you call or send a text every once in a while so we all know you're doing okay."

"All right, map, car charger, and the occasional text. Anything else?" I ask, counting the short list off on my fingers.

Dad scratches at the back of his chestnut-colored hair, Mom gazes at me with glossy eyes, and James focuses on some game on his cell.

The pizza is delicious, of course, and after we go back to my apartment for one last look around, Dad climbs in the U-Haul and drives it to his and Mom's house. James and I follow in his car and Mom drives behind us. We're our own little caravan, something I can't imagine will ever happen again.

When I visited Reggie in July, I couldn't help but fall a little in love with the area. Warner, while considerably smaller than Phoenix, has a gothic charm. Old brick churches, even some with stone gargoyles on the steeples, are all over the sprawling city. I loved the river flowing through the center of the city and the friendliness of the people. And as an added bonus, the temperature never went over a hundred and five in the middle of July. Sometimes we top that in early May in Phoenix. Goodbye, stifling heat and sweaty knees.

My old room in my parents' house has long since been converted into a nice guest room with a sewing table for Mom's projects. There isn't a trace that I ever once lived here in this room. The full-size bed is adorned with a pink, shabby chic ruffled bedspread and white sheets with delicate roses. The white dresser looks like it's been rolled down the street a few times to reach that perfect aged quality. Even the curtains have ruffles.

I say good night to everyone and give James an extra long hug knowing he won't be here in the morning to see me off. He's roughly six inches taller than me and somehow got Dad's chestnut hair. I ended up with the bright red, almost orange hair that was the source of constant teasing in grade school. The teasing stopped in the fifth grade when my boobs showed up earlier than most of the other girls. After that, I used what I had to gather a different kind of attention. The wrong kind of attention I realized after graduating high school. I did a lot of growing up after Reggie found out she was pregnant and her parents kicked her out.

Goodbye, memories. Hello, new life.

In the morning, Mom and Dad greet me in the kitchen with a hot breakfast of scrambled eggs, bacon, and buttermilk pancakes. Mom's pancakes are simply amazing, better than any restaurant I've ever eaten in. She's taught me a lot over the years, but never how to make her pancakes.

"Mom?"

She glances up at me after taking a bite of eggs.

"Can I have your recipe for these pancakes?"

Her fork slips from her fingers and lands on her plate with a clatter. Mom's cheeks warm with a healthy blush and she looks to Dad, who is pressing his lips tightly together, obviously holding back a laugh.

"What? Did I say something funny?"

Both my parents burst into full-out, red-faced laughter and I sit back against my chair with my hands folded in my lap. Apparently, I've missed out on some strange pancake joke. After their uncontrollable laughter dies down, Mom dabs the tears from her eyes with her napkin and clears her throat.

"I'm sorry, honey. I guess you've never seen me make pancakes before." Mom replaces the napkin in her lap and continues. "It's just a buttermilk pancake mix, sweetie. There is nothing special about my pancakes."

My jaw drops. Remember those old cartoons where one of the character's jaws literally falls open and drops to the floor? Yeah, that's about what mine feels like.

"Really?"

Mom nods, her cheeks still flushed. "Really," she says, picking up her fork and cutting a bite of pancake. "I can show you which mix if you'd like?"

"My whole life is a lie," I mutter while finishing my breakfast. Makes me wonder what else of hers I love isn't homemade like I always assumed.

Chapter 6

Ace

"Remember when they imploded the Kingdome?" Ethan asks as our cab pulls up outside CenturyLink Field where the Seattle Seahawks now play. I think I was around twelve at the time and remember watching the broadcast on television with my dad. When the charges went off, it was like every metal rivet and cement joint just popped, spewing years of dust into the air. And then after thirty seconds nothing was left of the Dome other than a billowing cloud of gray-brown dust. It was just...gone.

"Yeah, I remember."

"Did you ever go to a game there with your dad?" Ethan's drumming his fingers on his thigh and staring out across the parking lot at a pair of brunettes wearing Seahawks tank tops and short black skirts.

"No, I wasn't interested enough in football for him to take me to a game then." By the time I was old enough, Dad was gone. Died of a heart attack while on duty when I was fourteen. Left Mom and me to raise Lexi, my eleven-year-old sister.

"But Alex took you to a few games, right?"

Mom remarried when I was almost sixteen and I gave the guy hell. I couldn't understand why my mom would choose to get married again and so soon. And now, here I am a widower at twenty-eight. I guess technically, I was twenty-three when it happened.

"Yeah, he did." Thank God for Alex. He saved my mom and has loved us like his own since the day they married. I wasn't the easiest kid to love given all the times I tried to push him away. But he stuck with us—with me—and is still happily married to my mom.

"Let's go catch up to those fine-looking ladies," Ethan says, swallowing up the thick emotion filling the car. Of course he's ready to go chase some tail, he's always hungry for some action. We climb out of his car, follow the path the girls took, and see them at the gates.

"Damn," he says, his shoulders dropping. "They've got rings on their hands. Suppose they're player's wives?"

I shrug as we move through the line, show our tickets for scanning, and then head inside. Vendors selling all kinds of Seahawks memorabilia line the walkways and various food carts make my stomach rumble. We grab cold beers and some popcorn and then take the stairs down to our seats.

We lucked out and ended up with upper field level seats near the twenty-yard line when we purchased our tickets two months ago. Opening home game against the Arizona Cardinals is sure to be good. A short round of fireworks blasts through the open roof of the stadium, signaling the start of the game. The Seahawks run through the tunnel, music blares over the massive speakers, and my pulse quickens. Once both teams are on the field, everyone stands for the National Anthem and then the announcer introduces the teams.

Cardinals kick off, the football sailing all the way to their end zone. Seattle catches the ball and runs it; Blackwood zigzags through the defense only to be tackled on the Cardinals' thirty-yard line. By the end of the first quarter, I'm nursing my third beer and the score is six to zero, Seattle.

"Hey, want another one?" I ask, leaning over so Ethan can hear me over the noise of the stadium. "I'm grabbing one from the guy over there."

"I'm good, I'll have a couple more at the hotel after the game," Ethan says, giving me the go ahead. I don't drink too often, but during a football game I enjoy myself and the slight buzz the amber ale gives me.

By halftime the Cardinals are up ten to six and my voice is growing hoarse from calling out all the shit plays happening on the field.

"Franklin needs to get his head out of his ass and throw the damn ball." The beer in my hand sloshes, spilling the cool liquid over my fingers. "Stop running through the middle!"

"You doing okay there, buddy?" Ethan asks, placing his hand on my shoulder. His brow is raised and his brown eyes drill into me.

I shrug away from his touch and say, "I'm pissed, Franklin's going to lose the game if he keeps having the team play like this."

Ethan's gaze drifts over the field and then lands right back on me. "How about we cut you off after you finish this beer? What is that, number five?"

"Six," I say, then belch loudly, earning myself a few head turns in my direction. Yeah, okay. It's time to switch to water until we return to the hotel

The final play of the night has everyone on their feet, holding their breath as Gunderson runs the ball through the line and narrowly avoids being tackled in a two-point conversion attempt. He leaps over the Cardinals' defense, holds the football in the crook of his left elbow, and tucks into a ball as he flips over the other team, crossing the line. *Touchdown!* The fans erupt in screaming, "We Are the Champions" by Queen plays over the speakers, and Seattle wins twenty to nineteen.

"A cab was a good idea," I say when a yellow taxi finally pulls up. My buzz is gone, but there is no way I'd get behind the wheel regardless of how I feel right now. We climb inside, instruct the driver to take us to the hotel, and sit in silence during the fifteen-minute drive. The lights of Seattle glow like Christmas lights; they're bright, shiny, and always appear festive even in the drizzling rain. Today, however, the weather was perfect for a football game.

Ethan and I pass through the automatic doors of the hotel and head straight for the bar. The lobby is dark and moody with burgundy furniture, dark tiled floors, and mahogany check-in desks. Sparkling antique brass chandeliers light the large space and direct us toward the bar in the back. The bar is just as moody as the lobby, except the lights glow blue and cast almost a cold feeling over the room.

The small round tables scattered across the floor are mostly filled, some with couples, most, however, are groups of two or three singles. Ethan and I take a couple chairs at the bar and order our drinks. He likes Scotch on the rocks, I'm sticking with beer.

"Check out the chicks at seven o'clock," Ethan says casually.

Looking at a woman has never been an issue—but for me they're like pieces of fine art. Look, but don't touch. Admire from afar and enjoy the beauty because a fleeting glance is all I'm going to take. Ethan, on the other hand, has no qualms about making his intentions clear. And tonight, he has his sights set on a leggy blond wearing black, six-inch stilettos and a short black dress that could barely pass as a towel. Her friend keeps glancing over at us and I start to count down from twenty knowing both girls will make their way over to us soon.

Seven, six...damn. Off by five seconds. Both women stand up, leaving their empty glasses, and walk over to us. Blondie sits next to Ethan, rests her elbow on the bar, and places her other hand on his thigh.

"You look like you need another drink," her friend says to me as she sits next to me, crosses her legs, and leans on the bar. She's good looking, with russet-colored hair, brown eyes, and full, pink lips. "I'm Rachel, that's Phoebe," she says, leaning closer to me. The top of her strapless red dress slips lower over her ample chest as she leans even closer. Any more of that and she'll be sitting on my lap.

"Rachel and Phoebe, huh?" I've seen *Friends*; these chicks are fake naming us. Rachel nods, a smile growing across her flushed cheeks. "Nice to meet you, *Rachel*. I'm Chandler and that's Joey." Everyone knows Joey's the one bringing home the chicks, whereas Chandler's the awkward one who lives vicariously through his friend.

Rachel orders a Big Red Hooter from the bartender and I ask for another beer. When our drinks arrive, Rachel plucks the cherry from her drink by the stem, brings it to her lips, and slowly licks the liquid off of it. Damn, this woman knows what she's doing and something in my stomach tightens each time the tip of her tongue lands on the surface of the bright red cherry. Finally, she pops the little fruit from the stem, swirls it in her mouth, and swallows.

Why, hello there, friend. He hasn't come out to play with a chick since meeting Stacey, and before that it had been years.

Rachel sucks the stem into her mouth and within seconds pulls it out and it's twisted into a knot. Corny, really. But her intentions, as unwanted as they are, have stirred up a desire I shoved down five years ago. And as tight as my shorts are getting, I'm heading up to my hotel room alone.

Glancing at my watch, I ignore whatever Rachel is saying and turn to Ethan. "It's after midnight, I'm going to head upstairs." A wide grin spreads across his face and I know what he's thinking. "Dude. I'm heading up there alone."

He shrugs and then says, "See ya on the flipside."

I return my focus back to Rachel, her flushed cheeks and pink lips almost make me reconsider. *Almost.*

"Thanks for the company, Rachel. I'm heading to my room."

Her plump lips part, her tongue slides over her bottom lip, and she stares at me with wide eyes. Like she's trying to find something to say that will make me change my mind about returning to my room alone.

"My name's not really Rachel," she blurts out, sliding off the barstool. Her six-inch stilettos make her stand at eye level, which, oddly, I find is a turn-off. I like a girl who is confident enough in herself not to have to wear shoes like hers. Short or tall, doesn't matter—but embrace it.

I laugh at her confession, place my hands on her shoulders, and she visibly softens at my touch. I lean in as if to kiss her, but at the last second move to her ear and whisper, "It was nice to meet you, Not Rachel. It doesn't matter what your name is or isn't, I'm returning to my room alone. Nothing you can do or—" My voice suddenly cracks and my brain starts misfiring. Her freaking hand is cupping my Johnson. Who the hell does that?

"What you're saying and what I'm feeling are telling me two different things," she whispers at my neck, sending a shock of chills down my back and straight to my groin.

I stumble backward, shoving her hand off my

junk, and clear my throat. "Jesus, Rachel." I turn around and storm out of the bar. At the elevator, I press the up button and wait for the doors to slide open. A soft ding indicates the arrival of the lift, and I check over my shoulder to make sure the psycho hasn't followed me. The coast is clear, and I step inside the small space.

The reflective brass walls distort my image, though it almost appears more real than it should. What I see is rippled, imperfect, and broken—I guess the reflection isn't distorted after all. The ride to the fourth floor is slow and leaves me time to compartmentalize what happened in the bar. What caused me to practically race out of there like a dog with its tail between its legs? A good-looking woman came on to me, and I freaking got turned on. It's not like women haven't made advances toward me. I work hard at keeping myself in check so shit like that doesn't happen.

Chapter 7

Stacey

I'm paying by the day to keep the U-Haul truck.
I need to find a job and a place to live. I've been
staying with Reggie and Jordan since I arrived on
Wednesday and today's Friday. I'm going to run
out of money sooner than later if I don't do
something.

"Still job searching?" Reggie asks over her bowl
of cereal. Micah already got on the bus for school
and Jordan's out taking care of the horses.
Apparently, now that he's retired from the music
industry, he finds manual labor appealing and
relaxing.

"Should I just go up to Warner and drive around
until I find something?" The internet is not proving
helpful in my search.

Reggie shrugs, places her empty bowl into the
sink, and moves to hug me from behind.

"Just unload your stuff here and stay with us.
You can probably find a job in town and it will be

like old times." She releases me from the hug and we both laugh. I'd love to room with Reggie again, but now that she's married, I think I'll pass.

"Okay, I'm going to get dressed and go find myself a job."

An hour later, I'm in my car driving a little over an hour to Warner and racking my brain for jobs I would consider taking. I've worked in retail for several years and while the clothing discount was always nice, I'm twenty-seven and ready to have the kind of job that can turn into a career.

Three hours and two iced caramel lattes later, I still don't have any leads. It looks like either I'll be working back in a mall or serving fast food through a window. Not that there's anything wrong with either, I was just hoping for something...more. Stopping at a red light, I see a bookstore on the corner. It's cute with its pale gray stone exterior and large windows with charming displays of books and gifts. I spot the door and gasp—there's a help wanted sign! Quickly signaling to change lanes, I turn the corner and find a parking spot on the side of the building. It's still retail, but it's a *book* store. I like books; I like them a lot, actually.

An old-fashioned bell dings as I walk through the glass door and I'm greeted with the heady scents of paper and leather, along with a mix of something sweet and floral, gardenias maybe? Floor-to-ceiling light oak bookshelves line the walls and each shelf is packed with books. Each shelf is organized by genre—it's like a book addict's dream store. Books, books, and more books. All that along with fresh pastries and a coffee bar. I quite possibly have died and gone to heaven.

"Good afternoon," a woman with mousy brown hair pulled into a low ponytail says from behind the counter. She wears a pair of elegant glasses over her brown eyes. "Can I help you find something?"

I clear my throat and fight back my eagerness to work here. No one likes to be jumped like a lioness attacking her prey.

"I'm actually here about a job? My name's Stacey and I've just moved here from Phoenix and would love to work in a bookstore."

The woman's eyes light up and a warm smile pushes her glasses up a little higher on the bridge of her nose.

"I'm Julia, it's nice to meet you." Her hand passes over the counter and I take it in mine and shake it in greeting. "Do you have a resume?" I pull it from my purse and hand it to her, watching anxiously as she reads it thoroughly. She pulls her glasses from her face and places the end of one of the earpieces between her teeth. Julia nods a couple times and finally directs her gaze to me.

"So tell me, Stacey. What made you move all the way north to Warner?" Julia smiles, places my resume on the counter, and leans toward me. Her eyes are warm and kind and I feel a little tug in my chest—like an ache for my own mother. I like this woman already.

We talk for quite some time about me moving up here to be closer to Reggie and how I'm currently staying with her. Julia frowns a little when I explain that I'm still paying for my U-Haul because I haven't looked for a place to live yet. My stomach twists into a ball of nerves thinking she won't offer me the job because I'm technically homeless right now.

"I assure you, I will find an apartment or house to rent this weekend. For me, it's find a job first and then a place to live. Reggie says I can stay with her as long as I need, but I don't want to drive over an hour each day back and forth, you know?" The nerves in my stomach sneak out of my mouth in the form of a word-train. Once you tug on the first car, the rest follow in one quick word-vomit. It's not pretty.

"You know," Julia begins, standing to her full height. She walks around the counter toward me and takes me around the store. "I know we don't know each other, but I like you. A small house on my street was actually just put up for rent. I can write down the phone number and call you with it later tonight if you'd like."

A house would be amazing to live in, but somehow I don't think it would be in my price range. But I accept her offer since I have no other options at the moment. When Julia has shown me nearly every square inch of the two-story bookstore, she walks me to the door with an encouraging smile.

"I will call you later this evening with that phone number and my decision about the job," she says, shaking my hand once again. "It was really good to meet you, Stacey."

"Thank you, Julia. It was nice to meet you too."

The drive back to Reggie's house was calming. The landscape of rolling amber-colored fields and the bright blue sky gave me the overwhelming sense that I made the right decision in moving here. I have to admit, I do miss James and my parents, but they will be flying up for Thanksgiving and that's only a little over two months away. Maybe I'll actually be living in that small house on Julia's street.

Reggie, Jordan, and Micah are sitting at their kitchen table eating dinner when I walk through the front door and I feel as though I've just intruded on their family time.

"There's a plate next to the pot of noodles," Reggie says, pointing to a large stock pot on the stove.

"Thanks, but I grabbed a hamburger from the diner in town. I'm going to head upstairs and make a couple phone calls." Before Reggie has time to argue, I jog up the stairs, feeling like a teenager caught sneaking in after curfew. Silently, I pray that I will be able to afford this house. I love Reggie and Micah, and sometimes Jordan, but I need my own space. Actually, they need their space to be a family. I'm the one cutting in on their family dynamics.

After sending a few emails, checking Facebook, and playing a game on my phone, I huff out a sigh. I'm bored out of my mind and Julia still hasn't called. Back to Facebook, I scan through James's profile when my phone finally rings.

"Hello?" *Breathe.* "This is Stacey."

"Hi, Stacey, this is Julia...from the bookstore?"

"Thank you for calling me back," I say, crossing my fingers and holding my breath. *Please let me get the job...and the house!*

"First, I wanted to give you the phone number to the house for rent. It's not much from the looks of it, but maybe it will work out." She rattles off the number and as I write it down, I release the breath I was holding and then cross my fingers about the job.

"I've got to tell you, I was really glad you stopped in today. I had actually only posted the sign about twenty minutes before you showed up. Are you still interested in the job?"

"Yes. Definitely." If it's at all possible, I cross my fingers even tighter.

"Then I would love to offer it to you. I just know you and I will get along wonderfully. You're perfect for the job and I'd love for you to start on Monday. Will that work for you?"

As calmly as I can, I say, "Yes. Monday is great." We talk a little more about the job before finally hanging up. On my bed, I jump around on my knees and then fall into my pillow and squeal as loud as I can.

When I've calmed down, I retrieve the phone number from the top of the dresser and dial. It rings four times and goes to voice mail, and after leaving a message, I run downstairs to tell Reggie the good news.

She and Jordan are seated next to each other on the couch, her cheeks are flushed and her lips are swollen. She looks like I've just caught her and her husband making out. Yet another reason to quickly find a place of my own. I sit down on the love seat across from them and throw a pillow across the room, hitting my best friend on the forehead.

"What was that for?" she squeals, throwing it back.

Jordan laughs and flips through the television channels.

"For making out in the open when anyone could walk in on you. You do have a son, may I remind you. And a houseguest. Thank goodness you both have all your clothes on."

Reggie's cheeks flush even brighter as she turns and punches Jordan in the shoulder.

"That's spousal abuse," he teases, digging into her sides, tickling her.

"So, I have some news," I say, tucking my legs underneath me. "You are looking at your newly employed best friend."

Reggie and Jordan offer me congratulations as I tell them about the bookstore and Julia. I'm actually really excited to start working there, even though getting out of retail would be ideal. But something about the job and Julia makes it all okay. When I mention the house for rent, I can't help but catch the spark of excitement from them both about having their home to themselves again.

"Hopefully, I'll hear back soon and be out of your hair before too long," I say, slightly wounded but excited at the same time. I can handle an hour's drive to come see my best friend over fifteen hundred miles any day.

Saturday passes with no word from the owner of the house for rent, and when Sunday afternoon comes and still nothing, I begin to lose hope and kick myself for not apartment hunting all weekend. Why did I think this was going to work out? Oh yeah, because my name is Stacey and I don't believe in backup plans.

When my phone rings Sunday evening, I expect it to be my mom calling. "Hello?" I say, not recognizing the phone number.

The voice, distinctly male, clears his throat before speaking. "Yeah, this is Chase Steele. You called about the house I have for rent."

The breath catches in my throat as my nerves start twisting into a knot in my stomach. I really want to get this house I haven't even seen yet.

"Yes, thanks for calling me back. I was beginning to worry that maybe you already rented it out."

"You're the first person to call about it. I just put the sign in the window a couple days ago. How did you find out about it? Were you driving through the neighborhood?" I like the sound of his voice, it's a little gravelly but smooth at the same time.

"Actually, I just moved here and got a job. The woman who hired me saw the sign and gave me your number." We talk a bit more about the house and when he tells me the cost of the rent, I nearly choke. It's actually in my price range, and since it's vacant, I can move in right away.

"Can I meet you there tomorrow to see it? I'm like ninety percent certain I want it, but I just need to see it first."

We arrange to meet at the house tomorrow at 7 p.m. and then hang up. I can't believe it—I may have just rented a house!

Chapter 8

Ace

It's possible I'm going to throw up. Like spew all over the front yard of my house in front of neighbors I don't know anymore. I haven't set foot on this property in five years and I have no intention of stepping inside the faded blue front door today or ever again. The day I buried my wife was the day I handed over keys to a housekeeper and a landscape maintenance company. Ethan and a couple of his buddies packed up our things and furniture, put it all in storage, and I pay the monthly bill like clockwork.

I couldn't even park my motorcycle in the cracked driveway, which, if I examine closely, resembles my heart with the numerous fracture lines. Even the exterior of the house needs a little love, not that I plan on personally taking care of the chipping gray paint or the dusty windowsills. Huffing out a sigh, I walk up the driveway that leads to the garage in the back of the property. How am I going to show this chick a house I can't step foot in?

Marley and I were on cloud nine over the fact that we'd bought a house—with her parents' help since they co-signed on the loan. She was nineteen and I was twenty and we had just married. We dated in high school and when I graduated, leaving her with one more year left, I knew she was it for me. I went right into the police academy, graduated six months later, and started out behind a desk. After Marley graduated and I got promoted to a patrol car, we got married.

And bought this damn house I can't go inside or sell.

Ethan's been working on me for a couple years to rent it, and over the summer it finally felt like it was time. Like maybe the house deserved to have some happy memories made within its walls. I shudder recalling the state in which I'd left the house—I should have just burned it to the ground.

Walking back toward the front yard, a silver car with Arizona plates pulls to a stop behind my motorcycle, snapping me back to the present. The driver cuts the engine, opens the door, and steps out, revealing fiery red hair and a pair of creamy white shoulders. The breath in my lungs catches as she turns around to take in the view of the house. Her name floats off my lips in a whisper. "*Stacey*."

Pulling my phone from the back pocket of my jeans, I check the number she called from, noting the 602 area code. *Phoenix*. Shit.

She hasn't noticed me standing at the corner of the house yet, so I take a second to replay her message on my phone. How did I not connect the voice on the message to the voice of the girl I spent a couple crazy days with in July? Dancing with her at the club and then attending her friend's wedding weren't exactly what I had planned, but after Stacey left, I found myself thinking about her a lot. Hell, as she practically glides up the front walk, her bare shoulders taunt me, reminding me of how much I had wanted to run my lips over her soft skin.

That's dangerous ground right there.

Feeling like a creeper, I clear my throat, announcing my presence just as she climbs the three steps to the small front porch. Stacey's nose scrunches up as she glances at me, then her eyes widen in recognition.

"Ace?" A smile graces her lips and suddenly she leaps off the porch, runs to me, and our bodies collide in a warm embrace. On instinct, my arms snake under hers and wrap her in a hug and my eyes close as I breathe her in: peaches and lilies—I don't think I could ever tire of that scent.

"What are you doing here?" she asks as her arms slip off me after a brief pause of awkward silence. I'm sure I looked like a stalker hiding out behind the corner of the house, but what else could I do? I wasn't exactly expecting *her*. Sure, she left her name with the message, and said it again when we spoke yesterday, but Stacey's a fairly common name. How was I supposed to know it was the same Stacey from this summer?

I clear my throat and take a step backward. "This is, uh…" Why is this so hard for me to say? I own the damn house and should have no issue stating the fact. "My house. This is my house." Stacey's head jerks back at the roughness of my voice. I didn't mean for it to come out sounding like I'm a territorial caveman beating his club on the land surrounding the house.

"Sorry," I say, once again clearing my throat. "More to the point…what are you doing here?" Last I knew, she was in Arizona. Not that we'd ever exchanged numbers or anything. I had no way to keep track of her—legally.

Stacey's hands ball into fists and land on her hips, more so in a playful way than her being obstinate. A smile forms, revealing the creases on her cheeks that resemble cavernous dimples.

"I decided to move here, Mr. Officer." Damn, those brown eyes of hers draw me in, making me want to glide my fingers down her bare arms and pull her close. That tank top she's wearing hugs all her curves, revealing more of her body than she probably intended. Tugging on my right earlobe and running my tongue over my bottom lip while I stare at her is probably not the best idea right about now considering her cheeks have taken on a rosy hue and she's turning away toward the house.

"Will you show me around?" she asks, walking toward the porch steps. For a brief moment, my legs begin to move to do what she's asked, but then my brain catches up with me. "I really like the house from the out—" Stacey pauses when she turns and notices me still standing in the spot she left me. "You coming?" Her head tilts to the side, her hair drapes over her shoulder, and a hesitant smile forms on her lips.

I shake my head, fold my arms across my chest, and stand at attention—feet firmly planted shoulder-width apart. A muscle in my jaw ticks while my heart thunders in my chest in fear. I'm freaking terrified of stepping foot on that porch and I can't tell her that or why. She would leave the property running and never glance my way again.

Not that I want her attention.

Right. I don't want anything to do with her; I don't want her smiles, the chirp of a laugh she offers when she's on the verge of being nervous, or her velvety touch. I don't want any of that.

I can't have any of that.

Stacey steps off the porch and stops in front of me. My nose fills with the scent of peaches and lilies and I want to close my eyes and savor it. Memorize how it floats in the air and warms me from the inside. But I don't. My eyes instead focus on hers as she brings her warm hand to rest on my forearm.

"Did you change your mind about renting your house to me? If you did, please just tell me." She drops her hand when I say nothing, pulls her bottom lip between her teeth, and lowers her head. "It was good to see you, Ace. See you around." Stacey skirts around me and slowly makes her way back to her car. She steals one more glance at the house and then me, and when our eyes connect, my stomach flips and feels like it drops to my knees. She raises her hand to chest level and offers me a wave.

"Stacey, wait," I say, shaking my head at my stupidity as I jog up to her. "This is just really hard. Take the keys and go look inside. I'll stay outside while you look around." The gold key dangles from my hand and when her palm opens to me, I drop it into her waiting hand.

"Thanks," she says, avoiding eye contact. She steps around me, walks up the cement walkway, which coincidentally also needs repair, and ascends the three steps to the front porch. She pushes the key into the lock, turns it, and then glances over her shoulder at me before opening the door.

I don't exactly know what I expected when she walked through the door. Maybe I thought the house would spit her back out, or maybe the ghost of Marley would come rushing out to greet me and then yell at me for letting another woman inside our house. But nothing happened. Absolutely. Freaking. Nothing.

No lightning strikes, storm clouds, slamming doors, or shattering glass. Not even any sign of my deceased wife—not that I truly believe in ghosts or that Marley would be haunting the house. Her *memories* haunt me wherever I am.

Glancing at the ground at my feet, I notice a small anthill with dozens of tiny black ants crawling around. As Stacey exits the house, she locks the door, turns back to me wearing a smile. I scatter the small dirt hill, covering the ants with the loose earth, and meet her in the middle of the walkway. Damn, the ants only multiply.

"Ace, it's perfect," she says, beaming. My heart flutters in my chest remembering those exact words spilling from Marley's lips so long ago. "When can I move in?" she asks, holding out the key.

I swallow hard around the lump forming in my

throat and shake my head. "I don't want the key back. You keep it. You can move in as soon as you want."

"Really?" she squeals, and then leaps at me with her arms outspread and then pulls me in for another hug.

I can't return the embrace this time, because for the briefest moment, I swear I saw Marley standing at the door wearing her favorite white sundress and a serene smile on her face. Blinking several times, when I glance back, she's no longer there and I'm ready to get the hell back to Ethan's place and drown Marley's memories in a couple beers. Stacey and I exchange information so she can mail me her rent checks and the deposit, and then part ways.

While driving back to Ethan's, I decide I've probably just done the stupidest thing I ever could. There's no question that Stacey makes me feel things I don't want to feel, but knowing she's living in my house will make it easy to stay away.

Chapter 9

Stacey

I've got the keys to the house! Never would have thought this day would come, but here it is and now I get to move in. As soon as Ace pulls away on his motorcycle, I call Reggie and tell her the great news. In the background I can hear Jordan offering to help me move in tomorrow. Not that I don't want to move in right away, but my bed's not even cold yet. Sheesh.

The house is super cute with its large windows, wood floors, and old brick fireplace in the living room. The three bedrooms are all upstairs, along with two small bathrooms. Downstairs there is a half bath with cute white hexagonal tiles on the floor and a fancy pedestal sink. The galley kitchen is older but in good condition and has all the appliances I would need. It even has a small backyard with a couple giant trees and soft green grass.

Why Ace doesn't live here is beyond me. Maybe

he owns a couple houses and keeps this one as a rental. Though when I asked him if he was coming inside to show it to me, his face paled and his eyes looked like he'd seen a ghost. When I first met him on the airplane, his icy blue eyes are what drew me to him. They hold so much emotion in them, but today what I saw was pain and sadness. And it crushed me. Why someone like him carries that around is beyond me, and I find myself wanting to help him. I want to heal his wounds and see those eyes of his when he's truly happy and no longer hurting.

True to his word, Jordan has me up at the crack of dawn the next morning, helping me pack up what little I unpacked, and wants to be on our way before 9 a.m. He even has Reggie helping me tape up boxes in between making Micah breakfast and packing his lunch for school. I don't know if I've ever felt so unwanted.

Thirty minutes before Jordan wants to leave, Vic shows up with Jemma and their baby girl. Does everyone want me out of this house? Completely flustered and a little bitter, I shove my bathroom items into a small duffle bag, hoist it over my shoulder, and head downstairs and out the door. I shove the bag in my car, send a quick text off to Jordan giving him the address of the house, and then hop in my car. I'm outta here. I can take the hint.

Halfway to Warner, Reggie calls, but I ignore it and turn the radio louder. Several songs and a scratchy throat later, a White Shadow song begins to play, making me groan and change to a different radio station. I really don't need the reminder that Jordan used to be the freaking lead singer of White Shadow and how he's stolen my best friend. I kind of hate men at the moment.

The house looks just as cute today as it did last night, which means I know I made the right decision in renting it. I have no idea how far Jordan and Vic are behind me, but I don't care, this gives me time to do a little more exploring. Julia, my new boss, was kind enough to give me the day off so I could move in today. I assured her I wouldn't need another day off for a long time, but she said it was no problem.

The faded blue front door of the house reminds me of a mottled stormy blue sky back in Phoenix. In the summers during monsoon season, the sky can turn so many shades of blue and it's beautiful. And the sunsets? You've not seen a real sunset until you've been in Arizona. Vibrant pinks, purples, oranges, and yellows line the sky, looking like an abstract painting. They're so amazing you'd almost think they were fake. Something else I'm going to miss, I guess.

Key in hand, I walk up the path to the front door and see a note taped to the handle. It's from Ace and it reads:

Stacey,

I forgot to mention that your key will open the garage in the back and you'll find everything you need to care for the yard. I will cancel the landscape

maintenance company and the
housecleaner since you will be living
here. If you need anything, just shoot me
a text.

–Ace

I re-read the note. He's cancelling the landscape
company? Um…yeah, that doesn't work for me. I
have no idea how to mow the grass. We didn't have
grass in the backyard growing up in Phoenix. We
had a pool and rocks. Lots of rocks. In a rush,
hoping to stop him from making the call, I send Ace
a text.

Me: You cannot cancel the landscape company.

A heartbeat later, the ellipsis flashes on my
iPhone, letting me know he's typing a response.
When it doesn't come and the ellipsis keep flashing,
I almost give up and call him. He must be writing a
novel, a simple okay doesn't take this long to type.

Ace: Why not?

Me: I'm from Phoenix, remember?

Ace: So?

I grumble to myself as I type my response.

**Me: I have no idea how to work a lawnmower.
I'll pay for the maintenance, just don't cancel**

it. Let me know who I need to pay.

Ace: OK.

With that taken care of, I step inside the house, close the door, and let out a happy sigh. This place is mine, I get to live here! I would roll around on the carpet if there was any just because I could. No more pot smoking neighbors, no more sharing a wall and having to listen to a bed thumping against it in the middle of the night. It's mine!

Jordan and Vic show up forty-five minutes later and begin bringing boxes into the house. They drop off a box, I bring it to the room I want it in, and we repeat the process until they start bringing in the furniture. I direct them to the master bedroom and where to set up my bed and dresser. They bring my old couch and drop it off in the living room and then bring in my small table and chairs. When the U-Haul is finally empty, I look up the nearest dealer and follow behind the guys in my car as we drive across Warner to drop off the truck.

On the way back to the house, we stop off and grab a couple pizzas to eat. Even though I'm hurt by Jordan wanting me out of his house, I'm grateful for his and Vic's helping me to unpack.

Standing in the kitchen and devouring the pizza, I finally decide to find out what Jordan's issue is with me.

"Was it really that bad having me as a temporary roommate?" I ask with a laugh, trying hard to keep eye contact with him. Vic glances at me and then to Jordan with his hand partially raised to his mouth.

Suddenly I feel about an inch tall, thinking my best friend and her husband talk about me to Vic and Jemma.

"Reggie and I just needed our space," Jordan says in between bites of pizza. "It's nothing personal."

Nothing personal? This just got personal. "Did I do something to piss Reggie off? Ever since I came up in July for your wedding, things have been off between her and me. It's never been like this before."

Jordan shrugs, shoves another bite into his mouth. "As far as I know, the two of you are fine," he says when he finishes chewing. "You should talk to Reggie if you think something's wrong." Typical guy answer not making me feel any better.

After the pizza is devoured, Vic and Jordan take off and I collapse on my couch. Actually, first, I lean over the back of the couch, stretch out my arms, and pretty much hug the comfy thing. I love my couch. And I love this house, and can't believe I get to live here. The brick fireplace makes a great focal point in the living room, and if the television sits on the secondhand dresser used for storage, it will complete the space. TV and a fireplace, you can't get better than that.

I spend the rest of the day unpacking boxes and putting my things away. The downstairs feels cozy and fresh with my furnishings—not that I have a lot of stuff—but it looks like me and makes me happy. By the time my stomach growls, demanding food, I'm done for the day and have numerous flattened boxes scattered around the house. Grabbing a pad of paper from a drawer in the kitchen, I begin to make a list of questions I have for Ace about the house as well as a grocery and shopping list. According to the maps app on my phone, the nearest Wal-Mart is about five miles away. I should be able to purchase everything I need there, including dinner.

I shove my phone in my purse, pull the keys out, and head out the front door, locking it before walking to my car. Once inside, my phone alerts me to a text.

Ace: How did moving go? Need any help?

Me: All done. Heading to the store to grab a few things to make some dinner. I'm starving.

It's after seven and truly I have no desire to cook, but I don't want to drive around aimlessly looking for a place to eat. Besides, I'll need food for breakfast.

Me: I have some questions about the house, when would be a good time to talk?

Ace: You want to meet up for dinner?

Me: Um, now? Sure. Where?

Ace texts me the name of a burger joint a couple miles from the house and I whisper up a prayer of thanks. A burger sounds perfect right now. Thank goodness for GPS because the streets in Warner are like a squiggly maze and make no sense whatsoever. Back home in Phoenix, the main roads are all straight, forming a grid pattern, and make navigating the massive city a breeze. Warner is less than half the size of Phoenix and I could easily find myself lost.

The restaurant is not much more than a small brick and glass building with an old-fashioned drive-thru in the back and a few small tables inside. I spot Ace sitting at a table near the door, offer up a smile, and tuck my hair behind my ear. He looks good in dark jeans, a faded blue v-neck t-shirt, and a pair of navy Converse shoes. He strides toward me and I find myself staring at the way the t-shirt stretches across his chest and hugs his biceps, which tease me with the hint of his tattoo. If he looks this good with clothes on, he must be a vision nude.

My cheeks heat as he approaches, tugging on his ear and ducking his head like he's unsure what he's doing here.

"Hi," he says, stopping right in front of me. Citrus and rosemary invade my senses and wrap around me like a warm blanket.

"Hi, yourself." Neither one of us moves, our eyes are locked on one another and our ragged breaths meet for a secret kiss in between us. Ace breaks eye contact only to dip his gaze to my lips, which part on their own. His hand rises near my cheek but then as if he remembers something, he steps backward, drops his hand, and turns his gaze to the food counter.

"Let's get dinner, yeah?" He steps around me and practically runs to order his dinner.

Chapter 10

Ace

I almost kissed her. Standing in front of her, watching her chest rise and fall in sync with mine, was almost too much. Hell, it *was* too much. Another five seconds of standing so close to her and my lips would have found hers, and I think a part of me would have enjoyed it. And then I would have hated myself. Kind of like I hate myself right now sitting across from her at this small square table having no other place to look than right at her. Underneath the table, the tips of our shoes keep bumping into each other and we both continue to apologize after each touch.

When our food finally arrives, we focus on the fries and burgers, avoiding awkward conversation and pointed stares. Funny things happen when you concentrate on eating and don't speak in between bites of food. For instance, my burger quickly disappears, as do Stacey's fries. Three quarters of the way finished with her burger, Stacey wraps it in the white parchment paper and pushes it away. I finish my fries, pile my garbage into the paper basket, and sit once again staring at the girl in front of me. She picks up her soda, wraps her lips around the clear straw, and sucks up the beverage. Her eyes find mine and dip back to her cup before she places it back on the table.

"I have a lot of boxes," she says out of the blue. Her fingertips rest on the edge of the table as though she's hanging off the edge for dear life. Do I make her nervous? She glances up at me, her cheeks flush, and then her right hand moves from the table to the parchment paper that has sprung open from around the burger. "Is there a place I can take them and throw them away? And when is garbage day?"

She's asking about...I shake my head, clearing the laugh trying to break free. "Tuesdays are garbage day," I say, finding a smile on my lips. "And I'm sure you could dump the boxes in one of those large bins behind Wal-Mart or a grocery store."

"Right, that's what I was thinking." Her shoulders slump as she relaxes in the chair, though I'm not sure how anyone could really feel comfortable on the hard plastic seat with the metal spindles poking into your back. "Well, thanks for meeting me for dinner. I should probably find Wal-Mart so I can put some food in that fridge of yours."

My entire body tenses up at the mention of my fridge. It's stupid, I know, but when Marley and I moved in, there wasn't a square inch of the house we didn't christen. Which included the doors of the fridge—more than once I had her pressed against

73

the stainless steel surface while kissing her or nibbling on her ear. Not one room in that house was left untouched by us, which is possibly one reason I can't go inside. Of course the real reason is the worst of them all, and I shudder at the memory. Some days I wish I could forget them, every single freaking memory of my wife. I wonder if it would be easier then.

But then I would be erasing the happy memories of her and I, and that might be even worse than reliving the bad.

"Good luck at the store, and if you need anything, just call or text." My offer sounds genuine, but in truth, there is not much she could say or do that would make me set foot inside that house.

Twenty minutes later, I step through the front door of Ethan's home to find him sitting on the couch with an Xbox controller in his hand and a game of Halo Reach blowing up the sound system. I pull two beers from the fridge, walk into the living room, and grab another controller before sitting on the couch. Ethan snatches a beer from my hand and restarts the game so I can join in.

There is something mind-numbing about video games. Sure, you get drawn into the beauty of the actual art in the game, but after a while you're wholly immersed in the objectives. Killing aliens, finding new guns and ammo, along with taking control of the base becomes your life. And before you know it, it's after midnight and both of us have to be at work early.

"You got home late," Ethan says, turning off

Halo Reach and flipping on the cable. He scrolls through the guide and settles on sports highlights. This is the other thing playing video games does: removes any and all conversation about impromptu dinners with the girl who briefly turned your world upside down in July and is now renting the house in which your wife died. His statement is meant to draw out what I did on my way home. But I really don't know if I'm comfortable talking to him about dinner with Stacey.

"I had dinner with Stacey." Apparently, my mouth is controlled by something other than my brain.

Ethan's eyes nearly pop out of his head as a smile begins to take shape. "As in *Stacey*, Stacey? The chick you went out with twice this summer? The Stacey who is currently living in *your* house?"

"Nothing gets past you, does it?" I shrug my shoulders and roll my eyes in annoyance. I seriously don't want to have this conversation with my brother-in-law.

"So, this date…how'd it go?" He leans back on the couch, resting his arms on top of the pillows.

"It wasn't a date," I grumble, then grab my empty beer from the coffee table, stand, and take it to the trash in the kitchen.

"Okay. How did the not-a-date go?" Ethan laughs, obviously taking great pleasure in my discomfort. Why did I decide living with him was a good idea?

"Listen, I'm glad you find this so funny. But I really don't want to talk to you about it. It's weird, and I don't think talking about some chick with my dead wife's brother is a great idea."

That shut him up. I never joke about Marley's death, let alone speak so bluntly about her. I'm irritated to the point of becoming angry, but for what reason? I'm the idiot who asked her to meet me for dinner and then almost kissed her. For the briefest moment, I got lost in the way her jaw curves, meeting her graceful neck, how her skin looks so soft and smooth. I found myself wanting to feel the warmth of her lips on mine, to know if they are as pillowy soft as they look.

But then I caught myself moving in to touch her cheek and stopped before it was too late. Before I did something that would fill me with guilt and regret. I have enough remorse swirling around inside me, I don't have room for any other feelings.

"All I'm saying is it's been five years, bro. It's time to move on," Ethan says. Shame burns through me at his words because, yes, on the rare occasion I do think about it. I've wondered what moving on would feel like and how it would affect Ethan and his parents. Being faithful to Marley's memory hasn't been hard, especially when you don't give yourself the opportunity to stray.

"I'm honoring my marriage to your sister," I argue from the kitchen. I'm standing over the sink, my hands gripping the counter with my head bent low.

"You're honoring your marriage to a ghost," Ethan says, suddenly standing behind me. "Marley wouldn't want you to be miserable."

"I'm not miserable." I turn around and fold my arms across my chest. He doesn't know how I feel.

How it feels to be unable to save your own wife.

"Just think about it, okay? No one would think any less of you if you were to start dating again." Ethan claps a hand on my shoulder before walking away. His bedroom door closes and I stand in the kitchen trying to determine if what he said has any merit. By the twisting in my gut and the sudden change in the tempo of my heartbeat, I'd say Ethan doesn't have a clue what he's talking about.

For the next hour, I spend my time in the basement lifting weights and running on the elliptical. I'm dog-tired, but unable to control the racing thoughts streaming through my head. Flashes of Marley and me making love in the living room or in the shower haunt me. How her body felt pressed up against mine, her soft settling against my hard. What we had was amazing and terrifying all at the same time. When we were good, we were great. But when it was bad...it was explosive. And I had no freaking clue how to deal with that. And by the time we started to figure it out...it was too late.

It's been five Goddamn years and it still stings like a hot knife when I think about her. It cuts so deep that some days I wonder how she could handle the pain of what she had done.

Collapsing against the handles of the elliptical, I let the tears slide down my cheeks. I hate these tears and I hate her for leaving me. And worst of all...I hate myself for hating her.

Chapter 11

Stacey

I really love working at Julia's bookstore. I love the scent of paper and new books and making the shelves look pretty after someone has come in the store and browsed. It doesn't even bother me when a customer has taken a book off the shelf and set it down someplace else. It's kind of like a scavenger hunt where the books are the prize—and who doesn't like book prizes?

Okay, maybe I'm being a little dramatic. I do really love working here and Julia is an amazing boss. She reminds me a bit of my mom, which makes me a tiny bit homesick. But I'm good. Warner is good. I just wish it were great. Like here it is Friday night and I have no plans to go out or to do anything fun this weekend. If I were back in Phoenix, I'd be calling up Jade and Bianca and we'd be going out to the clubs tonight. A little drinking, a little dancing, and a whole lot of flirting. It would be the perfect end to a great workweek.

But nope. Other than Julia, I don't know anyone here. And Reggie doesn't count because she lives an hour away and is no longer single. I'm beginning to think it really sucks being the *single* friend.

After I tidy up the non-fiction books, I wander over to where Julia is going through new inventory and pricing the little trinkets and gifts. She's about my mom's age, maybe she has a daughter.

"Do you have any kids?" I ask, standing in front of Julia.

She glances up from underneath her glasses, smiles kindly, and returns to her task. "I do," she says, placing a price tag on a small figurine. "Grady is seventeen, Chris is twenty-one, and Alisha is twenty-six."

"Do you think Alisha would ever want to hang out with me? I don't have many friends yet and would love to meet some new people." I cross my fingers behind my back, hoping Julia thinks we'd get along. Yes...I still cross my fingers at twenty-seven. Julia's fingers still over another figurine and then she shrugs.

"Alisha and I don't talk a whole lot right now. But I could give you her number if you wanted to call her." Julia's shoulders sag as she places the price tag on the trinket. I feel like I should ask her more, but the small amount of moisture around her eyes indicates the subject may be too fresh to pry. So instead, I offer to help price the new inventory and then get to work setting up displays.

Julia heads out for lunch, leaving me in control of the store. Times where I'm alone are nice, because as much as I like her, I don't have to watch everything I do. If I want to break out into a mini dance session because an awesome song comes on the radio, then I do it. If she's here, I make sure to keep myself in check.

So when a song I love comes on and the store is empty, I don't hesitate to jump around and shake my stuff, letting my hair fly around me. Halfway through the song, someone clears their throat behind me and I freeze with my hands over my head and my hips cocked to one side.

"You get paid to dance like that?"

My eyes clamp shut as I cringe and slowly turn around. Ace is standing near the door wearing his uniform, looking damn tasty. I haven't seen him dressed in his police gear yet, and I start to wonder when I developed a thing for a guy in uniform.

"Don't stop on my account," he says, smiling one of his rare real smiles. Those are my favorite. The ones he gives that can hardly be counted as a smile and don't reach his eyes are painful. They're filled with hurt and sadness, making his pale blue eyes the saddest pair of eyes I've ever seen.

But right now, they don't look anywhere close to sad. In fact, if I had to guess, I'd say they hold a hint of humor with a side of hunger. As though he was enjoying watching me dance. When we danced at Reggie's wedding in July, he surprised me with how well he moved. Actually, he blew me away. His moves were precise, steady, and sure, and made me feel desired. Ace's hands on me were warm and held me tight to his chest, and by the end of the night, I would have gladly invited him back to my place.

Except, I wasn't at my place, and I've been trying to change the way I live my life. I've done those random hookups way too many times. I don't want to be that girl who brings just any guy home anymore. Or who hooks up in the guy's car because she has a roommate who has a kid.

And so I said good night to Ace, and we parted ways. Never in a million years did I ever think I'd run into him again, let alone be living in a house he owns.

"What are you doing here?" I ask, trying to fight the blush creeping up my neck.

Ace glances around the bookstore, taking in the upper loft with its iron railing and oak bookcases. When his gaze settles back on me, I see hesitation and confusion drawn on his brow.

"Truthfully," he says, taking a deep breath. "I really don't know why I'm here. I was on my lunch break and in the area. I guess I kind of just ended up here." He shoves his hands in the pockets of his navy blue uniform pants that cling to his thighs, highlighting the strength in them.

"Do you like to read?" I ask, and immediately want to slap my palm to my forehead. *Do you like to read?* What kind of conversation starter is that? "I mean, this is a bookstore after all. Maybe I could recommend something to you?"

Ace raises a brow as his lips narrow into a half smile. His icy blue eyes hold a glimmer of a sparkle and I take it as a challenge. "A book? Sure…I could read something."

"Any particular genre?"

He shrugs a shoulder. "Surprise me," he says

with a faint grin.

Yes, Mr. Officer, I accept this challenge. He follows me through the store as I make my way back to the romance section. I turn before we get to the shelves and stop; Ace nearly collides with my chest.

"Whatever I pick, you have to promise to buy," I say, raising my brow as I place the challenge before him. He nods and opens his mouth to speak, but I hold up a finger and continue. "You also have to promise to *read* it."

"You're not going to make me read some boring historical fiction book, are you?" he asks, and it's a valid question since that's currently where we are standing.

I shake my head and walk him two shelves over, scan the titles, and pull out one of my favorite romance books. It's about a girl who gets her heart broken by her boyfriend and then moves in with a neighbor temporarily and ends up falling in love with him. But the twist is she doesn't know the roommate is deaf until after she moves in because he plays the most beautiful music on his guitar. It's one of those books that, sure, it has romance in it, but it also makes your heart swell and your knees weak.

"What are we doing in the romance section? That's just as bad as historical fiction," he says, tugging on his left ear. "I don't want to read that crap."

I pull the book from the shelf and hold it against his firm chest. "This," I say, patting his shoulder. Okay, maybe it was more of my hand slipping down his bicep to his elbow. Holy muscles under that navy blue uniform! I clear my throat and finish my thought. "This book is not crap. It's beautiful."

Ace turns the book around, reads the title, and groans, tilting his head back. "What kind of book title is *Maybe Someday* anyway? God, I'm going to turn into a chick, aren't I?"

Laughing, I pull him by the elbow up to the counter where he regretfully pays. He leaves with the promise that he will actually read the book and then he'll call or text me to discuss it. I can't hide the girly giggle escaping my throat as he walks out the door. Julia walks in just as Ace walks out and she gives me a quizzical look through her glasses. She scurries up to the counter, her lips pinched together.

"Is everything okay?" she asks in a rush. She glances around the store and returns her gaze to me. "I saw that cop leaving, did something happen?"

"Relax, Julia. That was my friend Ace. He came in to see me and ended up buying a book." The smile on my lips keeps growing and I don't want to do a darn thing about it. I like that he put it on my face.

She visibly relaxes, her shoulder dropping and lips stretching out into her typical pleasant grin.

"Okay, that's...good, then. Did you eat while I was gone?" she asks, stepping around me to settle behind the counter. I shake my head and she continues. "Well, I can handle things here if you want to take your lunch break."

I pull my purse from underneath the counter, tell her thanks, and head out the door. I shoot off a text to Ace telling him not to let me down, and then while I'm at it, send one to Reggie asking if we could talk when she had some time. I ate my lunch alone without a response from either.

Chapter 12

Ace

I spent the weekend reading that damn book Stacey made me buy and two things happened. The first is I realized being around her makes me feel something other than pain. Guilt settles in a little later when I have time to think, but not feeling hurt and angry is…nice. The second one is I found out I actually enjoyed reading that book. So as I sit here at 9:30 p.m. on Sunday night, I find myself sending her a text stating as much.

Me: Okay, so you were right about the book.

She doesn't need to know exactly how much I liked it, but enough to know it wasn't terrible like I'd assumed it would be. A few minutes pass with no response so I decide to grab a quick shower and wash the day off me. Being a police officer is extremely rewarding, and when paired with riding around in my patrol car with Duke, it's even better.

He and I make a great team.

The warm water soothes the tight muscles in my back and for a fleeting moment I let my mind wander. Showing up at the bookstore where she worked wasn't something I'd planned. Honestly, during my lunch break, it was like the car had a mind of its own. Like it was suddenly on autopilot, headed straight for Stacey, and there was nothing I could do to stop it. When I walked inside and saw her dancing uninhibitedly to whatever song was on the radio, I wanted so badly to take her in my arms, pull her face to mine, and kiss her until she begged me to strip off her leggings and take her behind the counter. She brings out something primal in me—a hunger—I haven't felt…in a very long time. If ever.

My relationship with Marley was great. We were high school sweethearts and horny as hell. She could turn me on with just a passing glance. I loved her fiercely and I loved her hard. The hunger I feel toward Stacey is animalistic. I almost feel like a predator laying claim to my next meal, and if I weren't so wrapped up in the guilt dragging me down, I'd eat Stacey for breakfast.

And lunch and dinner.

But none of that matters because my will power is holding fast. I won't be tempted. I won't be swayed. But hell if I won't take care of Mr. Willy here in the shower.

Fifteen minutes later, shower over and slightly more relaxed, I dry off, toss the towel over the shower rod, and head to bed. Duke whines from his kennel, asking for a quick scratch behind the ear, which I indulge him in. In fact, a little romp around the room and a quick game of tug-o-war is in order. He snarls with his teeth clamped on his end of the rope and jerks back until a ping from my cell makes me lose my grip.

Like a teenager, I spring across the bed and snatch my phone off the nightstand. Pressing the center button, the screen lights up, revealing a text from Stacey.

Stacey: *I told you so! Now call me to discuss.*

I glance over to Duke, who is lying on the floor with the rope dangling over his front paws and his big brown eyes gazing up at me longingly.

"Do I call her back, boy, or just send her a text?" After receiving no reply from my dog, I take a deep breath and call her. What will it hurt to talk to her about a book? It's not like we can't be friends. So I do maybe the third most idiotic thing since meeting her.

I call.

"I wasn't sure if you were going to call," she says when she answers.

I take a deep breath and slowly let it out, hoping to calm my racing heart.

"I wasn't sure either." There. The truth. It's always best to lead with it regardless of the situation. "But if you start telling me how dreamy the deaf guy is, I'm hanging up." Her laugh could revive a sleepy room with its tender sound and comforting warmth. For the better part of an hour we talk about the book, and as we dive deeper into it, I admit I actually was a little angry with the guy for staying with his girlfriend out of guilt. But as Stacey and I spoke more, I wondered if maybe she knows more about me than she's let on. I'm still holding on to my wife and she's dead. Could Stacey know about what happened? Or why I am who I am today?

"So you see, it's possible to love two people, but in different ways," she says, bringing me back to the present. I really have no idea what she was talking about, but my comfort level has diminished significantly. I won't do love…ever again. Hell, I don't even know if I'll do *like*. That in and of itself is dangerous.

"Hey, my dog needs to go out. I'd better get going."

"Oh," she says quietly. I feel her disappointment tugging at my chest. "I didn't know you had a dog."

My cheeks puff out as I release a breath and my hand tugs at the back of my neck. "Yeah. I'm a K-9 Officer. But he's more like family than my partner." My hands are beginning to twitch from the need to hang up the phone.

"That's nice. I'd love to meet him," Stacey says, the pitch of her voice climbing higher in tone. She's looking for an invite or something, and, sadly, she's not going to get one.

"Yeah, maybe someday. But right now, I've got to go and take him outside. I'll talk to you later." Before she can object or keep me talking longer, I tap the end call icon, silence my phone, and lay it facedown on the nightstand. Because I don't like to lie, I throw on a pair of boxer briefs and a white t-shirt and take Duke outside. Of course he does his business like the good dog he is and then scoops up a ragged tennis ball from near a tree, bringing it straight to my hand. I rub the scruff at his neck, sit on the back steps, and throw the ball at least a dozen times.

Thirty-seven. Thirty-seven is the number of times I thought about Stacey over the next three days. Sometimes it was the joyous sound of her laughter. Others it was her creamy white skin and soft shoulders I still wanted to nibble on. But like right now, right now as her name pops up on my caller ID at 7:30 a.m., all I can think about is how fast my heart is beating in my chest.

I've spent years honing my body, training it to respond how I need it to, especially in the line of duty. Why the hell can't I stop it from reacting like a hormonal teenager whenever she's involved?

"Hello?" My hand is on the door of my police SUV, Duke's in the rear, secured, and I need to get to work.

"Ace," Stacey pants, sending inappropriate thoughts straight to Mr. Willy. My hand fists around the door handle, pulls open the door, and I slip inside. "The garage door won't open and I need to get to work." She's in full panic mode now, her voice an octave higher than normal.

"I need to get to work too, sweetheart." *Shit.* I didn't mean for it to sound clipped and irritated, nor did I intend to call her sweetheart.

"I'm working alone today," she pleads; my resolve is fading. "Could you please come fix it?"

I slam my hand down on the steering wheel, fire up the SUV, and pull out of Ethan's driveway like

I'm running from Hell. The house is only about a ten-minute drive from here, but I'll be late to work now.

"Fine. I'll be there in ten minutes. But I don't have time to fix it; you're going to have to settle for me driving you to work."

"Okay, that's—"

I hang up before she finishes, call the captain, and let him know I'll be late, and then, because I'm a freaking police officer, obey all the posted signs and stop lights between Ethan's house and hers.

Stacey's sitting on the front porch steps when I pull up to the curb in front of the house. Her hair is twisted into a messy bun on the top of her head, the dark jeans she's wearing draw my eye to her long legs, making me think about how they'd feel wrapped around me. *Dammit!* She jogs up to the passenger side of the SUV, climbs inside, and immediately the scent of peaches and lilies swirls around me.

She buckles up, turns to me with a giant grin on her face, and says, "Thank you so much for doing this." I grit my teeth and pull away from the curb while I try to ignore the way her perfume makes me want to lean across the center console and lick her neck to see if she tastes anything like she smells. "So, I think I locked the keys to the house inside."

My foot slips off the gas and stomps on the brake pedal, lurching her forward in the seat. Duke whines in the back from losing his balance.

"Are you trying to kill me?" I ask, breathing hard through my nose. Thank God we're at a stop sign with no one behind us because I can't physically remove my foot from the brake pedal at the moment.

Stacey's jaw falls open, then snaps shut as her eyes narrow in confusion. "You're the one who slammed on the brakes, not me. Shouldn't it be me yelling at you?" She leans back in the seat, folds her arms across her chest, and rolls her eyes.

"Sorry," I mumble, then proceed through the stop sign. "I have a spare key you can borrow when I drop you off after work tonight."

"Fine," she says, turning her gaze to the passenger window. That suits me just fine…silence and the occasional sigh.

I really hate the occasional sigh.

Chapter 13

Stacey

I don't know what's worse, pissing off Ace or not knowing *what I did* to anger him. Either way, he's mad—I guess—and won't answer my texts asking if he wants me to pick out another book for him. It's not that I really want to pick out another book, but he's really the only person I know in Warner and consider a friend. He's been avoiding me for ten days and it sucks.

After a long day at work, the last thing I expected to come home to is a woman wearing a knee-length floral skirt and a soft pink sweater standing on the front porch, holding some sort of casserole dish. She's around my age, maybe, with a fringy blond bob, eyes the color of ivy, and a hesitant smile.

"I'm Lucy," she says, walking to meet me near the driveway. "I'd wave but..." She glances down at the foil-covered glass pan and then expectantly back at me.

"Stacey. And you have your hands full."

"My mother always says you should bring a new neighbor some food after they move in, and since it's been a while, I thought maybe you'd be out of casseroles from neighbors and I'd bring you over one of hers." Her hands are covered in lilac-colored oven mitts, and when I move to accept the dish, she pulls it back. "It's super hot, and Mom would kill me if you burned yourself."

"Your mom made this?" We step inside the house, Lucy following me through to the kitchen. Thank goodness I had the sense to clean the dishes last night before bed.

"I can't cook to save my life," she admits, setting the casserole on the counter on top of the trivet I pulled out of a drawer. "Mother tells me no man will ever want to marry me if I don't know how to cook." We both laugh and fall into easy conversation as she joins me to eat the chicken and noodle casserole. It's amazing and I help myself to a second portion.

Turns out Lucy is a year younger than I am, single—since she can't cook, apparently—and teaches third grade at a nearby elementary school. She's easygoing and I think I've made my first girl friend here in Warner. Inside, my inner fourteen-year-old self is doing an awkward happy dance because I really needed this.

"I'm so glad you came over today," I say while gathering our plates. "I could really use a single friend right now."

"Can I see the house? I've been dying to look around since it came up for rent." Lucy stands, straightens the hem of her floral skirt that looks like it belongs in the 1950s, and stares, wide-eyed, at me.

"Sure, I guess. I'm still not quite unpacked. So if you don't mind the occasional mess, I'll start the tour."

"Mother says the man who used to live here lost his wife about five years ago," she says, and it sends chills down my arms, like a breath of frozen air has settled around me, puckering my skin in goose bumps. As we tour the house, Lucy peers into each room and when she sees an empty bedroom upstairs, a goofy grin works its way onto her oval face.

"This house is amazing. I wish Mother would let me move out, then you and I could be roommates." Actually, that would be pretty nice, rooming with someone again.

"Maybe Ace would let you move in. I'll ask him the next time we speak," I say, crossing my fingers he says yes. I'm not making a whole lot at the bookstore, and adding someone else to pay for rent would more than make me feel comfortable.

Lucy's eyes fall, like she's been given terrible news. "I really don't think Mother would allow it."

A bark of a laugh slips from my mouth but I cut it short when her eyes narrow—she's being totally serious.

"Lucy, you're twenty-six years old. I'm pretty sure you can move out if you want to."

She shakes her head, clasps her hands together at her waist, and then slowly descends the stairs. "You don't know my mother, she can be…very persuasive."

Before she opens the front door to leave, I grab her elbow and pull her around to face me. I let go when I see the telltale signs of tears.

"Do you want to move out? Because if you do, I can help you. No one should feel trapped, even if it's their own mother doing the smothering."

Lucy sniffs, blinks away the tears on her bottom eyelashes, and smiles sweetly. "I would like that very much," she says, and then slips out the door. She scurries, like a little mouse, down the walkway to the sidewalk and then quickly walks down the street toward her mother's house. As much as I loved the casserole that woman made, I'm not sure she's a person I ever want to meet. Not only does she seem to know about some history with this house, but who doesn't let their grown daughter move out if she wants?

I said I would help Lucy, and I'm starting right now.

Me: Met a neighbor who is being held hostage in her mother's house ;) Would it be okay if I asked her to be my roommate? She'll pay half the rent...

Ace: No.

I guess something finally grabbed his attention, though it wasn't the response I was expecting or hoping for.

Me: Why not?

Ace: I said no.

My finger hovers over the send button, but calling him a jerk, I suppose, is a little juvenile. Instead, I ask him another question that's been bugging me.

Me: Why are you mad at me?

The familiar ellipsis flashes on my screen and then fades away. This guy…he is infuriating with his inability to answer questions. I don't even know why I bother. I don't hear a word from Ace the rest of the week, and as I pack an overnight bag, I'm pretty sure I could finish out my lease and not care if I heard from him again. I don't need to see those piercing blue eyes or the three-day-old beard he always sports. And I really don't care if I never see him in his police uniform again either. Because even though he is completely drool-worthy in that thing, I don't need the drama that seems to follow him.

By the time I pull up outside Reggie's house I've convinced myself that I'm better off not having Ace in my life. And if Lucy ends up moving in without him knowing, what does it matter? I've always lived by the principle of it's better to ask for forgiveness rather than permission. And in this case, I can't see how he'd ever even know if she moved in.

A mop of floppy brown hair peeks out the front door, followed by a very toothless Micah. He runs down the steps and wraps his arms around my waist, squeezing as tight as he can.

"Stacey!" he says with gusto. "You're here! I've missed you so much."

"I've missed you too," I say, running my hand through his soft hair. "Is your momma home?"

He nods enthusiastically, twines his fingers through mine, and pulls me up the stairs and through the front door. Reggie's in the kitchen scrubbing a pan and smiles when she sees me. I texted her a couple days after moving into the house and we both apologized for being short with each other. She'd been stressed over the wedding and putting Micah into a school. I admitted to feeling a little jealous over her meeting Jemma and becoming instant friends. Hopefully, we're good now, since I'm staying the night to hang out with her.

"I'd totally hug you, but my hands are gross from cleaning this pan," Reggie says, holding up soapy hands.

"I'm good, you just finish what you're doing. Micah and I are going to hang out in his room for a while."

"I want to show you my new Lego set Mom bought me," Micah says, again pulling me up the stairs. Once in his room, he pulls out the chair at his desk for me to sit on and pulls out three unopened boxes of Star Wars Lego sets. "Can we build this one?" he asks, holding up some sort of fighter ship.

"Dude, it has, like, six hundred pieces. It will take us all night." I would build Legos with him all night if I didn't have plans with Reggie. Instead, I point to the small set and we start in on it. After thirty minutes, we have a good portion of it built and Reggie joins us. Together, the three of us work on it, finishing the pirate ship. Micah beams up at us and then practically pushes us out of his room so he can play with the finished product.

"So, Jordan is taking Micah out for dinner and then a movie, so we have the house to ourselves for a few hours," Reggie says when we're back downstairs. "I've rented two movies and picked up a couple bottles of wine."

Wine and movies with Reggie is just what I need. When Jordan and Micah leave for the night, Reggie and I drive into town to pick up some Chinese food and then head back to her house to start our night. We pull a couple forks from the kitchen in case we need them, and then bring our food to the living room where Reggie puts on the first movie—*Robin Hood*, the Kevin Costner version, and one of my favorites. Halfway through the movie, Reggie and I get to talking, nearly forgetting about what's happening on the television.

"Tell me about your house," she says eagerly. She leans toward me like a kid trying hard not to open Christmas presents early. "Tell me about Ace. I still can't believe you're renting *his* house."

"I know, right? It was really weird at first, and awkward. Like, he didn't go inside to show it to me and still hasn't come inside since I moved in. The garage door even stopped working one day and I asked him to come fix it, but he wouldn't. Instead, he called a repair company that came and took care of it."

We talk more about how he and I went to dinner that first night and how he showed up at the bookstore. When I mention Lucy and the possibility of me asking her to move in with me, Reggie seems surprised but says nothing.

"And Lucy says her mother told her that the man living in the house five years ago lost his wife. You know I don't do well with ghost stories, but I swear the temperature dropped, like, twenty degrees when she brought it up." I still feel the chills talking about it now.

"You think it was Ace who lost his wife?" Reggie asks, eyes wide with curiosity.

I shrug and say, "I guess it's possible. But he doesn't seem old enough to have been married and then have his wife die five years ago."

"Well, I'm glad you've found a friend up there. And I'm sorry Ace is…weird," she says, giggling. "I think the wine is going to my head." We've finished off the first bottle and the second is sitting on the coffee table in front of us. We glance at each other, raise our brows, and then lunge for the bottle. I beat Reggie to it, giving me the first glass. I pour the dark red liquid into my wine glass and then fill hers.

"To best friends," I say, holding up my glass. Reggie clinks hers against mine and we giggle and finish watching *Robin Hood*.

We're both yawning by the time the movie is over, but Jordan and Micah haven't returned yet so she pops the second movie in and presses play. The title screen appears and I pull my lips between my teeth as I see the nearly naked images of several really good-looking men dancing seductively on the screen.

"I'll be right back," Reggie singsongs from behind the couch.

"Just so you know, I don't have a hot guy to return home to, so this is really unfair," I say, pressing *play* on the remote.

"Yes, but I brought Jack to join our party." Reggie holds up a bottle of Jack Daniels whiskey and smiles brightly. I have missed living with her so much.

"This still doesn't excuse your choice of movie. You've got rock God extraordinaire coming home soon, you could have picked something tamer." A movie about male dancers—mostly naked male dancers—is so unfair to watch as a single lady.

The movie begins and we take shots of Jack Daniels each time one of the dancers removes his shirt, and two for each time he removes his pants. Best night and best friend ever.

Chapter 14

Ace

Some days it would be so nice if I were a dog. Duke has the day off, which means he gets to hang out with the guys at the station while I answer domestic calls. It's not that I mind the domestics, it's the partner riding along with me on these days. Officer Chuck Kilty is about forty-five years old, has a dun-lop—a belly that has dun-lopped over his belt—and smells like mothballs. Who freaking uses mothballs anymore? Chuck's a good guy, but sometimes, because of his age, he thinks he can order me around.

I've never put him in his place, even though I outrank him, but one of these days a blood vessel is going to burst in my forehead from holding back.

"What has your panties in a bunch, Steele?" Chuck refuses to call me Ace like everyone else and it's yet another thing about him that grates on my nerves. He plops one of those powdered sugar mini donuts into his mouth, making me cringe at the realization that it's police officers like him who give the rest of us a bad reputation. Not all officers like to sit around and eat donuts.

"Cut the crap, Chuck. We've got rounds to do."

He shrugs his shoulders, pulls another mini donut from its plastic wrapper, and powdered sugar sprinkles over the front of his navy blues. Chuck shoves the donut into his mouth then tries to brush away the white powder, but only spreads it further.

"You spill any of that in the car and you're paying to have it vacuumed," I say, shooting him a warning glare.

"Relax, Steele," he says, crinkling the plastic wrapper and tossing it into the small trash bin I keep up front. "What's on the docket for today, anything better than patrols?"

Chuck opens the in-car computer, scrolls through the open cases, but a call comes in over the radio that pulls both our attention from the computer.

"Possible domestic disturbance at 1708 West Elm Street. Cross streets are North Kempton and West Hampshire."

Chuck pulls the CB from the dash and answers the call. "Roger that. Officers Steele and Kilty responding."

"Thank you, Kilty. Proceed with caution and call for backup if needed."

"Roger that." Chuck's face lights up in excitement and I turn on the lights and siren. We're only about six blocks from the call location, and when we pull up to the house, a man is sitting on the porch steps with his hands gripping the back of his neck. His black hair is unkempt and it bleeds into a patchy week-old black beard. I stop the car diagonally in the driveway to prevent anyone from leaving and Kelty and I step out of the patrol car.

"Sir, we received a call about a possible domestic violence situation," I say, slowly approaching the man.

He doesn't look up as we step in front of him. Instead, he shakes his head side to side and grips the back of his neck tighter.

"Sir, can you hear me?" I ask, hoping he's outside working on controlling his temper and that whoever is inside is still breathing. Calls like this many times go one of two ways—smoothly, where the couple will cool off and go to counseling or maybe even go their separate ways. The other way sends a shiver down my spine.

"My sister's inside in pretty rough shape," the man says, his voice shaking with…confusion, not guilt or anger. I swallow the lump in my throat, debating whether to go inside or send Kilty. Before making the call, Kilty pulls his cuffs from the clip on his side, moves around the man, and proceeds to slowly stand him up and cuff his hands behind his back.

"Can you tell me your name, son?" Kilty asks, and then walks him to the patrol car. Somehow, I think he got the better end of the deal. Steeling myself to walk into a nightmare, one hand falls to the baton on my hip and the other on the radio on my chest.

"Officer Steele, ma'am. I'm here to help you." The house is a disaster, and filthy. A lingering scent of cigarette smoke burns my nose and there's an underlying putrid smell of rotten food; I have to breathe through my mouth in order to keep from gagging. In one corner of a living room sits a mangy gray cat with tufts of hair missing and frightened green eyes that follow me around the room.

The kitchen is clear, except for the empty takeout containers lining the counters and overflowing trash spilling over the can and onto the stained tile floor. I keep moving toward the back of the house, stepping over piles of dirty laundry and cat feces and have to wonder how someone can live like this.

"Holy shit," Kilty says, suddenly right behind me. "The guy's story is this is his sister's house and she's a little unstable...mentally."

I nod, understanding coursing through me. "What's his sister's name?" I ask, preparing to knock on what I assume is a bedroom door.

"Gloria Stevens, thirty-three and meaner than the devil." When I glance back with narrowed eyes, Kilty says, "His words, not mine."

There's no answer from behind the door after I knock, so I turn the handle and slowly open the door. It's stuck on something pretty heavy, so I push harder, but whatever's on the other side pushes back, slamming it closed.

"Miss Stevens, I'm officer Steele, and my partner is Officer Kilty. Your brother contacted us and we're here to help you. Will you please open the door?"

"Go away," a shrill voice shouts from the other side. "I don't want you here."

"We're only here to help, ma'am. Will you

please open the door so we can talk to you?" I ask, and watch as Kilty's nose scrunches up from the acrid scent of urine coming from under the door. "You gotta breathe through your mouth." My whispered words are lost in the shriek of the woman on the other side of the door.

"I've got a knife, I'll slit my throat if you come through that door," Gloria threatens, making my heart thump hard and fast in my chest. When someone threatens their own life, we have to act and quickly. With a mentally unstable person, you never know if they're serious or bluffing, hoping you'll go away. This is one situation where I won't take any chances.

I can save her. *I have to.*

"Miss Stevens, I'm going to ask one more time for you to open the door. If you don't, I'll have no other choice than to enter the room by force…though I'd rather not have to." Using my hand to count down from five, we wait for the door to open. At one, the door still remains closed and a click of the lock tells me she's not budging.

Turning to Kilty, I say, "Get prepared to grab her if she runs out of the room. If she stays inside, I'll grab the knife and get her to the floor. Take my cuffs and be ready to detain her if needed." Kilty nods, pulls my cuffs from their clip, and stands at the ready.

"Miss Stevens, I suggest you stand back. I'm going to open this door and don't want you to get hurt."

"Go away!" she screams, though I hear her move across the room. I brace my hands on the doorjamb,

105

raise my leg, and kick the door with great force. The jamb splinters and the door groans open, revealing a mostly dark room covered in clothing, boxes, food containers, and bodily fluids. Standing in a nightgown near the back wall of the room is Gloria Stevens. Thick dark red stains dot the front of her nightdress and my vision blurs momentarily. Before I have time to act, Gloria raises her arms over her head, brandishing a knife, and rushes toward me. Adrenaline kicks in and I sidestep her attack, pull the knife from her hand, and hope to God Kilty catches her on her way out. I turn quickly to see Kilty's arms wrap around the woman's upper body and hold on tightly. He wriggles the cuffs until they are clamped around her wrists and then stands to his full height.

"Miss Stevens, please come with us," he says, helping her down the hall and outside the house. I follow them outside and collapse on the front porch. The woman had cut her wrists, and let them bleed. Obviously they weren't deep wounds and no longer bleeding when we arrived, but all I could see when she lunged toward me was *Marley*.

Marley in the bathtub with blood-red water.

Marley in my lap bleeding out.

Marley's lifeless eyes staring back at me.

Chapter 15

Stacey

It feels good to be back at work, especially with all the new products Julia had come in over the weekend. I love creating new displays in the window and on the shelves. There's something therapeutic about it, making me get lost in the work. I'm so engrossed in a particular shelf I don't notice the door chime or the person standing beside me looking over my shoulder. I turn and jump back, holding my hand over my heart.

"Lucy! What are you doing here?" I stand upright and pull her in for a hug. She hesitantly returns the embrace and then steps back. "Why aren't you at work?"

She shrugs and smiles. "End of the quarter, no school."

"So you thought you'd just come say hi? How sweet," I tease, putting the last of the display together.

"Actually, I was going to see if you wanted to go

to lunch with me. Mother is out of the house today and I thought I'd get out too."

I glance at the clock on the wall and realize the morning has disappeared and it is actually time for my lunch break. "Sure, let me make sure Julia's fine here and we can go." I find her heating up her lunch in the back room and she shoos me out, telling me to go and enjoy lunch with a friend. Lucy and I make our way out of the bookstore and walk down the street to a little Thai food restaurant I like. We order up at the counter, take our seats at a small table near the window, and wait for them to bring our food.

When I first met Lucy, she looked like she was transported straight from the '50s with her knee-length floral skirt and pink sweater. Today, she's dressed in a pair of skinny jeans and a black cotton shirt. Her shaggy blond bob is a little wild and carefree. She totally needs to leave her mother's nest.

"So I talked to Ace about you moving in," I say, sipping my soda through a straw. Lucy's eyes nearly pop out of her head in surprise. "He said no."

Her shoulders drop, as does the excitement in her eyes. "It's okay. Mother wouldn't let me anyway."

I laugh at the awkwardness of her controlling mother and continue. "I've never really been one to ask permission though. So, I figure you just move in anyway. If he kicks us out, he kicks us out. We can find another place."

"But he already said no. I don't think it's a good idea."

"Oh, sure it is. Besides, I've always lived by the

ask for forgiveness way of life. It's harder to say no when it's already happened." Lucy and I glance up as our food arrives. We both breathe in the rich peanut scent of our food and start eating. Thai food is one of those foods you have to try before you say you don't like it. It may sound strange with the different curries or crushed peanuts, but add all the noodles and sauces and it's mouthwatering. My Pad Thai is amazing and makes for great leftovers.

"I still don't know if I should," Lucy says after a while. "I just don't know how to ask my mother."

"Don't ask her. You're twenty-six and have the right to do as you please." I finish my soda, stand, and walk over to the machine and refill my cup. I've never met anyone so afraid to stand up for themselves to their mother. Okay, scratch that, Reggie's always been somewhat of a pushover when it comes to her mom. But not this bad. This borders on abuse.

"I have it all worked out," I say, taking my seat at the table. Lucy glances up, eyes rapt and focused on me. "Start packing up your room and whatever else is yours in the house. Don't tell your mom until you're almost completely packed. Then you tell her you're moving in with me." I smile, feeling like I've solved a great mystery.

Lucy sighs, contemplates the plan while taking another bite of her lunch. I'm almost positive it will work, I just need to figure out how to convince her.

"Let's do it," she finally says, smiling ear to ear. We spend the rest of my lunch hour making plans to find boxes and get her packing. We settle on a move-in date of two weeks from now and head our separate ways after returning to the bookstore. The rest of the day I feel like I'm walking on a cloud. I'm excited to have a roommate again, because the truth is as much as I wanted my space a few months ago, I miss having someone around.

On the way home, I stop off at the store to grab a few groceries and a pint of ice cream to celebrate. Oh, who am I kidding? I eat ice cream all the time—I don't need a reason to buy it. I park outside the garage when I get home because I don't trust the garage door anymore, even though it's been fixed. I'd rather park outside and not risk getting stuck again.

I walk through the front door and immediately step into an inch of cold water. "What the…" There is water everywhere and I hear the sound of it spraying from somewhere inside. Groceries in hand, I wade through the pool my house has become and into the kitchen where I see the problem. The faucet has burst and water is spraying like a shower all over the place.

For a minute I can do nothing but stand in the middle of the kitchen, holding tight to my groceries, thinking about how I'm going to clean up the water. My jaw hangs open, tears float to the surface of my eyes, and I break down, dropping my bags of food…and ice cream. My furniture in the living room is going to be ruined, along with the kitchen cabinets and who knows what else. Tears slip down my cheeks, only adding to the flood at my feet, and I have no other option than to dial Ace. I don't even know how I'm going to make it through this call.

Voice mail. My call goes to his voice mail, but

this isn't the type of thing you leave a message about. Instead, I take a deep breath, snap a picture of the spraying faucet, and text it to him. That should get his attention.

Ace: What the hell?

That didn't take long. Neither did the ringing of my phone.

"Hello?" I say, holding back a sob.

"What did you do to my house?" he asks, sounding a notch above angry.

My nose is now running, mixing with my tears. Sniffing what I can away, I answer, "I don't know what to do. There's water everywhere. When I got home…Ace, everything is going to be ruined."

"Don't cry," he says quietly. "Have you turned the water off?"

"The faucet isn't turned on. It burst while I was at work." A sob breaks through and it's like a dam breaks loose. My shoulders and knees are shaking, making it impossible to stand. So I do the next best thing, and slide to the floor, only to sit in the cold water and then cry some more at my stupidity.

"Sweetheart, don't cry," he says. "I need you to listen, okay?" I nod, then manage to squeak out a yes. "Outside near the garage is the water shut off. I'll guide you through turning it off, okay?" He explains where the shut-off valve is and I'm able to turn off the water. Back inside, the faucet has stopped spraying, but there is so much water.

"There is no way I can clean all this up, Ace," I say, sniffing into the phone. "I'm so sorry. I don't know what to do."

"I'll be there in a few minutes, just hold tight," he says, and ends the call.

Wiping the tears from my eyes and snot from my nose, I walk upstairs to grab every single towel and blanket I own. It won't be enough to mop up the water, but it'll be a start. Arms full and back downstairs, I toe off my sandals and drop towels on the floor and repeat the process until everything I own that can soak up water is scattered around the main level. I feel sick about all the damage to Ace's house. The wood floors surely will be ruined, and the kitchen cabinets, not to mention my random pieces of furniture.

I just hope Ace doesn't kick me out.

Chapter 16

Ace

This girl is going to be the death of me. First the garage door, now a water leak—did I rent my house out to a walking disaster? I can only hope it's not as bad as she thinks it is. The picture she sent of the spraying faucet looked pretty serious, though. Grumbling to myself, I run through scenarios of what to do based on the possible situation.

I can stand outside while she soaks up the water and then have someone come in and assess the damage.

I can call for cleanup help and then have someone assess the damage.

I can tell her she'd better have renter's insurance and have her call someone to help clean up and then I can have someone come in and assess the damage.

Or…

There's always an "or" or a "but." I don't like "or" or "but." Not one bit.

Or, I could take a deep breath, go inside the

house, and check out the damage. I could be man enough to face my demons inside the house and help her like any normal man would do. Like a stronger man would do.

Everything in my body is fighting the right thing, my palms are sweating, and every couple minutes I have to swipe them across my jeans to keep the moisture at bay. My heart is racing in my chest and because of this I can't regulate my breathing. God, I think I'm going to pass out.

Get a grip, Ace. It's only a house. What happened in there are only memories now, floating around my head like dust motes looking for a place to settle. I wish I could blow them away, scattering the bad into the wind and never have to relive them. I don't want to dream about the things that haunt me. I just don't…anything.

I pull up against the curb outside the house and park my motorcycle. There is something understated about the small house sitting between two larger and statelier houses. Part of the draw for this house for Marley and me was how it looked like a blip in the road. Like it didn't quite belong with what's around it. We liked unusual and quaint.

Why didn't I just sell the damn house after she died? What was I trying to hold on to?

Deep breath after deep breath, I prepare myself to walk inside after five years. I haven't sweated this much since my first day at the police academy. Beads of sweat dot my forehead and back, and I shiver as they drop down my spine. My throat is parched and I didn't have the common sense to pack a bottle of water in the saddlebags.

Each step is like wading through molasses, and it only grows thicker the closer I come to the door. The first step onto the porch has my body ready to dry heave. I can't do this. My trembling hands are enough of a clue that I shouldn't be here. That I should have burned the house to the ground. I can almost feel it—the flames that would have engulfed the memories and the pain. It would have burnt them to ashes and I could have buried them with my wife.

My hand grips the post on the porch in order to keep myself upright. I'm here, and need to find the strength to push the front door open and step inside the place my nightmares take refuge. As I move my hand to the door, it opens on its own and the blotchy, tear-stained face of Stacey greets me. Her hair is wild, falling from a messy bun, and it makes the red color of her hair look like the flames I'm craving.

Fresh tears spill from her eyes as she rushes forward and collapses against me. Her arms wrap tightly around my waist and something crumbles in my chest as I breathe in the scent of peaches and lilies that is uniquely her. No longer needing the support of the porch post, I cage her in my arms and hold her while she cries. My hand moves in small circles on her back and slowly moves down toward the curve of her hip, a place I want to use to pull her against me.

"It's so bad, Ace," she says, sniffing against my t-shirt. "I don't have enough towels to mop up the water. I'm so sorry…I've ruined your house."

I ball the hem of her shirt in my fists, feeling her

pain and remorse. I know this is not her fault, and it kills me she thinks it is.

"Let's go inside, I'm sure it's not as bad as you think." I smile down at her when she finally glances up to me. Her eyes are puffy and bloodshot from crying, even her lips are swollen, and for a fleeting second, I wish they were like that from me kissing her. Swallowing back the thought, I release her from my arms and step backward.

Stacey swipes the tears away from her cheeks with the backs of her hands and then walks through the door. As I take yet another long, deep breath, I'm not prepared for the sight once I pass the threshold.

There is water. Everywhere. And at least an inch deep. I bring my hands up to the top of my head and run them through my hair and huff out the breath I was holding. Stacey's laid down towels and blankets wherever she can, and as I scan the living room, I see t-shirts, socks, and her...panties too. Everything is either floating or waterlogged and rumpled under the water.

When Stacey turns to me after I've had a chance to take in the sight, her bottom lip quivers and then she bursts into tears again.

"I'm so sorry," she says between sobs. "I broke your beautiful house." She crumples into a ball on her couch and continues to cry. The sight of the house and the flooding should piss me off. It should make me tremble with anger that the floors Marley and I refinished are now ruined, or that the brick fireplace will have to be repaired. But it doesn't. None of that matters at the moment.

Because at the moment, all I want to do is hold Stacey in my arms and laugh at the panties floating around the living room floor. I step over her floating clothes and sit down on her couch and pull her onto my lap. She tucks her head under my arm, leaving my hand free to brush the hair off her neck and softly stroke her arm.

"Everything is going to be okay," I say softly. "But, sweetheart, did you really think your panties would soak up the water?" And it's no use, the laugh won't quit bubbling up from my chest. It comes out almost like a bark, and it turns into something guttural and hearty from deep in my stomach.

Stacey sits up, swipes away her tears and narrows her eyes while studying me. "You're laughing?" she asks, her voice like a squeal. "I've flooded your house and you're laughing? What the hell is wrong with you?"

"Nothing's wrong with me," I say between laughing fits. I really can't control it, and, surprisingly, it feels really good to laugh. "I'm having a hard time keeping a straight face when I see your lacy underwear floating across the floor. It wasn't exactly how I pictured seeing your panties for the first time."

Stacey smacks my shoulder with the tips of her fingers and then stands, folding her arms across her chest. "I grabbed anything that would soak up water," she says defiantly. "What else was I supposed to do?"

I stand, towering over her, and pull her into my arms again and press a firm kiss to her forehead. It takes us both by surprise, her most likely more than me, since I can't seem to stop thinking about kissing her.

"You've done enough," I say, pushing far enough away so I can look her in the eyes. "Do you have any dry clothes?" She nods and rolls her eyes, blinking away more tears trying to start. "Pack a bag and you can come stay with me until all this is taken care of."

Stacey's eyes bug out as she backs away. "Are you sure that's a good idea?" she asks, biting the corner of her bottom lip. What I wouldn't give to be those teeth nibbling that plump bottom lip of hers. Is this a good idea? Probably not.

"Sure. There's a spare bedroom. You can just stay there until the house is fixed."

"All right," she says, then turns and bounds up the stairs. I watch as she jogs away and laugh at her wet pants, but curse how they hug her legs and butt, leaving little to the imagination. She returns a few minutes later carrying a purple duffle bag and has changed into dry clothes.

"You ready?" I ask as she pulls her purse from the kitchen counter.

Her smile is a little pathetic, almost floppy. "What should I do about all this?" she asks, gesturing to everything she used to try to soak up the water.

"Just leave it for now. I'll have a cleanup crew come in today and take care of everything. I'll have them set your clothing out to dry and then we can pick it up later. How's that?"

She nods and follows me out the door. Once

outside, I feel lighter and notice the weight of my memories haven't been present since Stacey threw herself into my arms. The panic attack I started to have disappeared as soon as Stacey opened the door.

"I'll follow behind you in my car since you drove your motorcycle," she says at the bottom of the porch. When I watch her walk to her car, I notice it's parked in the driveway and not in the garage. I know the door was fixed, so what's the deal with that?

"Hey, I had the garage door fixed. Why aren't you parking inside?" I ask, raising my voice loud enough for her to hear me.

A pink blush rises to her cheeks as she squints back at me and shrugs. "I don't trust it," she says plainly, and climbs inside her car.

Laughing to myself, I walk back to my motorcycle, start it up, and wait for her to pull out of the driveway.

Chapter 17

Stacey

Ace kissed me. This repeats in my head the entire drive to his house. He *kissed* me. Granted, it was only on the forehead and under great stress…but he kissed me. And I liked it—a lot. I liked the way I fit in his arms and the warmth radiating from his chest. I liked the way the stubbly beard on his chin scratched and poked my forehead as he pressed his lips against my skin.

Because I liked it all—too much—I asked him if it was a good idea for me to stay with him. When he said yes, my skin erupted in goose bumps. His yesses are like the still, calm waters of a river— *dangerous*—and I'm going to have to tread carefully. If I'm careless around him, I'll drown and suffer deeply for it. But I'll think about that tomorrow. Right now, I'm pulling to a stop along the curb outside a single-level brick home with a tidy front yard and manicured bushes along the front of the house. Ace climbs off his motorcycle and walks over to my car, then opens the door for me.

"This is your house?" I ask, taking in the large oak tree in the front yard. Ace tugs on his left ear as a faint smile crosses his lips.

"No, I live here with my buddy, Ethan. It's his house."

"You're looking a little green, Mr. Officer, you sure this is okay?"

He laughs, pulls my duffle bag from the backseat of the car, and walks with me to the front door. We walk into a small mudroom that opens to the living room, which looks nothing like I assumed it would. Sure, there's a massive television and sound system, but the furniture is nice, plush and clean.

"What's up, buttercup?" a guy—I'm assuming, Ethan—with shaggy brown hair says from the couch.

Ace's cheeks flush pale pink and then he clears his throat. "I've...uh, I brought—"

The guy turns around and his jaw drops. "Dude! You brought a girl home," he says, jumping up from the camel-colored couch. He leaps over the back like a runner jumping hurdles, and stops in front of us.

"It's not what it looks like," Ace says, stepping back and holding his hands up. "This is Stacey." Ethan's eyes narrow and he cocks his head to the side. "The girl I rented my house to?"

Ethan nods and then offers me his hand. "I'm Ethan, Ace's br—"

"Roommate," Ace says, interrupting his friend. "The house freaking flooded so I'm giving up my room until she can move back in."

My jaw drops as I gaze up at Ace. "You said there was a spare bedroom," I say, confused. "I'm not taking your room and sleeping in your bed."

"It's fine, the couch is really comfortable," Ace argues, then plants his hands on my shoulders and guides me to his bedroom. The room is sparse, with only a king-size bed on a metal frame, a tall dresser, a chair off in the corner, and a black wire dog crate, sans dog. The walls are bare and there are no pictures on the top of his dresser. The room is void of any personality whatsoever.

"Did you just move in here?" I ask, sitting in the chair.

Ace shakes his head and clears out two of his five drawers for me. "I've lived here for almost five years." He walks over to a door, which appears to be a small walk-in closet, and pushes his clothes to the side. "You can put your things in the dresser and in the closet while you stay here."

"Ace, I don't want your room," I say, standing from the chair and moving toward him. He steps out of the closet with his brows knitted together and drops his hands at his sides. "I'm totally fine with the couch. Besides, it would be weird sleeping in your bed." *Without you*, I don't add.

"You're sleeping in my bed, end of discussion," Ace deadpans. He moves to the bed, pulls back the gray comforter, and tears off the sheets and tosses them into a hamper in the closet. "There's a spare set of sheets in the closet outside the bedroom, can you grab them for me?"

Nodding, I walk out of the room and run right

into Ethan's chest. His hands grip my arms to steady me, then he steps back, releasing me.

"Sorry about that," he says with a smile playing on his lips. He's not as tall as Ace, but he's still good looking with his shaggy brown hair and chocolate brown eyes. He's broad in the shoulders and narrow at the waist. "Everything okay in there?" he asks, jerking his chin toward Ace's bedroom.

"Yeah," I say, feeling deflated. "He won't let me take the couch, though. I feel weird taking his bed."

Ethan shrugs and then says, "Yeah, get used to it. He can be pretty damn stubborn." He rubs the back of his neck, peers over my shoulder into Ace's room, and then claps his hands together at his waist, making me jump. "Well, it was nice to meet you. I'm heading to bed."

"Nice meeting you too," I say, then open the door to a surprisingly organized linen closet. I pull a set of gray sheets from a shelf and return to Ace's bedroom. He's standing at the dresser without a shirt on and I'll be honest, my eyes are glued to his toned back and the tattoo on his left arm that wraps completely around his impressive bicep and down past his elbow. Licking my lips and then pulling my bottom lip between my teeth, I watch as he pulls a white t-shirt from a drawer and pulls it on over his head.

Ace turns to me, his eyebrow raised, and I realize I just freaking groaned. Out loud. Because he covered his glorious body with a t-shirt. Heat rushes up my neck and settles on my cheeks, and like a blubbering idiot I push off the doorframe and start putting the clean sheets on his bed. From the corner of my eye, I catch a smile work its way onto Ace's lips but it soon disappears as he helps me with the sheets.

"Where's your dog?" I ask after the bed is made.

Ace glances at the kennel, then back to me. "He's doing some training."

"Oh. I was hoping to meet him."

Ace shrugs and leaves the room. Mr. Quiet and Brooding is back. Awesome.

***

Poor Julia and my inconsistent work schedule. I hated calling in today, but she understood and even offered to help with cleanup. When I explained that Ace has it covered, she wished me luck.

Ace refused to let me sleep on the couch last night, and as much as I fought him on it, he won and I slept like a baby. His bed may just be the most comfortable thing I've ever slept in, and I might steal it when I move back into my house. Both Ethan and Ace are at work, and while they both said to make myself at home, it's strange staying someplace where nothing belongs to you. I grab a quick bowl of cereal, take a shower, and try to figure out how to work the TV and sound system. Guys and their stupid surround sound…why does it take a degree in electrical engineering to figure out how it works? I struggle for almost ten minutes then give up and decide a trip to my house is in order.

When I pull up along the curb, I gasp at the sight before me. Dozens of workers are scurrying around the house, pulling out furniture, Ace's kitchen cabinets, and…shit, all my clothes. They've strung them up over low branches to dry them out. There are bras and panties all over my front yard. I let my head fall onto the steering wheel, which only produces a loud, annoying honk and adds to my embarrassment. This is one way to get back at me for breaking his house.

I step outside my car and slowly walk up the path to the front door. Men nod and continue sucking up the water with long hoses, and circulating fans are drying out the house. I step inside only to be greeted by a young, dimpled man with sandy blond hair and gray-green eyes.

"Morning," he says, smiling ear to ear, giving me a good shot of his deep dimples. "You the owner of all the clothes outside?"

Heat rises to my cheeks while I nod and watch the men working.

"Is there a garbage bag around here?" I ask, scanning the bare rooms.

"I'm not sure, but you don't need to help. This is our job." Dimples smiles again and leans against the wall. I don't miss how his eyes travel the length of my body.

"I wasn't planning on helping. Just need something to put my clothes in so I can wash and dry them."

"I'm Braden," he says to my boobs. "I'll see what I can find." He walks to the small pantry and pulls out a trash bag and brings it to me. "Want some help?" he asks, glancing at my red lace bra dangling from a branch.

I shrug, turn around, and start gathering clothes. I can feel Braden right behind me, and when I look back, he's holding up one of my black bras and smiling like a teenager.

"What I wouldn't give to see you in this," he says, a smirk playing on his lips. He tosses the bra into the garbage bag and I roll my eyes. We work in tandem until the bag is full. As I prepare to tie it up, Braden holds up my red lace bra and runs it through his fingers.

"Can't quite say I've ever seen anyone try to soak up a flood with their bra. Quick thinking, but this…" He twists it in his hand. "This isn't going to soak up anything."

We both laugh and I pull my bra from his hand, but he catches my wrist and pulls me close. A little too close, but I don't pull away. He's funny and not bad looking. I glance up at him and watch his thick lashes flutter as he licks his lips.

"How about I take you out to dinner tonight?" His thumb brushes my palm and I think he expects it to do something to me. Instead, it makes me reconsider my proximity to him.

"I'm sorry," I say, then step back. "I'm not available."

"As in you're busy tonight, or…?"

"As in she's unavailable." My eyes close at the sound of his voice and my heart thuds against my chest, like it's trapped and trying to escape. Ace's hand rests on my shoulder and the heat from it shoots through me, piercing me to my core.

"If you're going to flirt on the job, then you can take your sorry ass home," he says to Braden.

Braden tosses his hands up and backs away. He retreats inside the house, leaving Ace and me standing at odds in the front yard.

Chapter 18

Ace

His freaking hands were on her bra. Shit! My temper is spiking and it pisses me off to no end. I can't let myself get worked up over this girl, but damn it was killing me to watch him flirt with her. What's worse is how her fingers kept tucking her hair behind her ear like she was gobbling up his attention. The jerk walked back inside the house, hopefully returning to do the job I'm paying for.

Stacey pulls away, turns around, and places her hands on her hips. Her brown eyes narrow at me and her jaw works in a slow, angry circle.

"What the hell was that, Ace?" she asks, cocking her hip to one side. Her cheeks blush a rose-red color and I'm fighting everything within myself not to pull her close and kiss the hell out of her.

Instead, I shove my hands in my pockets, keeping them safe. Keeping *me* safe, and say, "I'm paying him to clean up this mess, not flirt with you."

"He was helping me gather up my clothes, which were hanging all over the yard for everyone to see. So, thank you for that."

I yank my hands out of my pockets and scrub them over my face. "You think I told them to hang your bras and panties outside? Seriously, what kind of guy do you think I am?"

Stacey rolls her eyes and folds her arms across her chest. Her hair is once again falling out of her messy bun and with the sun behind her, she looks like an angel bathed in light.

"I really don't know," she says, her eyes looking anywhere but at me. And it's in this very moment the pull is too much.

My feet betray the distance I'm forcing between us and they step closer to her. It's quick, the way my hands cup her cheeks and gently turn her head so her eyes are locked on mine. Her long lashes flutter, her lips part like she's preparing to say something. But mine have their own agenda and it includes consuming anything she might say and swallowing the words like my next meal.

My tongue glides across my lips just before I press them to hers. Her eyes close as her body melts into mine and the gentle touch is gone. I pull away, lick my lips again, and dive back down, a hunger for more taking over. I'm not a patient man, so when Stacey's hands run up my back and fist in the fabric of my shirt, I press forward and groan into her mouth. There's no waiting or asking permission, my tongue parts her lips and takes what it wants.

I'm a man starved, and devouring the feel and taste of her like she's my last meal. My hand grips the back of her neck, tugging on the loose strands of hair falling from her bun. Her tongue swirls around mine and I want more of her. So. Much. More.

The realization hits me of what I'm doing and I jerk away, taking three steps backward, and run my hands through my hair. Stacey's lips are swollen and red, her hair is almost completely hanging loose from her bun, and she's staring up at me with watery eyes.

"Dammit," I growl, then stalk back to my motorcycle and drive away. What the hell did I just do? My lips still feel the heat of hers on mine and it's driving me freaking crazy. Everything about this girl turns me inside out and makes me forget myself. Forgetting is not an option; I don't deserve to have a clean slate or to be free of the memories that haunt me.

The entire ride to work I can't concentrate on anything but the way Stacey was looking at me as I left. I know I hurt her when I walked away, but what else was I supposed to do? I shouldn't have kissed her.

I shouldn't have liked it.

I shouldn't want more. But God, do I want more.

I sit in the precinct filling out paperwork, fielding calls all while trying to keep my mind occupied on anything but Stacey. Kilty's sitting at the desk in front of mine, eating those damn powdered sugar donuts again, and which each bite, the white powder falls onto his uniform. At noon, I head out to grab a bite to eat and wind up receiving a call to go out in the field. Thank the stars because I'm not sure I can handle any more deskwork today.

Duke's been at training for the past week and he's needed for this job, so I scoop him up from the kennels and drive across town to the railroad district. It's a shady part of Warner and a lot of shit goes down here, especially in the abandoned warehouses. A tip was called in about a drug deal going down this afternoon, and this is what I live for. Busting the idiots who supply the youth with drugs and keep them high enough they always come back for more.

Six patrol cars and our two K-9 units meet up at a location several blocks away to discuss the options. Kilty, Rogers, and Phillips will go in on the east side and sweep through the lower warehouse sector. Hamilton, Black, and Andrews will take the west, while Fredricks and Matthews will man the south. Duke and I, along with Coulter and his dog Bruno, will work our way in on the north side. The rest of the crew will hold back and wait for further instruction.

Busts like this usually end up either successful or a complete flop due to lookouts or misinformation. I need a freaking success if I'm going to make it through the day. The crews disperse, making their way to the check-in points while Coulter and I pull on our gear and then help the dogs into theirs. Duke hasn't been on a bust in over three months and as well-trained as he is, he's as anxious as I am to move. His big brown eyes stare up at me, begging for us to get to work.

"Just a little while longer, boy," I say, scratching behind his ear. He whines, then sits beside me like the good dog he is.

131

"East checkpoint secure," Kilty says over the radio. Soon, all the check points are set and the captain tells us to advance and calls for radio silence.

"Let's go, boy. Let's go," I say, and Duke lurches into a jog as we make our way to the warehouse district.

***

Two hours later, the warehouses are clear and all we manage to detain is a juvenile dealer trying to sell marijuana. Phillips cuffs him and escorts him to the patrol car while reading the boy his rights. Duke looks at me and I swear he and I are thinking the same thing, and feeling the same disappointment. Adrenaline is pumping through my body and there is no way I'm going to be able to sit at the desk the rest of the day without doing something about it.

"Hey, Captain," I say, walking up to him. "I need to blow off some steam. I'm heading to the gym and then I'll be back."

"Sure thing, Ace. Good work out there today," he says through his bushy gray mustache. "Hey, I need another man on the floor tonight, you feel up to working a double?"

Damn. "Yeah, I can do that. See ya later." Back at my SUV, I remove Duke's gear and he jumps in. I scratch his ears and tell him he's a good boy. He walks in a circle then lies down, his eyes trained on me. "You waiting for your treat, boy?" His ears perk up and I pull a treat from my pocket and let him have it.

I drop Duke off at the kennels at the precinct then head to the gym all while grumbling to myself about my disappointing day. I don't mind working a double, but double desk duty is not my idea of productive. Nor is it the cure for my overactive brain when it comes to thinking about Stacey and the piss-poor bust. At the gym, I start on the elliptical to run off the feel of her hands on my chest, on my back, and behind my neck. When that doesn't work, I turn to the weight bench and try to push all thoughts of her from my mind.

"Dammit!" I say, dropping the weights back on their shelves. I need to get a freaking grip. I'm not a violent man, but right now I need to hit something. Glancing around the gym, I notice the hanging bag in the corner. That. I need to punch that.

Over and over. And over.

"Hey, Marty!" I shout over the music to the gym owner. He glances up from the leg press and I call him over. His bald head glistens with sweat that drips onto his black muscle shirt. "I need help wrapping my hands." I hold up my hands, hoping he'll tape them so I don't hurt myself.

"You gonna start fighting?" he asks, pulling the tape from a nearby cart.

"Nah, I just need to hit something."

"I could hook you up in the light heavyweight competitions if you're interested. You've got the build for it." Marty wraps my hands while trying to convince me to start fighting, and as tempting as it is at this very moment, I don't have the heart for it. Nor the pain tolerance.

"I'm good, man. I'm just going to hit this bag for

a while."

Marty jerks his head in acknowledgement and returns to his workout, leaving me to fight my demons in the form of this blue hanging bag.

Chapter 19

Stacey

I spent the day reeling from Ace's kiss and the way I felt it in my toes. A kiss like that doesn't happen every day, and Heaven knows it's been a while for me. I could have stood in the front yard all day with his lips on mine and not cared what the neighbors thought. So when he pulled away, looking like he just made a huge mistake, I couldn't help the stabbing pain pulsing in my chest.

The Wash-n-Fold and I became really good friends considering I spent almost four hours there washing and drying my clothes and towels. And on the plus side, I met Hank, a homeless veteran who shares his time here and at another laundromat a few blocks away. He told me about fighting in Vietnam and how when he came home his wife had left him and taken their two children with her. When I asked him if he ever sees his boys, a far-off look washed over his face as a single tear slid down his scruffy cheek. After all my things were folded, he helped put them in my car and I offered him one of my heavy blankets. He smiled when he took it, revealing two missing front teeth.

After the laundromat, I drove around Warner, familiarizing myself with the roads and city, and stopped off at a large, hilly park. I walked around for a while and even sat on a swing, letting myself become reacquainted with my inner-child. Young children laughed and screamed while playing tag or climbing the massive play structure. I made a mental note to tell Reggie about this place so she can bring Micah next time they're up here.

When I've exhausted all my ideas to keep myself away from Ace's house, I gather my courage and do what I do best when I'm nervous or stressed: cook. Finding the nearest grocery store on the GPS on my phone, I drive a few miles and head inside. Scanning the shelves and fresh produce, I come up with a menu any man would love to eat. I make my purchases then smile as I walk out of the store with the makings of a great dinner.

Twenty minutes later, I have the chilled steaks resting on the counter and seasoned with salt and pepper and a little bit of granulated garlic. While those warm up to room temperature, I peel and dice potatoes, tossing them into a large stockpot with a dash of salt. Next, I prepare asparagus by rolling them in olive oil and salt and pepper, and then lay them out on a baking sheet.

Ethan steps through the front door as the potatoes start to boil and stares at me like he's died and gone to Heaven.

"You cook?" he asks, dropping to his knees.

"She cooks!" I laugh and slide the asparagus into the oven before helping him to his feet.

"Are you always this melodramatic?" I roll my eyes, press a finger to the steaks, and then start heating the cast iron skillet. "How do you like your steak?"

"I'll eat it however you cook it," Ethan says, sliding a satchel off his shoulder. He's wearing blue scrubs and I realize I have no idea what he does for work. "I'm going to go change. Don't eat without me."

Fifteen minutes later, a freshly showered Ethan walks into the kitchen wearing a pair of black gym shorts and a white t-shirt. His shaggy hair curls at the edges and flops over his eyes.

"Dinner will be ready in about five minutes," I say, stirring the gravy. Three place settings are on the table, along with the mashed potatoes, horseradish sauce, and asparagus. "What time does Ace usually get home?"

Ethan's jaw clenches as he sits down at the table. He dips a finger into the potatoes then brings a small scoop to his mouth. He groans, licks his finger clean, and then opens the beer I set out for him.

"Actually, he texted me and said he's working a double shift tonight. Something about being swamped at work."

In other words, he's avoiding me. That's just great. I finish up the gravy and join Ethan at the table.

"Dig in," I say, pulling a steak off the platter along with some asparagus. We eat almost in silence, except for the appreciative groans coming from Ethan's mouth.

"This is so good," he says between bites. "You got any dessert?"

I smile—he's such a man. "Yes, actually, I do. But we're going to play a little game before you get to eat any."

Ethan's smile falls as he considers my words. "What kind of game? Does it involve removing articles of clothing?" His smile returns while his brown eyes roam my upper body.

"All clothing will remain on," I answer, swatting my napkin in his direction. "I'm playing for information."

"That's not fair. What do I get?" he whines, pushing his plate away.

"Um…dessert?"

I quickly gather up the dishes, making sure to save a plate for Ace and cover it with plastic wrap. Just because he's avoiding me doesn't mean I can't still take care of him. Somehow I feel like he needs someone watching over him.

"All right, I want to see this dessert," Ethan says, glancing around the kitchen. I point to the fridge and he jumps up like an eager puppy waiting for a treat. His eyes widen in excitement as he pulls out the large pan of brownies. "This smells incredible."

"Thanks. You ready to play?"

He nods, but grabs a knife from the drawer before returning to the table.

"I'll make a deal with you," he says, smiling ear to ear. "For every question of yours I answer, I get to cut a piece of this and eat it."

"Sure," I say, shrugging my shoulders. "You'd just better leave some for Ace." I sit back in my chair, fold my arms across my chest, and decide to start with the easy questions first. "You came in the house wearing scrubs, what do you do for work?"

"You want to know what my job is?" he asks, his brows drawn together. I nod and smile, knowing I've surprised him. "I'm an ER nurse. And before you go and start making fun of me, let me say that I actually really love what I do."

"I wasn't going to make fun of you." I'm actually pretty impressed, but I do laugh when Ethan cuts a small square of brownie and then plops it into his mouth. His eyes roll back in his head as he groans some more.

"These are incredible. Are they homemade?"

"Um...yeah. I can't stand the way boxed brownies taste."

"Next question," he says, waggling his eyebrows and scoping out the brownie pan.

"How old are you?"

"Twenty-eight. Next." He cuts another brownie and gobbles it up quickly.

"How long have you known Ace?"

"I was wondering if this is where your questions would end up." He smiles like he has me pegged. Maybe he does, because truthfully, I'll take whatever information he's willing to share about Ace.

"We went to high school together...so about fourteen years." Another question, another brownie.

"Why does he live with you and not in his own house?"

Ethan's back grows rigid and his Adam's apple bobs in his throat. He lays the knife on the table and sits back in his chair. Did the room just grow cold, or is it just me? When it's obvious he's not sure how to answer, or that he won't answer, I decide to retract the question.

"Never mind. Obviously it's none of my business. Forget I asked."

"How much has he told you about himself?" he asks, staring straight at me with haunted eyes.

"Honestly…pretty much nothing. He's pretty closed off. I don't think he really likes me." I must be stupid for thinking this since he kissed me today. Though, I suppose you could kiss someone you don't like, but I imagine it wouldn't set my lips on fire and reverberate in my toes if there wasn't some kind of connection between us.

"Ace is…he's punishing himself for something he had no control over. He doesn't talk about it and I suppose he may never. But he was married…to my sister." Ethan pauses, glances out the kitchen window, and slowly closes his eyes. So he and Ace are more than friends, they're brothers. Or brothers-in-law, but still.

"What happened? You said was. Did they divorce?"

"Marley passed away five years ago and Ace blames himself. He had nothing to do with it, yet he constantly pushes people away, not willing to grow close because he's afraid he'll somehow hurt them."

"I'm really sorry," I say, sniffing back the wide range of emotions rolling through me. Not only did Ace lose his wife, but his best friend also lost a sister. "Can I ask how she died?"

Ethan's cheeks puff out as he releases a long breath. When his gaze returns to me, I can see the pain etched around his eyes and how it still affects him after five years. If he's still hurting like this, I can't imagine how Ace must feel. Oh God, what he must be feeling after our kiss this morning.

"Marley wasn't well. She suffered from depression, we just didn't know it was as bad as it was." My hand flies to my mouth, scared of where this story ends. I'm not sure I can handle it. "One day while Ace was at work, she tried to kill herself. Ace found her when he got home and she was pretty much gone."

"Oh my God," I whisper against my palm. Tears burn my eyes as I try to hold them back, but it's no use. They fall and my heart breaks for both Ace and Ethan. I feel horrible for accepting his kiss when it's obvious he's not ready to move on. He's tried to tell me in his own ways, but I've ignored the signs. And now we've crossed a line and I'm afraid of what it means.

"Hey, don't cry," Ethan says softly, moving to stand next to me. "I miss my sister, Ace misses his wife, but time heals all wounds, right? It's not his fault she's gone and it's not your fault Ace can be a jerk. He's still dealing with the guilt he carries because he thinks he could have saved her. He blames himself for not seeing the signs or getting her the help she needed."

"He kissed me today," I whisper as I look up at Ethan. His eyes bug out, most likely from shock, and his hand squeezes my shoulder.

"It's about damn time someone breaks through the walls he's built. Don't give up on him, Stacey. He needs you more than you and he know." We talk a bit more before Ethan heads off to bed, but not before I have him show me how to work the TV and surround sound. When he closes his door, I finish up the dishes and then change into a pair of shorts and a tank top in Ace's room. I bring a blanket with me to the couch where I proceed to watch television until I fall asleep.

Chapter 20

Ace

Working a double shift because I'm a fool and angry with myself for kissing Stacey probably isn't the best idea I've ever had. In fact, I'd say it ranks right up there with streaking through my parents' neighborhood when I was seventeen. I'm so tired I could fall asleep at my desk and probably will if I don't stand up and walk around.

Standing at the vending machine with my forearm pressed against the glass, all my brain can do is run circles around my lips on hers, her fingers at the nape of my neck, and how if we would have been alone, I would have had her naked beneath me. This fantasy of her and me has got to stop. It's not fair to either of us to go down this road that will lead to nowhere. The last thing I want to do is hurt her more than I already did today by walking away.

My shift ends at 2 a.m., and since eating an energy bar, I've woken up enough to safely ride my motorcycle home. Weaving through the streets of

Warner is nice this late at night…or this early in the morning, whichever way you look at it. Traffic is almost nonexistent, making my normal twenty-minute drive only twelve.

Based on the flickering faint blue light reflecting through the front window, I assume Ethan fell asleep watching TV again. Slowly opening the front door so as not to disturb him, I creep toward the couch and stop dead in my tracks. Stacey's curled up on her side, her red hair spilling over the pillow she's resting on, and one arm is draped over the cushion, nearly touching the floor. She's wearing a pair of short shorts and a thin white tank top that seriously should be illegal. It shows off every curve and peak and I'm going to lose my freaking mind. I move around the couch, pull the blanket from around her ankles, and drag it up to her shoulders.

There. At least her…assets are more concealed.

If I were a different man, there would be nothing stopping me from claiming her soft, plump lips again and making her mine. As I stand over her, my fingers twitch with the desire to touch her. Before my brain has time to catch up, I sit on the coffee table facing her and slowly push a thick strand of hair from her cheek. The tips of my fingers tingle at the mere touch and my resolve is crumbling.

Her skin is warm and smooth and, moving on their own, my fingers trail down her neck to her shoulders. Stacey shifts at my touch, rolling from her side to her back, making the blanket slip down past her breasts. Why in the hell is she wearing such a revealing tank top? And why in the hell am I still sitting here with my hand hovering over her pert breasts?

Groaning, I move to stand, but her husky voice, scratchy due to sleep, halts me. "Ace? What are you doing?" Damn. She's even sexier waking up with her hair askew.

I clear my throat, trying to get the image of her breasts out of my head. "Sorry, I was getting ready to turn the TV off, but covered you with a blanket first. You, uh...looked cold." Without meaning to, I glance at her tank top, only to be greeted with two firm buds taunting me.

"What time is it?" she asks, sitting upright and pulling the blanket over her long legs. I search the room quickly, wishing for another blanket to cover her top half.

"It's almost two thirty. I didn't mean to wake you." Finally, I find the remote behind me and turn off the television, cloaking the room in darkness. In hindsight, maybe it wasn't the brightest idea. The conscience often disappears in the dark after midnight. "Why aren't you in my bed?" I don't recognize the low register of my own voice, nor the twinge in my throat at how much I *want* her in my bed. With me.

"It's your bed, Ace. I'm fine sleeping on the couch while I stay here. Really, I don't mind."

There is no freaking way I'm coming home every day to her sleeping on the couch in next to nothing. "I want you in my bed," I say, and then immediately realize my poor choice of words. "I mean—"

"I know what you mean," Stacey says, a light blush settling on her cheeks.

Nodding, I move to stand, but decide to stifle any further thoughts of her and I sharing a bed instead.

"I also wanted to apologize for this morning. It was wrong of me to kiss you and I hope you understand it can't happen again." By the wide-eyed expression she's offering me, this is coming as a shock to her and I don't know why, but it irritates me. She's looking at me like I've pulled the rug out from under her, when, in fact, it is she who has surprised me. I didn't want someone like her in my life causing me to question the past five years.

"Ace, I'm sorry," she says, laying her hand on mine.

A shock of heat rushes up my arm, settling in my chest, making me even more certain whatever this is needs to stop. I jerk my hand from hers, and clasp my hands behind my neck.

"I never meant to make you uncomfortable. It's not my intention to try to replace your wife."

What the…?

I nearly knock the coffee table over as I jump to my feet and try to scramble away. My confusion turns to red-hot anger and it's bubbling dangerously close to the surface. A tremor works its way down my arms and to my fingers, and in order to keep from breaking the closest inanimate object, I ball my hands into fists and shove them in my pockets. My blood is boiling, sweat is beading on my brow, and my chest is constricting, making it hard to breathe. How the hell did she find out about Marley? And what the hell am I going to do with her?

My legs carry me back and forth across the living room while Stacey follows my every move. She doesn't offer any further apologies for bringing up my wife or overstepping her bounds. And at this moment, I don't know what I'd say to her if she did. I've not felt blind rage like this in years and it makes me feel weak and small. Some men feed off anger, I cower at it because anger is an evil thing that pollutes everyone around you.

Stacey stands, the blanket falls completely away, revealing her shapely body, and I turn my back to her. In a flash, her warmth surrounds me and her arms clasp together around my chest. My body quakes under her touch, my heart stutters then slips through the cracks made by her embrace. And in this moment I have to do damage control. Cut off the head before we're in too deep.

My hands peel her arms off me and I move away, my rage diminishing but not forgotten. "I don't know why you think it's okay to talk about my wife, but it's not. I'm guessing you talked to Ethan, and the fact that you asked about me pisses me off, not to mention the things he must have told you." I pause to take a breath, knowing I have to prepare the final blow. "Just leave me the hell alone. I don't need your help, and I don't want you. And that kiss...forget about it because it's never happening again."

Lies. They're slick little devils that burn as they're spoken. I turn to face her and what I see crumbles what's left of my already shattered heart. There are no tears, no trembling lips, no far-off looks of hurt. Instead, her brown eyes cut into me like razor sharp steel. It's like I can see the barrier she's built in a hurry around herself and it's fortified with an anger so thick it fills the room.

"You're an asshole," she whispers, quickly moving back to the couch where she gathers the blanket from the floor and then disappears down the hallway. The door to my room opens with a squeal and closes with a snick. I stand in the middle of the room, rebuilding walls of my own, realizing they weren't as impenetrable as I thought they were. Thicker, higher, and more resilient, that's what they need to be.

That's what I need to be.

Chapter 21

Stacey

I will not cry or show weakness in front of him. I will not...cry. *Shit*. Why is it I always screw everything up? I knew how fragile Ace was, yet my big mouth had to go and say something stupid. Of course I'm not trying to replace his dead wife. I'm not even trying to start a relationship with him—other than a friendship. But no. I had to go and poke the lion and get bitten in the worst kind of way.

Inside his room, I pull my duffle bag down from the top of the closet and start throwing what I can into it. I thought maybe it could work—staying here—but I see now there's no way. Not with the anger seething off Ace. It's so thick and heavy, no wonder he can't move on. I gather my makeup, hair dryer, and curling wand from the bathroom, tossing them into the bag as well, and then sit on the edge of Ace's bed. A defeated sigh floats from my lips as a tear slips down my cheek. It seems no matter how hard I try to hold them back they're determined to

149

fall.

And I let them. What's the use in keeping them inside now? Where one falls, several others follow until I climb across the bed and bury my head in the pillows. Tomorrow, I'll move my things to a hotel and deal with the exorbitant fees. Losing a bit of money is less painful than staying someplace you're not wanted.

***

Showered, dressed, and ready for work, I grab my duffle bag, step out of Ace's room, and walk to the kitchen. He's still sleeping on the couch, so instead of grabbing myself a bowl of cereal for breakfast, I scour the kitchen for a pad of paper and a pen. The scratchy drawl of the pencil on the paper grates on me as I scribble a note letting him know I'll stay at a hotel from here on out. It's what I need to do because the tension between us is growing more and more awkward as the minutes tick by. As much as he's trying to help me out, it's only confusing me and hurting what could be a great friendship.

At the door, I glance back to the couch and gulp back a gasp—he's wearing only a pair of black boxer briefs. He was fully covered five minutes ago with a navy plaid blanket. My eyes peruse his mostly naked form and realize he's a work of art. Every muscle is defined, thick and corded, even in his sleep. The tattoo on his left arm starts at his shoulder and wraps around his bicep, stopping just below his elbow. As my eyes work their way down his body, it's quite apparent his circulation is working well. My cheeks flame as his hand moves over his boxers briefs to adjust himself.

I am totally busted.

I fumble for the door handle, unable to take my eyes off him. Finally, I connect with the handle, turn, and slowly open the door. His eyes flutter open and he takes in the sight before him, a knowing smile passing over his lips.

"Like what you see?" he asks, his hand resting over his junk. Oh. My. God. Not only are my cheeks glowing, my chest feels like it's on fire.

"You may want to take care of...you know..." Unable to finish a thought, I glance at his boxers, turning yet another shade darker, and then return my gaze to his face. "I've got to go to work."

I step outside, quickly shut the door, and make a dash to my car. No one should look as good as he does and sleep almost naked where anyone can stumble upon him. It's a good thing I'm moving to a hotel tonight.

The drive to work consists of stop-and-go traffic and images of a nearly naked Ace invading my thoughts. It's going to be a long freaking day if I can't get him out of my head. My cheeks burn once again and my stomach lurches as I recall the status of his boxer briefs and what lurked underneath. I'm not a prude, I've had my share of one-night stands and short relationships. But seeing...*that* has my nerves totally buzzing, reminding me exactly how long it's been since I've had *that* near me. In any capacity.

The conversation with Ethan also runs through

my head, making me wonder how long it's been for Ace. If he's unwilling to get close to anyone, does he pick up random women and take them home to satisfy his needs? No. A hotel maybe. I can't picture him bringing anyone to Ethan's house. Especially remembering the look he gave Ace when I followed him through the door. Whatever he does, it's none of my business, and truthfully, I don't think I really want to know.

I pull through the McDonald's drive-thru, grabbing a quick breakfast to eat in the car, and arrive five minutes early to work. Once inside, I flip on all the lights, clock in, and start a pot of coffee in the back room. Julia wanders in a couple hours later wearing a big grin, flowing cotton pants, and a loose linen shirt that ties at the collar. She looks ready for a beach vacation sans the big floppy hat.

"So, I have some news," she says, setting her purse under the front counter. Her eyes scan the store with love and admiration before settling back on me.

"Let me guess," I say, grinning. "You're leaving for Hawaii and taking me with you?" I laugh, secretly wishing it were true. I'd love to visit Hawaii.

"Sadly, no. But my news is almost as good." Julia unfolds a chair from behind the counter and asks for me to sit. She unfolds another and sits in front of me. Why do I feel like I'm about to receive an unwelcome lecture?

"My husband has finally retired," she says, unable to stop the smile that lights up her face. She's never mentioned her husband and I never thought to ask if she was married, so this is news to me. "He wants us to move to Florida and I've agreed."

Um...what? My jaw falls and I have no idea where to look because I'm suddenly feeling like I'm about to lose my job.

"Wow. That's...great?" My voice is thick with confusion and threatening to quake with hurt.

"I know! I can hardly believe it. He's been saying he would retire for almost five years now. But he's done it and he's ready to move. I've always wanted to live there and this is the opportunity we've been waiting for."

My cheeks puff out as I exhale a deep breath. "So what will you do with the bookstore?" In other words, I guess I'll be job hunting...again.

"That's the best part," she says, practically squealing. "Nothing. I have you now. You can run the store!"

If my jaw drops any more, I'll be eating flies for lunch. "You want me to run the store? Like...be the boss?" Julia nods eagerly. "I'm honored, but are you sure? I mean, I've only worked for you about a month. I don't know everything there is to running the store."

Julia playfully slaps my knee and laughs at my outburst. "Of course I'll train you for the next two weeks, but then if you're up for it, the store is yours. You'll need to hire someone to come in part time and I can help you with that."

"Why would you leave me in charge? I just don't understand." Stuff like this never happens in the real world, which is why I probably sound like the most ungrateful person alive.

"When you stepped inside that first day, I knew there was something special about you. You're a great person, Stacey, and I know you're way more capable of running this place than you believe. I trust you and think you deserve this."

Julia retrieves her purse from under the counter, stands, and folds the chair back up. Her eyes travel the store once again and then she turns back to me.

"Tell you what. I have some errands to run today but will be back before you leave. Take the day to think about it and tell me your decision tomorrow. Okay?"

I slowly nod my head, still in shock. Julia smiles graciously, pats my shoulder, and leaves me alone in the store with my head spinning. Never in my life would I have guessed something like this would happen. That being said, do I want to run a bookstore the rest of my life? Or at least for the foreseeable future? She didn't say I had to stay forever, yet what else would I do? The thought of going back to college makes my stomach turn. But if I accept, it means staying here in Warner for who knows how long.

Sure, I moved here to be closer to Reggie, and I'm grateful to be here. But can I see calling Warner my home for the next five years or longer? So far, I don't have anything tying me here, and technically I'm homeless since the house I'm renting is torn apart.

Holy crap, my life is a mess.

Chapter 22

Ace

Getting caught with your hand moving over your morning wood isn't particularly how I envisioned my day starting. Nor, as my vision clears, is the note sitting on the kitchen cabinet. Like hell she's going to stay at a hotel until the house is finished. My fist crumples the paper and I toss it in the trash. Not freaking happening. Back in the living room, I pull my phone from off the end table and shoot off a text to Stacey.

Me: Your ass had better be sleeping in my bed when I get back home tonight.

Shit! Why is it everything I say always comes out wrong? And why has no one invented a text-retracting feature? Like somehow you should be able to cancel or edit a text up to two minutes after you've sent it. Because shit like what I've just texted will always be interpreted wrong.

Me: You know what I mean.

There. Maybe that will clear the air.

Stacey: (…)

Damn that ellipsis. In the end, she doesn't respond, and it pisses me off. I head to the basement to run off some steam instead of stewing about how this girl has found her way under my skin and how it terrifies me. I tried so hard last night to push her away, and in the end, I obviously got what I wanted. But it sure as hell doesn't feel very good. In fact, my chest is so tight it's making running on the elliptical very difficult.

Sufficiently worked up after trying to run and then weight lifting, I head back upstairs to shower. Since working a double, I have the day off, but I need to run to the station and bring Duke home. His training will be done today and I miss him. That dog has saved me in more ways than I can count.

I shrug on a vintage t-shirt and a pair of loose-fitting sweats and head to the kitchen for a quick bite to eat. Ethan sits at the table eating some toast and scrolling through texts or something on his phone.

"You missed an amazing dinner," he says with a mouthful of toast.

"Yeah?" I pull open the door to the fridge and can't help the twinge in my throat at the plate of food sitting on the shelf covered in plastic wrap. Damn, she saved me some dinner and I essentially made her so uncomfortable she moved out.

"I'm an asshole," I mumble, which makes Ethan's head pop up.

"You just figuring that out?" he asks with a smirk.

"Shut up." I pull off the plastic wrap and stick the plate in the microwave. Nothing wrong with a little steak and potatoes for breakfast, especially when it smells as good as this does. By the time the food is heated through, my mouth is watering. I grab a knife and fork and join Ethan at the table. The first bite of steak has me moaning like a man starved. "Holy shit, this is good."

Ethan smiles, nodding his head. "She also made brownies. Homemade." He jerks his chin toward the fridge and I jump up, grabbing the pan, practically salivating. "Can we keep her?" Ethan bats his eyelashes and rests his chin on the backs of his hands on the table.

"We can't make her live here just to feed your fat ass," I say between bites of steak and potato. "Besides, she's not coming back."

Ethan sits ramrod straight in his chair and narrows his eyes at me. "You gonna tell me what you did to make her leave? Because you really are an asshole if you did something to hurt her." He abandons the last half of his piece of toast, eyeing me like he's challenging me to tell him just how cruel I was to her last night. My breakfast eaten and my attitude tanking, I stand and move to the counter.

"I kissed her," I say, tossing my fork into the sink.

"Yeah, so what?" The look on his face tells me

he's not surprised.

"She told you?" Of course she told him. Apparently, my life has suddenly become an open forum. "Oh, and thanks for telling her about Marley, you ass."

"So you kissed her. What's the big deal?"

"She's not Marley," I answer with a huff. "Besides, I told her it wouldn't happen again and that it was a mistake."

"Jesus. Are you really still that effed up over what happened?" He gathers his plate and discards the remnants of his breakfast in the trash. He stands beside me at the counter with his arms folded across his chest. "Man, you need to move on. Marley's gone and it wasn't freaking your fault."

"I should have seen the signs," I say, feeling the breath catching in my lungs. "So, yeah. It was my fault."

"What are you going to do about Stacey? I see the way you look at her and I know you wouldn't have kissed her if there wasn't something there."

I push off the counter and release a shaky breath. "I'm not going to do anything about her. I'm no good for her—you and I both know that."

"That's a crap excuse, Ace. She's good for you and you for her. Girls like her don't come around every day, and if you don't do something about this, she's going to get away from you. Hell, I'd ask her out if I thought she'd go for it."

The hell he will. The hairs on my neck raise and my muscles tense just thinking about Ethan and Stacey together.

"Why haven't you asked her out? She means

nothing to me." *Lies. Godawful lies.* My only saving grace is Stacey's not here listening to us go back and forth. If saying this sends a shooting pain throughout my body, I can only imagine what it would do to her. To be fair, it would be the end of this thing between us.

"You're not only an asshole, but you're the dumbest dude I know. That girl's crazy about you and I'm fairly certain you know it."

I shrug and stalk out of the kitchen. I'm done talking about this with Ethan. He's my brother-in-law and I won't disrespect Marley or her family by discussing another woman.

My keys are in my room and when I step inside, Stacey's scent wraps around me and I silently curse myself for putting her in my bed. Peaches and lilies have stained my sheets, my pillows, and my soul. Shit. Not my soul…just…ah hell. In a burst of frustration, I yank off the sheets and toss them into the dirty clothes, noting the other set of sheets already in there. More laundry, more peaches and lilies, and more thoughts of Stacey.

Stacey. Stacey. *Stacey.*

***

By the time I'm at the station, my nerves are shot. I park my motorcycle, storm into the building, and breeze past reception without so much as a passing glance. Heads turn my way as I cut through the desks and make my way to the rear of the building where the kennels are. Duke's there. He'll make everything better.

159

"Hey, Blevins, I'm here to pick up Duke," I say to the paunchy older man sitting at the kennel desk. He shoves his glasses up over his nose and waves me through. As soon as I see my dog's eyes, my pulse lowers and I can finally breathe. I slide the lock open, clip the leash to his collar, and thank Blevins. Every few months, Duke undergoes a week of intensive training, which is more like a refresher course, and I miss him terribly when he's gone. I've learned to not only put my life in his hands when we're out on a bust together, but he's my family.

Outside the building, I trade my motorcycle for the K-9 SUV and drive home to spend some much needed time with Duke.

After a run in the park, a few games of fetch, and wrestling, Duke's worn out and I'm starved. It's after six, which means Stacey will be done working for the day, and if I wasn't such a jerk, she'd be on her way here. But I'm a jerk and she's not coming here.

I really want her here.

And so it's time to apologize and pull off my biggest lie yet.

Me: You can have the couch.

Me: I don't want you to stay at a hotel.

Stacey: I'm fine, Ace. Gonna stay at the Motel 6 down the street.

I want to beat my phone on my forehead and yell at her at the same time. Why is she acting so stubborn?

Me: Fine. I'll come steal your room key so you can't stay there. Such a waste of money.

Stacey: You wouldn't.

Me: Try me.

Stacey: (…)

Me: Please.

Stacey: Fine. But you're cooking dinner tonight.

Dinner. I can do dinner.

Stacey pulls up outside the house twenty minutes later and my pulse skyrockets. Duke whines when her car door shuts and he races to the window. Ethan's head pops up from the back of the couch and he eyes me suspiciously. When she knocks, I remember the lie I've promised myself and take a couple deep breaths before pulling the door open. *Friends.* We're just going to be friends.

"Hey," she says through a whispered breath, and my heart lurches in my chest. Her hand moves to tuck a stray hair behind her ear and then my dog nudges her thigh, making her shriek. "Sorry, I wasn't expecting that."

"Duke, away," I order. He obeys, leaving Stacey and me standing awkwardly at the front door. She steps around and I close it, and then follow her to the couch. Ethan, Stacey, and I all sit stiffly while we wait on the pizza to be delivered.

"So that's Duke?" she asks, turning her head to the pile of black and brown fur curled in a ball in the corner of the room. At the sound of his name, his ears perk up and he lifts his head, looking for permission to come meet our guest.

"Here," I say, and Duke jumps to his feet and saunters over. His big brown eyes look Stacey over before he sits at my feet.

"Can I pet him?" she asks, tentatively holding out her hand. I nod and she falls to her knees on the floor getting on Duke's level. My throat clenches as her hand absentmindedly falls to my thigh.

"He's beautiful. I've always thought German Shepherds were amazing dogs," she says, scratching behind his ears.

"Thanks, he came all the way from Germany as a pup." I stifle a laugh threatening to burst from my lips as I remember teasing Marley about Duke's language skills. "He didn't understand a lick of English when I first got him so I had to give him all his commands in German."

"Really? I never thought about dogs understanding different languages." She's running her hand down his back now and has finally removed her other hand from my thigh, leaving a warm tingle that's quickly turning cold. Ethan and I laugh, both knowing where this conversation is headed.

"What?" Stacey glances up at Ethan and then me, her brown eyes dancing with curiosity.

"Oh, nothing," Ethan says, balling his fist on the

couch. He's trying to contain his laughter as much as I am. "Why don't you teach her some of those German phrases, Ace?"

I shoot him a death glare, but cave, knowing the phrases I'm about to say are nothing short of vulgar. I shrug, sit up straight, and scoot my back against the couch as I bring out my best German accent. *"Kommen Sie auf meinem Schoß sitzen. Zeig mir deine Brüste."* I pull my lips between my teeth, holding in the laugh, but can't fight my spreading lips.

"What do those mean?"

"Come. And lay down," I lie, totally unable to contain my laughter.

"Wow. That's a lot of German words compared to their English counterparts," she says, totally oblivious that I just asked her to come sit on my lap and show me her boobs.

Chapter 23

Stacey

Ace makes me dizzy with how much he flip-flops. One minute he's hot, the next cold—I swear he's going to give me whiplash from his mood changes. This Ace, the relaxed and laid back version, is good and I like him very much. The way his eyes shine with love for his dog brings out an almost childish quality in him, like maybe he never had a dog as a kid and now he has one.

Eventually, Duke grows tired of me scratching behind his ears and nuzzling him and he returns to the corner of the living room. My duffle bag is still in my car but when I mention I need to grab it, Ace jumps off the couch and asks for my keys. Both Ethan and I glance up, wondering where the fire is.

"This has got to be one of the most awkward situations I've ever been in," Ethan says when Ace disappears out the front door. He huffs a breath and clasps his hands together behind his head, bumping my head with his elbow. "Sorry. How are you holding up?"

"Does it matter? I just want to have my own place again and not be in anyone's way." I scoot over about a foot, steering clear of Ethan's spear-like elbows. Ace returns, my duffle bag slung over his shoulder, and his eyes travel between Ethan and me before he grunts and stalks back to his bedroom.

"As long as you cook more food like last night, you sure as heck won't be in my way," Ethan teases, flashing a wide, toothy grin.

"I see how it is. You talked Ace into letting me stay so you could use me for my mad skills in the kitchen."

"You know it," he says before standing and saying good night. His shift starts early in the morning so he makes his excuses to get to bed early. And by early, I mean 9 p.m. early.

"You scare him off?" Ace teases from the hall. He takes the cushion next to me, leaving little space between us. My body doesn't realize we're just doing the whole "friends" thing and it warms at his proximity. If body heat had fingers, mine would be tracing the muscles in Ace's arms and abs and possibly dipping lower.

But we're just friends.

"No, he needed to go to bed," I say, scooting to the other end of the couch. "Duke is pretty cool." Body, meet distraction in the form of Duke the police dog.

Ace gives me one of his rare real smiles and scoops the remote off the coffee table. For the next forty minutes we stare at the TV, watching some spy show I can't follow. Julia's offer is running around in my mind and I'm working out the pros and cons of accepting.

"Keep that up and you'll have nothing left of your fingers," Ace says, startling me out of concentration. I glance down at my hands and realize I've chewed off all my fingernails and have come dangerously close to the quick. "You okay? Not sure I've ever seen you so focused on giving yourself a manicure using your teeth."

I twist on the couch so I'm facing Ace and tuck my feet under a pillow, warming my cold toes. "My boss offered to let me run the bookstore so she and her husband can retire in Florida." I shiver from the slight chill in the room and pull another pillow over my chest.

"Get over here," he says, tossing the pillow off my feet and body. His eyes flicker to mine and his normal glacier blue eyes darken to a foggy blue. But when he blinks, the color fades and he reaches across the couch to pull me closer. What can I say, my body still hasn't received the message about us being just friends. I curl into him, resting my head on his chest while his arms drape over me. Friends, Stacey. *Just friends. Ha! Friends who cuddle?*

"What did you tell her?" he asks, resting his chin on my head. "You're obviously torn about the offer."

Since we're friends, I have no idea what to do with my free hand. Do I let it rest limply at my side or do I drape it over his chest and let it settle where it lands? My hand raises on its own, but I force it down to rest on my thigh. Ace has other plans apparently, since his hand just took mine and placed it on his firm stomach. A few inches lower and I'd get up close and personal with Ace Jr., or whatever he calls it.

Deep breath. Or maybe I should just breathe normally because my head is starting to tingle.

"I asked her to let me think about it," I say, returning to the conversation. "She's leaving in two weeks and wants me to tell her my decision tomorrow."

"Do you want the job?" Ace's fingers trace circles on the back of my hand and I have to close my eyes tightly to talk myself down from doing something really stupid. Instead, I shrug and release a heavy sigh.

"Yes, but no. If I say yes, then I'm stuck running a bookstore forever. And I don't even know if I want to stay here in Warner."

Ace's hand stops moving over mine. "And if you say no?"

"Then I have to hunt for a job or go back home to Phoenix."

"You signed a six-month lease."

I laugh at the situation. "Yeah, well, I doubt you could hold me to the lease considering the house is currently uninhabitable."

"Do you want to go back to Phoenix? Have you always planned to leave here?" His fingers once again begin to move across my hand, lulling me into a relaxed state.

"I haven't really thought about it much. I only moved here to be closer to Reggie, but it's not the same now that she's married and lives an hour away. I guess I didn't realize it would never be the same since we're no longer roommates. I really miss her."

"Would you stay if I changed my mind about you sharing the house with someone else?" I tilt my head up, trying to determine if he's serious. When he glances down, everything is so clear in his eyes—sadness, hurt, and fear. I wish it could be me who erases it all and gives him the love he so clearly needs. "Do you still want that girl to move in with you?" The softness of his voice alone feels like a kiss. Like the words floated from his lips and settled on my cheek like the gentle fluttering from the wings of a butterfly.

If I rose up two inches, our lips would meet. They'd softly touch like we were testing the waters to see if proceeding further is safe. I'd feel the kiss in my toes and my heart would beat against my ribs. It would be magic.

But we're just friends.

The moment is interrupted by a whiny growl from Duke, who is still asleep in the corner of the room. Ace's arm pulls me closer and the TV distracts me enough that I forget how close we are and how easy it would be to kiss him.

***

Over the next few days, most of our nights consist of sitting together on the couch with Ace's arm draped over my shoulders. Ha! Like that's not confusing. And, obviously, I like being a glutton for punishment because each time his hand finds its way to my shoulder, I slide in next to him without question. After we spoke that first night about my job and Julia's proposal, I fell asleep with the image of Ace's haunted eyes burned into mine. Tossing and turning the whole night, when Julia arrived at work the next day, I let her know I would accept the job. She was so pleased she jumped up and down like a child and I couldn't help but join in with her.

Tonight, not wanting to put myself through any more torture by snuggling up to Ace, I've dubbed it video game night. I know they enjoy playing some alien hunting thing. It seems pretty straightforward so I'll join in too. Like peas in a pod, the three of us take our spots on the couch; the only difference tonight are the black game controllers in our hands.

"So I just move this thing to walk and push this button to shoot the gun?" I ask, holding the bulky object in my hand. Ace's lips curl into a cocky grin as he nods then starts the game. I'm not sure if I've ever mentioned my brother to him or Ethan, and for them to think I've never held a game controller is laughable. I'm pretty sure ninety percent of the world's population has held one of these.

"Take that, alien scum!" I shout as I shoot down another grotesque creature. Both Ace and Ethan sit stone still while playing, the only things moving are their fingers and eyes. I, on the other hand, can't sit still. My hands jerk back each time someone comes up from behind my avatar or shoots at me. When I kill an alien, I practically leap off the couch. I'm pretty much kicking ass and taking names.

By the start of the third game, Ethan turns his entire body toward me and stares at me while I eagerly await the alien ship's landing.

"I thought you said you never played before," Ethan says, scowling.

"What's the matter? Can't handle being beaten by a girl?" My laugh is partnered with Ace's chuckle and the hairs on my arms stand on end. His laugh is glorious—deep and guttural—like he saves up each laugh for just the right moment. "I have a brother. I've played plenty of Xbox. Just never this game." My smile falters as Ethan's face turns down in a frown and I try to hold in my laughter.

"Yeah, well, next time, don't play so dumb," he grumbles. "I'm no longer taking it easy on you. Game is on."

Chapter 24

Ace

It's been five days since I convinced Stacey to stay here after she left that note. *Five. Agonizing. Days.* Whenever she's near, my arms grow brains of their own and find any excuse to touch her or pull her close. My body freaking loves it. My head feels like it's the ball in a ping-pong match. I thought this game night idea of hers was brilliant. There would be no touching, no close calls with a slip of my lips accidentally finding hers. I could concentrate on the screen in front of me, the game controller in my hand, and my avatar on the screen. Kill aliens. I can do that.

Except when *she's* playing. Stacey brings a whole new responsibility to the game, like it's my job to watch out for her avatar and keep it safe. And then she goes and creams Ethan, jumping enthusiastically off the couch, allowing a sliver of her creamy white skin to show between the hem of her shirt and the top of her shorts. The freaking controller slips from my hands, landing on the carpet with a thud. My fingers twitch to touch her, to feel that slice of smooth skin beneath my hands. My lips long to graze across her midsection, my tongue dances in my mouth, needing a taste.

I'm so screwed.

Yanking the controller off the floor, I stand abruptly, trying desperately to discreetly adjust myself in my sweats, and then toss the game piece in the basket near the TV. I'm so done tonight.

"Duke, kennel," I say sharply. My tone startles my poor dog and brings Ethan's and Stacey's attention to me. "I'm going to bed." Duke whines then trots across the floor toward my bedroom. Love that dog.

"Dude, one more game," Ethan says, holding up his controller like a peace offering. If he knew the thoughts running through my mind, he'd understand. The problem isn't the game, it's the girl sitting between us who unknowingly threatens the walls I've built around my heart. One more day, one more brick crumbles, creating a fissure that will one day make the entire wall tumble to the ground. I can't afford to lose any more bricks.

I need to be a robot. Turn off the switch that controls emotion and desire. A switch that allows me to go to and from work each day and ignore this magnetic pull I feel toward Stacey.

Another day, another struggle.

In the patrol car today, Kilty earned an earful from me about the donuts he eats. I'm biting everyone's head off and there's nothing I can do about it except move out or kick her out. And my stupid conscience won't let me make her leave. And I'm sure as hell not staying in a hotel.

I'm so screwed. Screwed. Screwed.

Ten days into our living situation and I'm a ticking time bomb. I'm not sleeping well because every time my eyes close, all I can see is Stacey's soft lips and the sway of her hips as she cooks in the kitchen, unaware of her private little happy dance. In my bed, in the dark, my body craves something I haven't had in so long.

Ethan's gone for the night, covering a night shift for a coworker, and Stacey's in the kitchen swaying to some unknown song in her head and stirring something on the stovetop. The shirt she has on is nothing more than a piece of fabric draped over one shoulder, leaving the other bare and totally exposed. If I were a weaker man, I'd step up behind her and run my lips over the bare flesh and leave a mark on her so everyone knew she was mine.

"If you're just going to stand there, you could at least set the table instead of stare at me all night. It's kinda creepy." The flush on Stacey's cheeks makes me oddly proud. I put it there and it looks damn good on her. But I can't think like that. And she most definitely isn't mine. Why that thought ever crept into my brain is beyond me.

I push off the wall and set the table, and then stand next to her at the stove. The pot she's stirring has some sort of white sauce that's making my mouth water. It smells almost nutty and most definitely cheesy.

"What's for dinner?" I ask, leaning closer to the steaming pot.

"Alfredo noodles and chicken parmesan." Her smile lights up the room and flits across my chest. I want that smile to never fade; it's a smile free of hurt and loss. It's a smile I would have had years ago but don't remember how to make now. The timer on the oven buzzes, startling us both. "Can you pull out the breadsticks before they burn?" she asks, returning to stir the alfredo.

Once dinner is ready, we sit at the table and eat in silence. The sauce and noodles are incredible and the chicken perfectly breaded and moist.

"How did you learn to cook so well?" I ask, groaning through yet another bite. "Everything you make is amazing."

Stacey's lips curl into a shy smile and it's the first time I think she's ever shown a timid streak. Her brown eyes glance over the table and when she returns her gaze to me, my heart stutters in my chest. It seriously feels like it tripped over a rib, rolled three times, and then picked itself back up. There is nothing about Stacey that is fake—she's sincere, beautiful, intelligent, and kind. A perfect freaking package and it's incredibly hard to ignore the draw or the way my body reacts to her when she's near.

"Mom wasn't much of a cook, so I learned how as a teenager. I really love good food and enjoy making people happy when I cook for them." She rolls a noodle across her plate with the fork and pulls her bottom lip between her teeth and releases it quickly. "The sounds you make when you eat my food make me really happy." A flush rises up her neck, settling on her cheeks, and my walls, they're falling fast, crumbling before my eyes, and it terrifies me.

"Don't look at me like that," I say when her eyes settle on mine. They're full of hunger and longing and I have no doubt mine look just the same.

"Don't look at you like what?" she asks, her voice raspy and shallow.

"Like I'm everything you want." I stand up, knocking my hip on the table and sending our water glasses tumbling to their sides. Stacey reaches for the glasses, setting them upright. "I told you I wouldn't kiss you again. So don't you freaking look at me like it's all you want. Like it's all you think about."

"Ace, I—"

Before she can deny it, I cut her off with one parting blow. "Kissing you was the worst mistake I ever made."

She rears back like I slapped her instead of burning her with the words I've said. Everything inside of me is screaming about how wrong this is. How my words are poison and need to be sucked out before they kill whatever is left of my heart.

"How dare you," she says, no louder than a whisper. She clenches her jaw, stands up, and begins to clear the table. I want to apologize and beg her for forgiveness, because that kiss was hardly a mistake. If I could find it within myself to be the man she deserves, I would throw myself at her feet and kiss every inch of her body until she understood how she's turned my world upside down. How I finally feel awake after Marley died.

All of these feelings and realizations scare the

shit out of me. I thought I'd closed the door to my emotions five years ago, and since meeting Stacey, the door's been unlocked and is open a crack. I can see the bright lights behind the darkness I've been swimming in for so long, but I don't know how to move toward the warmth. I don't know how to let anyone in, and if somehow Stacey were able to be the one to bring me into the light, how do I know I wouldn't destroy her like I did Marley?

Stacey brushes past me to gather the leftover noodles and sauce at the table, and as she's covering the bowl with plastic wrap, I step up behind her. A crackle of energy snaps between us and her body stiffens. My hands settle on the counter on either side of her hips, caging her between my arms. Her breathing grows deep and ragged. Mine does the same, but along with it, my heart beats with the force of a ten-pound hammer in my chest.

"I shouldn't have said that," I whisper, moving my lips close to her ear so she can hear me. She gasps at my nearness and turns her head just enough that I can see her eyes flutter closed. I lean in closer, my front pressing against her back, and breathe her in. Her normal scent of peaches and lilies is faint, but it's there along with the smell of the meal she cooked for us.

"I'm sorry." Another whispered apology floats from my lips, landing on her cheek. She inhales sharply as my nose softly trails a line down the skin near her jaw.

"What are you doing?" Stacey asks, her voice trembling in a hushed whisper. Her shoulders relax as one of my hands moves from the counter to brush her cheek and glide down her arm. My fingers brush over hers and in one quick motion I grab her hand and twist her around to face me.

"Kissing you wasn't a mistake. Far from it," I admit, staring down at her pink lips. Her tongue darts out between her lips quickly, encouraging me to give in to what I want so badly.

"Ace, please don't kiss me again," Stacey whispers, averting her eyes from mine. A sharp pain stabs my chest, almost like the wind has been sucked from my lungs. I start to slowly push off the counter, but her hands land on mine, holding me in place. "Don't kiss me unless you mean it. I can't—"

I mean it. Every cell in my body means it.

My lips descend on hers and something in my chest bursts, flooding my body with raw emotion. My tongue runs along her lips, which finally— *finally!*—open to me. Her hands move from mine and reach behind my neck, pulling me closer. A low growl escapes as my tongue enters her mouth, seeking out hers. When they touch, my hand snakes around her waist, removing any distance between us. The other hand drags up her back until I reach her neck and then tilt her head so I can plunge deeper into her mouth.

I've spent five long years hiding from a woman's touch and in Stacey I've found the key to unlocking the door I closed long ago.

I pause for a breath, lay my forehead on hers, then quickly move my hands down her back, under her ass, and pick her up, wrapping her legs around my waist. My lips crash into hers again, but this time they open as though she's as hungry as I am. I walk us through the kitchen and into the living room where I sit down on the couch. Stacey rests on her knees, straddling my legs, and when her center drops over me, my body screams out for more. So much more.

Chapter 25

Stacey

When Ace kisses, he kisses with everything he has, with everything he is, and then more. I feel it in my chest, my fingers and toes, and in the way my stomach drops each time his tongue clashes against mine. Roaming hands skim beneath the hem of my shirt, slide up my back, sending a riot of chills to pebble across my skin. With a flick of his long, thick fingers, my bra is unclasped, letting the girls hang loose. His lips trail down my chin, to my neck, and then fall to my bare shoulder where he nips, kisses, and then devours me like I'm the last meal he'll ever eat. His warm hand pulls my chest to his, gaining him better access to my shoulder where his kiss grows sharp and persistent.

The feel of his beard, his hungry lips, and the press of our chests has my body aching for more. As his kiss deepens and his fingers dig harder into my flesh, I allow myself to settle farther into him. He's hard, hot, and pressing exactly where I need him to be. Slowly, I rock my hips against him, tilt my head back and to the right until his mouth finally moves back up my neck.

"I've wanted to kiss you right there since I saw you shaking your ass in the kitchen while you were cooking," he says, his breath hitching as I move against him, aching for the release my body is craving.

"God, you feel so good," I say, eyes closed and panting. When my eyes find his, they're dark, his lids are heavy and weighted down with fire and hunger. Ace's hands move to my hips where he pushes me further into him, gaining the friction I need. Our lips meet once again, crushing and bruising as we both take what we want, what we've denied each other since the day we met.

My arms snake around the back of his neck and pull him to me so the kiss breaks. I'm grinding on him, he's pushing me further down, and when his tongue glides down my neck, a moan tumbles from me, low and slow.

"Let go, sweetheart," Ace whispers at my ear. His gentle urging only intensifies the ache, and as one of his hands slides up my stomach to cup my breast, my eyes clamp shut, mouth opens in a silent scream. "Shit," he says, groaning as his hand stills on my breast. I'm shattering, collapsing on top of him, and feel his moist heat spreading through his jeans. For a minute neither one of us says anything, yet my head is resting on his shoulder and his hand hasn't moved from my right boob.

"You should probably…" he says finally, his cheeks flaming red. Before a cramp has time to settle in my calves, I slide off his lap and can't help but notice the state of his jeans.

"I'm sorry, I've never done that before," I say, looking around for something to help him clean up. Ace's eyes are closed, a hand rests over his eyes, and the muscles in his jaw flex and relax over and over. I can't tell if he's angry about the kiss or embarrassed that he just came in his pants.

"I'm just going to...um, finish cleaning up the kitchen." Quickly standing, I move around to the back of the couch, lean over, and press a kiss to the hand covering his eyes. "That was the most amazing make out session I've ever had." I need him to know it's okay, that it doesn't matter what happened in his jeans. It was really my fault anyway for getting a little carried away.

In the kitchen, quiet as can be, I fix my bra and work on the dishes, ignoring the ache in my chest. Maybe I shouldn't have walked away, giving him space, but I felt he needed it. Finally, food put away and dishwasher running, I return to an empty living room and my heart tumbles to my stomach.

He left.

I told him not to kiss me if he didn't mean it. I *told* him. Biting the inside of my cheeks to fight disappointed tears, I sit on the couch and fall into the pillows. I turn on the TV, force myself not to cry, and stare mindlessly at the flickering screen.

An hour and a half later, the door to the basement opens and out walks Ace, sweat slipping down his face and bare chest and back. He carefully approaches the couch, leans over the back, and presses a kiss to the top of my head.

"I needed to work out a few things," he says, his voice thick with apology. "I'm going to take a shower. Can I come back and watch TV with you?"

I shrug, trying to look like the last ninety minutes hasn't affected me so strongly. "Sure," I say, returning my concentration to the television. It's stupid of me to want something with him—he's obviously still grieving. The chemistry between us is electric, and flares like a sparkler bursting to life whenever we're near each other. The crackle from the sparks practically singes my skin like the popping embers from a raging campfire. When I'm not concentrating on the bookstore, my thoughts are filled with Ace and the first time we met on the plane.

He was different on the flight, still guarded but less tormented. Oh God, what if I'm the reason he's all over the place? The reason for his mood changes and flip-flopping emotions? Shaking my head to clear the truth from my mind, I snuggle further into the couch and bring a pillow onto my lap. Moments later, Ace joins me on the couch and pulls me to him like he's done every night since that first time.

***

Before going in to work the next morning, I stop by the house to check on the progress of the repairs. Ace let me choose the new cabinets and flooring. The hardwood was pretty much ruined after sitting under an inch of water overnight, so I put a neutral tile in the kitchen and new hardwood in the rest of the first level. Thankfully, the brick fireplace was spared, needing only minor repairs.

The workers have told us I can have the house back in about a week, which is both thrilling and sad because I know whatever this is between Ace and me will come to an end. And the sad truth is I don't want it to end. Yes, he's moody and temperamental, but he's worth the effort. I can see through his thick layers and know somewhere beneath them is a man needing somebody to love him. I want that person to be me.

On the drive to work, I pull through a drive-thru coffee shop and grab myself a caramel macchiato and a double Americano for Julia. My time is growing short with her and I'm growing more and more nervous as the days and hours tick down. She helped me place an ad for an employee and today I have the pleasure of holding interviews for two candidates. Being on this side of a business is completely different than what I've ever experienced before. It's both thrilling and terrifying at the same time.

"You ready for your first interview?" Julia asks as I barrel through the door to the bookstore holding the two coffees precariously in my hands. I blow a breath through my lips, sending my red hair floating to the side. "Your first one will hopefully be here in about fifteen minutes." She claps her hands, smiling eagerly, then accepts her Americano.

"You are a saint," she says, breathing in the rich aroma of coffee.

"Are you sure I'm ready for all of this? I still feel so nervous about running the business you love." I walk through the store to the back where I unload my purse and place my lunch in the fridge—leftover chicken parm and alfredo noodles. Yum!

"You'll do great," she says, smiling ear to ear. "I'll always be a phone call away. Oh! And my phone has that video call thingy."

"FaceTime?"

"Yes, that's it. We can do that if you need me." Over the next ten minutes, we run through some standard interview questions and then, when the bell over the door chimes, my stomach leaps into my throat.

Holy crap, I'm really going to do this. *I'm the boss!*

Forty minutes later, I'm thoroughly exhausted. And I still have one more interview to do before lunch. This girl—Ellery—would be fine; she's bubbly, loves to read, and has a high school diploma. She's young and could start tomorrow.

I glance at the clock, as does Julia; our next candidate is five minutes late. Punctuality is important to me, so, unfortunately, this is one strike against—I check the resume—Jodi. Seven minutes late and I'm ready to call Ellery and tell her she has the job. I really don't want to hold another interview.

"Well, that was disappointing," Julia says as we both check the clock again. "I guess she didn't really want the job."

"I think Ellery would do great here." After a brief phone call, she agrees to start on Monday, making the rest of my day fly by now that I've taken care of hiring someone to back me up. Now if I could just spend the weekend convincing myself

I'm fully capable of handling this job, everything would be perfect.

"Hey, wanna do something tonight?" I ask Ace when I step through the front door and see him and Ethan playing a video game. They pause the game and both glance back at me. Ethan welcomes me with his appreciative smile—I saved him some leftover chicken and pasta—and Ace greets me with an icy, tight-lipped twitch of his lips.

So…we're not as okay as he led me to believe last night when we were cuddling on the couch. Maybe spending this last week before the house is ready in separate spaces would be a good idea.

"Never mind. I think I'm going to grab some stuff and head to Reggie and Jordan's for the weekend." I turn and jog up the stairs to grab my duffle bag and shoot off a text to my BFF.

Me: Want a weekend visitor? I need some Reggie time!

Reggie: Definitely! Bring wine!

Yep. This is what I need. Time away from the cause of this growing hole in my chest where my heart should be.

Chapter 26

Ace

Stacey blew into my life like a tornado, ripped me off my firm foundation, rocked me at my core, and then faded away like the end of any good storm. She breezed into my life, taking me by surprise, and after she left, I still found myself thinking about her and the way I held her when we danced at her friend's wedding last July. I knew I'd never see her again, yet when she showed up that day to rent my house, I let myself, for just that moment, feel the distant flutters of my heart trying to revive itself.

But then I turned it off as fast as it turned on. I made a promise to myself after Marley died that I would be faithful to her memory and honor our marriage despite her being gone. Fighting these feelings I have for Stacey is tearing me up from the inside out. She's everything I could want in a woman and more. But with each desiring glance or lust-filled kiss, the promise I made five years ago digs a wedge between us. And it's all my fault.

I'm the one who has kissed her. Twice. Yes, I wanted to taste her both times, press my lips to hers and feel her body against mine. But a promise is a promise. I just don't know what to do about it. Or Stacey.

Ethan and I spend the weekend holed up in the house playing video games or working out or drinking. When Stacey doesn't return Sunday night, fear bubbles in my chest, thinking maybe she was in a car accident on her way home. After pacing the length of the house a dozen times, I send her a text.

Me: Where are you? If you're driving, pull over and call me. Please.

Stacey: I'm still at Reggie's house. Gonna commute to work until the house is ready for me.

My hand wraps around my phone, holding it tightly. My other hand slides through my hair as I groan, fighting the urge to slam my head into a wall. Of course she left. I didn't give her a reason to stay and it's like I enjoy stabbing myself with a red-hot iron rod repeatedly through my chest. If there was any question I actually had any part of my heart remaining, there is the proof of it. It's burning through my ribs, falling to the floor for me to stomp on. Because I did this to myself.

"Dammit!" I toss my phone onto the counter and it slides into the backsplash. My hands scrub over my face before I lean over the counter, placing my palms on the cool surface.

"You want to talk about it?" Ethan says from behind. I turn to face him and he scowls at my pained expression. He folds his arms across his chest and leans on the counter, raising his eyebrows.

Do I want to talk to him about what a royal screwup I am? Not really. Do I want to share my feelings and hug it out over a pint of ice cream? Hell no. Am I going to talk? Yep.

"I kissed her and she left." I move to the kitchen table, pull out a chair, and sit down backward with my arms resting on the back. Apparently, this is the new me: lay it all out on the line in the most matter of fact way.

"That was, like, almost two weeks ago," he argues. "Besides, what makes you think she left? I thought she was having a girls' weekend or something."

I hold up my phone for him to see her text and his lips pull down in another scowl.

"I kissed her…again. The night before she left to stay at Reggie's."

"Obviously the girl has issues if she left because you kissed her." Ethan pushes off the counter, pulls out a chair, and echoes my posture, straddling the seat and arms folded over the back of the chair.

"She's not the one with the issues and you know it. We got a little carried away and I freaked out. That's why she left."

A wicked grin grows on Ethan's face before his hand falls to his thigh as he slaps it three times. "How carried away are we talking? Did our Stacey finally break your dry streak?"

I flip him the bird, shake my head, and tug on

my ear, hoping to ease the rapid beating of my heart.

"No, you ass. I didn't have sex with her. Sex is off the table and you know it."

"Sex can be on the table too. Or with her bending over the table and you—" Ethan tilts his head back and laughs when I cut him off.

"What the…Jesus, dude. She and I aren't having sex. I'm married to your sister." I scrub my hands over my face again and tug at the beard growing a little too bushy on my chin. Time for a trim.

"You're not married to Marley anymore. Marriage doesn't continue in this life when one person isn't alive any longer. You know this. You're just choosing not to believe it," Ethan says, resting his chin on his arms. "My sister would want you to be happy. She'd want you to move on."

"I wish it were that simple." My fingers pinch the bridge of my nose in an effort to stave off a brewing headache. "Every time something happens between Stacey and me, I'm flooded with guilt. Like I'm cheating on Marley. I *know* I'm not, but it doesn't change the tightening in my chest or the swirl of my stomach. It feels wrong, like I'm betraying my wife's memory."

"So that's it? You're just going to give up?" Ethan sits up, shrugs, and rubs his hand over his chin. "Is she not worth it?"

A frustrated huff blows from my lips as I roll my eyes.

"Seriously, Ace. Have you seen the way she looks at you?"

"Stop." I've seen it. I recognize the longing in

189

her brown eyes, the hope she's holding on to. But I don't want to hear it from my friend. My brother-in-law.

"No, I'm not going to stop. You need to know what I see in her. What I see in you." He stands up, the chair slides across the tile, and he walks to the fridge and pulls out two beers. "But first, I need a beer and so do you."

"I have to work in the morning," I say, accepting the glass bottle regardless. I have a feeling I'll need this if he's going to tell me things I already know.

"Dude, whatever. Just drink and shut your trap while I sound like a chick for a while and talk about feelings and shit."

We laugh, twist off the bottle caps, and take a swig of the cold amber liquid. I don't know what I would do without Ethan. He's been right here with me since the day after Marley died and truth be told, if it weren't for him, I may have drank myself to death. For the first month, I drank my meals. I wasn't even sober the day of her funeral—talk about guilt sinking its claws deep in my chest. I can honestly say that day is about as clear as mud in my memory.

After a month of drinking myself stupid, Ethan literally held my head up as he poured the rest of the alcohol in the house down my throat. I gagged, coughed, and eventually threw up. He left me lying in the mess and when I woke up the next day, he told me I was done drowning myself in liquid death. I was pissed but eventually realized he was right. Since that time, drinking has never been something I do to forget anymore.

But right about now, I'm considering it.

"You remember that first day last summer when you walked into the house with that stupid look on your face?" Ethan asks, knowing full well I know exactly what he's talking about. I had agreed to go out with her and her friends and was completely perplexed about what to do. "What about when you went to her friend's wedding? The next day you came home, you walked like you felt lighter. Like some invisible weight had been lifted."

Dancing with Stacey at the wedding had felt good, had made me lose myself in something other than the sad and painful memories of my life. Holding her so close and moving her around the dance floor was easy and natural, almost like breathing. Even now, a smile finds its way to my lips.

"See," Ethan says, a wide smile of his own taking over his face. "You're thinking about that night, aren't you?" I shrug as if it's no big deal, making Ethan roll his eyes. "She's good for you. You haven't kissed anyone in five years and I'm guessing you haven't seen any action either considering you don't put yourself out there. How anyone can go five years is beyond me."

Beer finished, Ethan stands and returns to the fridge. "Want another?"

I shake my head and finish off mine before laying it down on the table and spinning it. I watch the bottle until it stops and wait for more of Ethan's pep talk. Or whatever it is.

"Has it really been five years?" he asks, sitting on his chair again.

191

I nod once, stand the beer bottle up, and sigh. "And the other night I freaking came in my pants when she was grinding on me while we were making out."

Ethan stills, his beer halfway to his gaping mouth. "What the hell, man? That's just gross!" But then he laughs, making me feel like an idiot. "What did you do? I mean, that really sucks and must have been embarrassing." He's still laughing while I ball my hands into fists.

"Shut it, jerk-face. She obviously knew it happened, it wasn't like it was easy to hide. Neither of us said anything and she got up to do the dishes."

"You didn't explain to her about why it happened?" he asks. I shrug and begin to peel the label off the bottle. "Well, maybe that's the real reason she isn't coming back. She probably thinks you're not worth spending time on if you're too quick on the draw." Once again, Ethan erupts into laughter and a part of me wants to throw this bottle at his head just to see if he'll still think the situation is funny.

Chapter 27

Stacey

It's moving back in day and I couldn't be happier. I've spent the last week at Reggie's house and commuting to work—it's been pretty much terrible. Driving a little over an hour to and from work every day has me appreciating my short commute now that I'm back in the house. Everything looks and feels fresh and clean and for the first time in my adult life, I have brand new furniture. Ace's insurance covered the purchase of a new couch and kitchen table and a couple other small pieces. And I love them.

I stopped by Ethan's house when I knew Ace would be working to grab the rest of my things and then slid the key under the door. I needed to be done with that part of my life. Our relationship needs to stick within the realms of business only. He's my landlord and nothing more...no matter how much I wish it could be different. He's not ready for it and I can't handle the back and forth.

With everything back in my closet, cupboards, and cabinets, I sit down on my new soft couch and run my hands over the gray chenille fabric. Love this house, love my couch, and I can't wait to sleep in my own bed. Ace's couch, though comfortable, wasn't a bed, and Reggie's guest bed is lumpy. I feel a little like Goldilocks when she's trying out beds to nap in. This bed's too hard, this bed's too soft…Ace's bed was just right. I shake my head. No…my bed's just right.

Not wanting to dirty my pretty kitchen, I order pizza for delivery and realize Halloween is in three days. I have a newly remodeled house, and very few friends. What better way to meet people than to throw a party where everyone lives out their fantasies in one night? I scoop up my phone from the coffee table and call Ace, knowing I should make sure he's okay with me having a party.

"Hello?" he says, and my stomach tightens at the low tenor of his voice.

"Ace, it's Stacey," I say, then realize he knows it's me from caller ID. "Hey, Halloween is in three days and I was going to have a party and wanted to run it by you. Make sure you're cool with it." The span of three breaths passes before he answers.

"What time?"

"Oh. Um, like nine-ish, I guess."

"Who are you inviting? You need to be careful having people you don't know at your party." He's scolding me like a teenager, making anger flare in my chest.

"I'm almost twenty-eight years old, Ace. I'm pretty sure I can handle myself."

194

He sighs, and if I had to guess, he's either scrubbing a hand over his face or tugging on his ear. "Just be careful, okay? If it gets out of hand, call me and I'll be there." With that, the line goes dead. The man makes me either weak in the knees or deliriously angry—there's no middle ground with him.

As Monday approaches, my nerves begin to take flight. It's the last day Julia will be here to help me. All last week she worked with me and Ellery—who has been amazing to work with. In no way do I feel ready to take over the bookstore, but Julia assures me everything will be fine. I have the name and number of the accountant, payroll company, suppliers, and the list goes on and on. I'm so tense and nervous, sleep is nowhere in sight.

I don't remember falling asleep, but when the alarm on my phone goes off at 6 a.m., I wipe the sleep from my eyes, the drool from my chin, and stretch my arms over my head. I have kinks in my neck and back, sore muscles, and a scratchy throat. What the hell did I do last night, bedroom Olympics? Usually, that involves more than one player, and as far as I know, I was alone last night.

After a long, hot shower, some Tylenol, and a bowl of cereal, I leave the house and drive to work. Julia won't be in until the afternoon when she officially hands over the keys. I'm terrified, yet excited and sad. Julia's been a great friend and an even better boss. I hope I can make her proud.

Four coffees, a chocolate cake, and several tears later, Ellery and I say goodbye to Julia. She strides out of the building ready to move on to retirement with her husband and all I can think about is not screwing up and driving her bookstore into the ground. The next two days pass by with little incident, which grows my confidence in leaps and bounds. The evening of the Halloween party is upon me and as I finish the last of the food prep, someone knocks on the door.

Having no clue who it is, and not yet dressed in my costume, I wipe my hands on my apron and answer the door. A perky blond with a wide smile stands on the porch holding a tray of food and wearing a Catholic school girl uniform.

"Lucy!" I exclaim, throwing my arms around her. "I'm so glad you're here. Come in." She glides through the door, places the dish on the counter, and asks if I need help.

"I need to change into my costume and set out the food," I say, pacing the kitchen. "People should start arriving in about an hour."

"Go get dressed. I'll put the food out," Lucy says, shooing me up the stairs. "Go get your cute tushy up those stairs and don't worry about everything down here."

"Fine, fine. I'll go. Thank you so much."

Twenty minutes later, I'm dressed in a sexy librarian costume complete with a deep purple v-neck sweater that plunges to my belly button, a white push-up bra underneath and a tight, black pencil skirt. My hair is twisted up into a bun on the top of my head and I have on a pair of thick-rimmed black glasses. The theme of the party is to come dressed as a sexy version of what you do for work. I figured it was a great icebreaker.

Back downstairs, Lucy has the food laid out on the counters, the red plastic cups near the keg, and the bottles of alcohol lined up as though an actual bar was set up.

"Thanks for doing all this, it looks great," I say. "I love your costume, by the way. What did your mom think?"

Lucy's cheeks flare up and she tucks her hair behind her ear. "Will you kill me if I tell you that before I knocked on your door, I took off the clothes I was wearing over this?"

"Are you serious?" I ask, laughing. "Where are they?"

"I put them in your car, which you should lock by the way." Lucy and I walk outside, grab her clothes from my car, and I put them in the spare room upstairs.

"Hey, my landlord mentioned in passing that he'd be okay if you wanted to move in with me. I'd still love to have you as a roommate," I say, closing the door. "That could be your room."

"I'd really love to," she says hesitantly. "But I really don't think it's a good idea right now. Mom's health hasn't been that good and I wouldn't want to be the cause of something happening to her."

Sheesh, this girl seriously needs to cut the ties.

"Okay, but the offer is there." We end up downstairs just as someone knocks. I open the door to a sexy secretary, a sexy waiter, and a sexy...lawyer? Is there such a thing? Introductions are made and more people start to arrive. My little house quickly grows crowded and the party moves outside under the white lights I strung across the

197

yard. I love the glow they give and how it makes me feel like I'm in a fairy tale.

The party is in full swing when another knock on the door brings me out of the kitchen. I open the door and am greeted by Ace, dressed in a cop costume that isn't sexy. Like at all. It's more humorous than sexy because I know what he actually looks like in his uniform. And *dayum*, the man looks incredible in it.

"Ace, hi," I say, still surprised he's standing outside.

"Hey," he says, rubbing the back of his neck as his eyes travel down my body, stopping at my chest.

"Eyes up here, buddy," I say, lifting his chin with my finger. "Apparently, you didn't get the whole sexy costume memo."

He clears his throat, his lips turn up into a smirk that makes my insides turn to mush, and then he unbuttons his shirt down to where it's tucked into his pants. Then he rolls the sleeves up past his elbows, giving me a peek at the tattoo on his left arm.

"That better?" he asks, the smirk still planted on his lips.

"Come on in," I say, opening the door wider. He moves to enter, but then stops.

"I'll just go around to the back if that's okay," he says, walking off the porch. Oh. Kay. I close the door, follow him around back, and step through the gate he holds open for me.

"Is Ethan coming?" I ask, hoping to introduce him to Lucy. Even with her insecurities and crazy overprotective mother, I think they would hit it off.

"Yeah, he'll be here shortly. Should I let him know to rip his scrubs or something to make him look sexy?" he asks, taking in the crowd. I step back and scan the people, looking at them from his perspective. To be fair, when I said it was a come-as-your-sexy-working-self costume party, I didn't exactly know you could make any job look sexy. The women all wear next to nothing, which makes me feel overdressed.

"Nah, any single lady here will think he's sexy just because he's a nurse." And as if summoned from thin air, Ethan appears behind us dressed in a pair of blue scrubs and blue cloth hat.

"Looking good, Stacey," he says, his eyes roaming over my body. Also stopping at my chest.

"Eyes up here, asswipe," Ace says, practically growling.

Ethan shrugs, pulls me in for a hug, and whispers in my ear, "He's all yours. Just don't give up on him." He pats my shoulder then makes his way through the crowd.

"Do you know everyone here?" Ace asks, leaning against the fence with his arms crossed over his chest.

I shake my head and smile. "I pretty much know no one. Just Ellery from work and Lucy who lives down the street." I enjoy watching him squirm, and when he pushes off the fence to stand in front of me, my body reacts. Heat rises up my neck, flooding to my cheeks, and my pulse skyrockets. Damn this man for having this kind of power over me.

"You invited all these people here and you're

dressed like this?" he asks, his icy blue eyes once again traveling over my body. His tongue darts out of his mouth, wetting his lips and sending wickedly lusty thoughts to my brain.

"Are you trying to kill me?" He moves closer, backing me up against the fence. The back of his hand brushes over my cheek and the heat from his touch warms me through. The pad of his thumb moves over my bottom lip, making my heart knock against my ribs. "I've missed you," he admits, moving even closer. Each breath is like pulling teeth. It's painful and full of resistance because my body doesn't know how to let go. How to let him do this one thing I want him to do to me. His head drops, his eyes search mine, seeking permission. I want to deny him, tell him to take a hike. But most of all I want his lips on mine, hands on my body, and the heat from him holding me captive.

"I can't stop thinking about this," he says, his thumb still sliding over my lip. "It keeps me up at night. Makes it hard to concentrate. Makes me want to kiss you again."

I can't help it. I really can't. My tongue breaks through my lips to wet them and naturally quickly slides over the tip of his thumb. Ace tilts his head back and groans.

"Do you really want to kiss me, Ace?" I ask, placing my hands on his chest over his shirt. His heart is beating heavily, pounding against his ribs as hard as mine is. He closes his eyes, nods, and drops his thumb from my lips. "Then kiss me." His eyes snap open as if he can't believe I'm giving him the permission he's so afraid of asking for.

I slide my palms over the planes of his chest and up over his shoulders, bringing him closer. When his lips meet mine, he moans as if he can't get enough. His tongue quickly enters my mouth, seeking mine, and when they meet…oh God…it's like a fire is lit under Ace's hands and he can't keep them to himself. One finds its way to my waist and then snakes around to cup my ass and pull me into him. His hard meets the softness of my stomach, which is to say my bare stomach. The costume he's wearing is little more than glorified paper and I. Feel. Every. Ridge.

His other hand moves up my side, stopping at my partially exposed bra. His finger glides under the bottom wire, sneaking under my shirt before his palm rests over my left breast. I should care that anyone looking over at us might be getting quite the show, but I don't. Ace consumes me, my every waking thought, and right now, with his lips on mine, his hands cupping and kneading, nothing around me matters.

"I can't seem to stay away from you," Ace says breathlessly when he breaks the kiss.

"Then don't," I whisper, loving the look of his swollen lips and flushed cheeks. I move to kiss him again but he puts a small amount of space between us, signaling the end of our makeout session.

"I want to eat dinner with you," he says, bringing his hands up to cup my cheeks. I nod as he glances down at my chest and painfully, slowly, returns my left breast into my bra. "I want to eat dinner with you…here."

"Okay," I say, not underestimating the

significance of him eating with me here at his own house. But I'll take it. I'll take what Ace wants to give me because I want it all. I want dinners with him, cuddling on the couch, his kisses, warm touches, and hooded eyes. I want him even if it costs me everything.

Chapter 28

Ace

Stacey's party cleared out around 1 a.m., and after she walked a very tipsy Lucy home, I helped her clean up the backyard. People never have a problem leaving a mess when someone else has to clean it up. Now, as we sit on the back steps staring up at the night sky, a sense of calm washes over me. My arm is wrapped around Stacey's shoulders, holding her tight to my side, keeping her warm. The sky is dark with thick gray clouds and the chill in the air, and the smell of moisture tells me it's likely to snow pretty soon. Thank goodness she rented some outdoor heaters or her party would have been a bust.

"You going to be okay tonight, sweetheart?" I ask as she shivers against me. Instinctively, I pull her onto my lap and wrap my arms around her waist, drawing her arms around my neck. Sadly, her skirt is so damn tight she has to sit sideways rather than straddle me. The space between us is charged with a hungry current, and when her eyes find mine, her tongue slowly guides across her soft lips, dragging a groaning sigh from me.

"I'm glad you came tonight," she whispers, still gazing at me. "Did you have a good time?" Her fingers trace patterns on the back of my neck, drawing out goose bumps across my skin and sending Junior into a heightened state of awareness. Little separates us, in fact, it would be so easy to slide these ridiculous pants down my legs and push aside whatever she's wearing under that tight skirt and find release.

Truth be told, I have no idea if I could go through with it. I don't even own any condoms, and it's not like I'm going to make her buy some. We're not going there—I won't. Not tonight. Not...

"Ace? I asked if you had a good time, didn't you hear me?" Just like that, I'm back with her and enjoying the feel of her teasing the hair at the back of my neck.

"Yeah, I did." She lays her head on my shoulder and I place whisper light kisses on the top of her head. However, it's time to take out the bun—I'm done with the bun. I remove seven of those wavy pin things and then untwist the hair tie holding up the fiery red hair I've come to love. Her hair tumbles over her shoulders and back, making my fingers twitch with the desire to glide through the wavy strands.

Stacey moans softly as I run my fingers through her hair. As the minutes pass, she relaxes into me until I realize she's fallen asleep. A wave of panic stirs in my chest, causing my heart to rapid fire. I'm not sure carrying her inside to her room—*our room*—is within my power.

"Stacey, sweetheart. You need to wake up," I say, pressing a light kiss to her forehead. She mumbles something unintelligible as her head slips down my chest. Jesus, she's really out. I glance around, hoping someone has either come back because they forgot something, or at the very least someone is out for a 2 a.m. walk in the neighborhood.

Shit!

I rode my motorcycle here, so it's not like I can take her back to Ethan's house with me. And I have no idea where her car keys are. Dammit!

One deep breath in…one deep breath out.

I can't freaking do this. I can't go inside that house, up those stairs into the bedroom I shared with Marley. I. Can't. Do. It.

"Stacey, hon…please wake up." My arms hold her tighter and begin to shake with fear. This all feels too familiar, too raw, and it's gutting me, holding her in my arms like dead weight. My throat is closing up, tears are burning the corners of my eyes as beads of sweat drip down my back.

"Dammit, Stacey. Wake up!" I'm shaking her now, her head is bobbing back and forth and it's my worst nightmare on repeat. I can't lose her too, I just can't. She has to wake up because I can't go inside that house.

"Ace?" she says, her voice thick with sleep. "What are you doing?" She lifts her head, gazes up at me, and the shell around my heart cracks open and I kiss her. I freaking kiss the snot out of her because she's awake and alive and in my arms.

Stacey moans into my mouth and I wrap my hand behind her neck, tilting her head to give me better access. My tongue glides across hers in a frantic rhythm and desperate pace. She gives as I take and my other hand glides up her legs under the hem of her skirt to cup her little round ass. It's cold from the night air and...bare, making me break the kiss.

"Tell me you have something on under this tight black skirt," I say, staring into her eyes, secretly hoping she's going commando.

She shakes her head, pulls her bottom lip between her teeth, and gazes through her inky lashes. "Sorry to disappoint, but I'm mostly clothed underneath."

"Thong?" I ask, and she's nodding and I'm groaning in appreciation. "March yourself up to your bed, woman, before I lose myself in you."

"You could come with me," she says, pulling her hair over her shoulder. She makes me want to take her to bed. To peel her clothing off layer by layer, exposing the creamy, smooth white skin underneath. To run my lips over every inch of flesh before I delve in deep and let her consume all of me.

"I can't, sweetheart. But I'll come over for dinner tomorrow night, okay?" My fingers trail across her cheek before I place my lips on hers in a soft, slow kiss. "I'll see you tomorrow."

"Good night, Ace," she says before slipping inside the house that looks like it just ate the girl I'm having difficulties walking away from.

***

"Situation on Highway 75, all available cars please respond."

"Kilty and Steele, reporting," Kilty says over the radio. "What's the situation? Over."

"Possible high-speed chase with potential collisions."

"On our way, send coordinates. Over." As soon as dispatch sends coordinates, I turn on my lights and siren and navigate through the busy streets of Warner. Finally on the highway, three miles ahead of the oncoming car, we sit and wait for the blue late model Chrysler LeBaron. I have to laugh because that car hasn't been in production in years, how fast can they really be going? Sure enough, within two minutes, Kilty and I spot the car weaving through traffic at least twenty miles over the speed limit.

High speed is laughable when the driver is going seventy-five. Here I thought we were dealing with speeds up over a hundred miles an hour. Is it wrong I'm a little disappointed?

"Let's go get him," Kilty says, tightening his buckle and gripping the CB radio in his hand.

"Kilty and Steele in pursuit. Over."

"Proceed, Steel and Kilty. Two cars are one mile ahead and four are closing in from behind."

We pull out into traffic, siren blaring and lights flashing, and quickly match the speed of the LeBaron.

"Shit, Steele, it's a freaking granny driving. She can barely see over the steering wheel." Kilty slams the CB radio on his thigh and mutters a string of curses. "Dispatch, this is Kilty. Driver is an elderly woman. How should we proceed? Over."

"Attempt to pull over and stop by force if necessary. Go ahead."

"You heard dispatch," I say, waiting for Kilty to change over to the megaphone. He hates using that thing. Then again, I guess so do I. I pull the car up beside the LeBaron, matching her speed. Kilty swears again then holds the megaphone to his lips as I roll his window down using the automatic button.

"Ma'am, please slow your vehicle and pull over to the side of the road," he says, his cheeks burning red. His silvery hair is flopping in the wind the open window is causing and it reminds me of my great Uncle Henry's toupee. The woman pays us no attention and Kilty repeats his order. Still no response, he gets back on the CB.

"Suspect shows no signs of slowing down. Approaching mile marker ninety-five, requesting backup to stop by force." Kilty shakes his head and neither of us can hold in our laughter.

"Copy that, Kilty. Highway has been cleared and tack strips laid out. Proceed with caution."

A mile up the road, the woman finally drives over the nail strips, causing her to swerve right into my car, sending us spinning into the concrete median. The airbags deploy, sending out white powder and thick bags of air ramming into our faces and shoulders.

"Suspect has been detained, good work, officers. Sending medical units, sit tight."

An hour later, I'm sitting in the ER waiting to be cleared to go. Somehow Kilty weaseled his way out of being driven to the hospital in a freaking ambulance. I'm not so lucky.

A buxom nurse with a tight perm in her chocolate brown hair slides back the curtain to my little room and looks me over. She's in her mid-forties and smells like antiseptic.

"Chase Steele?" she asks, glancing down at my chart.

"That's me."

"I see you were in an auto accident." She reads through the papers on her clipboard then finally turns her attention to me. She winces at the sight of my face. "How are you feeling?"

"I'm great," I answer, only partially lying. My ribs are sore from the seatbelt and my eyes are burning from the powder in the airbags. But other than that, I'm fine.

"I'm pretty sure you've seen better days, Mr. Steele. I'm Veronica and will be reporting to the doctor on call. You mind if I check you over?"

I shake my head and let her run her tests of blood pressure, heart rate, and oxygen levels. All results are normal, well, at least normal for someone who's a little amped up on adrenaline.

"I'm supposed to be meeting someone for dinner tonight," I say, trying real hard to draw on all my patience. "Do you know when I can be discharged?"

"As soon as you see the doctor and he says you're good to go," Veronica says before stepping away and closing the curtain. I get off the bed and retrieve my phone from my coat pocket and send off a text to Stacey.

Me: Long day, going to be a little late. Should we reschedule?

Reschedule? I sound like a receptionist.

Stacey: No. Just come when you can.

Me: K. Sorry. Will explain when I get there.

Forty-five minutes later, the doctor finally comes in and clears me to leave with only bruised ribs and airbag burns to my face and arms. A cab picks me up and takes me to the station where I climb on my motorcycle and drive through town, stopping at a floral shop I used to go to when I worked late. Thankfully it's still open and I buy a bouquet of peach-colored lilies because they remind me of her. I drive the rest of the way with the flowers tucked into my jacket and curse myself for not having the forethought to have driven the SUV today.

Chapter 29

Stacey

I can't stop glancing at the clock on the microwave. Ace texted over an hour ago and he's still not here. Maybe he's not coming.

No. He said he's coming.

He'll be here.

He'll—the low rumble of his motorcycle sends a thrill through me and my heart beats heavily in my throat. He didn't park on the street. He always parks on the street. *Calm down, Stacey. You've got this.* Pep talks are for people who believe they work. I guess I'm not that kind of person because my palms are sweating and I keep checking my breath every ten seconds.

Will he knock or just come in? A hollow tapping on the front door answers my question and sends my pulse into a frenzy. When I open the door, a beautiful bouquet of peach lilies greets me and my stomach does a little flip in appreciation.

"They remind me of you," he says, handing them

to me. When I glance up at his face, I gasp in shock. His eyes are puffy and red, and he has some bruising along his cheekbones.

"Ace, what happened?" I grab his hand and pull him inside. He jerks his hand away before I can drag him into the kitchen.

"Can you just…give me a minute." He stands against the door, breathing hard enough through his nose that his nostrils flare. His hands ball into fists at his sides, then raise to his eyes as he pushes them hard against his sockets. His Adam's apple bobs up and down as though he's trying to control his emotions.

Crap. Maybe this was a really bad idea. Like a horrible, no good, really awful idea.

"Ace, we can go—" I start to say, but he cuts me off with a sudden kiss to my forehead.

"No. It's okay. I want to do this." His jaw clenches as though it pains him to admit what he wants.

"I'm serious. We could go out for dinner. Or if you're not up to it, we can try another time." I move away from him, giving him the choice to stay or go. After what feels like an eternity, he glances toward the kitchen, takes a deep breath, and with determined strides, walks into the newly remodeled room.

"Can I help you with anything?" he asks when I join him next to the fridge. I pull a vase from the cabinet and quickly put the flowers in water.

I shake my head, gaze up at his red, puffy eyes, and bring my fingers to his eyebrows and then trail them over his lids and down to his bruised cheeks.

"I'm just glad you came, Ace," I whisper as my fingers slowly move over his cheeks before settling on his lips. He kisses them then brings his hand up to mine and places it on his shoulder. "Please tell me what happened. Did you get into a fight?"

He laughs, forcing a smile as he shakes his head. "Hardly. It was a work-related car accident."

I look him over, trying to find injuries, but can't see anything. "Are you okay? What happened?"

"Some elderly woman was speeding down the highway thinking the highway signs were the speed limit. She was going seventy-five in a fifty-five zone and we had to bring out the nail strips to stop her. Poor thing blew her tires, swerved into my partner and me, and sent us spinning on the highway." He's laughing but I don't see the humor in it. On instinct, I playfully slap his chest and he buckles over, gasping for breath.

"Ace!" I fall to my knees, place my hands over his cheeks, and pull his head up to me. "Are you okay? What's going on?"

The jerk's still laughing, now harder than before, and he slips down to the floor, sitting on his ass. He pulls me with him, only to drag me over his legs.

"Are you going to tell me what happened or am I going to have to pull it out of you?" I ask, folding my arms across my chest. Gah! This man can drive a sane person crazy.

"Bruised…ribs," he says through gasps of breath. Oh. *Oh!*

"I'm so sorry." I'm such an idiot. I quickly untuck his shirt and work the buttons until I can slide it off his shoulders. He shrugs out of it, closes his eyes, and leans his head on the kitchen cabinet behind him.

"You know, taking your date's clothes off typically happens at the end of the date," he says, his voice thick and husky all of a sudden. When he opens his eyes, they're darker and filled with hunger. When my gaze locks on his, his brows raise, issuing a challenge.

"And here I thought you only wanted me for my cooking," I say, moving my hands slowly over his shoulders and down his arms, loving the way his muscles tighten under my touch. Ace in his navy blues is incredibly sexy, but in a white t-shirt where his tattoos on his left arm are on display…well, let's just say mouthwatering. That. Is. All.

Ace allows my playful exploration and closes his eyes while my fingers trail over his t-shirt and down to the bottom hem. His breathing grows quicker and the pulse at his throat picks up speed. When my fingertips glide across the skin above his pants, he hisses and sucks in a breath.

"Stacey," he says like a warning, but makes no move to stop me. I lean forward and press a kiss above his right eye and then his left. His hands move to my hips where they grip my jeans like a vise. My hands glide under his shirt, sliding it up over his stomach inch by inch. When it becomes clear I plan to take it off, he lifts his arms and pushes off from cabinet to allow me to slip the t-shirt over his head and arms.

My eyes fall to his rapidly rising chest and I pull my lips between my teeth when I see the angry purple and green bruise slicing across his chest in a diagonal direction.

"I'm so sorry I hit you," I say, returning my gaze to his face. He's staring back at me, his pale blue eyes growing darker by the second. Ace's hand moves to my chin as he guides me closer so he can feather kisses on my lips. We've had hungry kisses, angry kisses, and even lust-filled kisses. But *this* kiss. This kiss is something altogether on a higher plane. It's the start of a journey, the cost of a ride, a token for the train. It's slow, gentle, and filled with a carefree itinerary. There are no plans, no schedules, no places to go. Just a slow discovery of the feel of his lips on mine as his hands travel over the mountains and valleys of my body.

"What about dinner?" I ask, breaking the kiss and already missing the warmth from his lips.

"What dinner?" Ace playfully nips at my bottom lip, pulling it between his, and slides his tongue across it.

Three.

The number of breaths that pass between us before I slide off his lap and stand up, reaching my hand to help him off the kitchen floor.

Two.

The number of steps Ace takes before his hands land on my waist then trail behind to lift me into his arms.

One.

The number of doors standing in the way of a place both of us long to go but are unsure how to proceed.

Yes.

The answer to our unasked questions.

Ace's lips descend on mine as he effortlessly carries me up the stairs. At the top landing, he hesitates before dropping a hand from my butt to open the bedroom door, softly closing it behind us and cloaking the room in blackness.

"I don't have any condoms," Ace says when he sits me on the edge of my bed, standing between my legs. "But I can still make you feel good."

"I'm on the pill." I've never gone without a condom, so I'm not exactly sure why my mouth decides to blurt out this particular fact.

"Stacey," he says, but I hook my fingers in his belt loops and pull him down beside me, stopping his protest.

"We don't have to do anything, Ace. You could just sleep next to me and I'd be perfectly happy."

"I can't lay next to you and not touch you," he says, gliding his fingers through my hair as if to demonstrate. "I'm clean. I haven't been with anyone since—"

I quickly turn and throw my leg over his lap to straddle him again, pressing my lips to his. His words aren't necessary and will only stir up painful memories. My hands slide over his chest, snake behind his neck to tease the short hair at his nape. He tears his lips from mine and begins peppering kisses down my neck until his quiet attention turns frantic and desperate.

Gone is my shirt, but I'm wearing his kisses like fabric. Gone is my bra, but his hands hold me better than that old thing anyway. Pants and shorts are discarded in a pile on the floor. His legs twine between mine, hands grip bed sheets, my mouth catches his sobs, my skin absorbs his tears, and a small part of me dies while he releases into me and crumbles on top of me.

When he moves off me, he sits up, rests his elbows on his knees, and covers his face with his hands. He's shaking the bed with how hard his body is trembling and I don't have a clue how to make him feel better. Instead of rising to sit next to him, I pull the sheet over myself, turn my head away, and fight tears of my own that are threatening to spill.

"I won't ever love you," he admits when he finally stops shaking. He moves off the bed to gather his clothing and takes a part of me with him, ripping a hole in my chest. The hurt is dangerous and sickening, and my stomach is balling into such tight knots I feel like I'm going to throw up.

"You won't or you can't?" It's not a question, it's a demand, and the bitterness in my voice leaves out any doubt.

"What's the difference?" he asks, pulling on his pants and heading for the door. "You shouldn't fall in love with me." He leaves the bedroom. Leaves me. And I'm shattering into a million pieces.

His warning came too late—I fell a long time ago.

Chapter 30

Ace

As soon as I stumble out of the house, I turn and lose my dinner in the bushes beside the front porch. What I was thinking? I squeeze my eyes closed only to feel the burn of more tears slip down my cheeks. I made a promise to Marley, and tonight, not only did I break it. I freaking shattered it—and in our old bedroom.

My hands won't stop trembling, and if I can't get my heart rate under control, I risk going into cardiac arrest on the porch. Leaning over, supporting my weight on the porch post, I vomit again into the bushes, spilling more tears.

"I'm sorry," I say, falling to my knees on the grass. My hands grip the back of my neck as I pour out apology after apology to the one person who can't hear them instead of the one person who should be receiving them. But I can't help it.

"I'm so sorry, Marley. God, I'm so sorry." Crumbling further still, my forehead meets the grass as I tear at the soft green blades and scream curses into the ground. I hate this. I hate that she's dead and I can't move on. I hate myself for sleeping with Stacey, for betraying Marley. And I hate myself for running out on her and lying to push her away.

***

Somehow I made it home. Somehow I got undressed, showered to scrub the evidence of my betrayal off my body, and got in bed. I'm so screwed up that in the middle of the night I can smell peaches and lilies and feel the warmth from Stacey's body, holding me. *Cradling me*. Somehow I fall back to sleep, and when I wake up in the morning, she's lying in my bed looking like an angel with a fiery halo of red hair tossed over the pillow.

And for a minute, she's all I want to see. All I want to hold and kiss and...*love*.

The clanking of pans in the kitchen lets me know Ethan's up and cooking breakfast. He must know Stacey's here and last night was pretty much the second worst night of my life. Quietly slipping out of my bedroom, I pad barefoot down the hall and find him cracking eggs into a small mixing bowl.

"Hey," I say, my voice scratchy and raw.

"So, I think we need to talk," Ethan says without taking his focus off the eggs. "Sit."

I tread slowly through the kitchen, turn a chair around and sit, arms folded across my chest. "So talk," I say, sniffing while steeling myself for the lecture that's sure to come.

"You said you wouldn't hurt her." Ethan cracks two more eggs into the bowl then turns to face me. "The girl called me in tears after you left her house, begging me to let her know when you got home and if I thought you could use someone to watch over you last night. I invited her here because you need her more than you realize."

A stirring of jealousy rises in me over the fact that she called my best friend to console her. But then my rational side returns when I remember who caused her pain.

"Did she tell you what happened?" I ask, clenching my teeth until an ache in my jaw forces me to relax.

"She didn't have to tell me. Ace, believe it or not, I know you probably better than you know yourself. For the life of me, I can't figure out what your problem is." Ethan tosses the fork he was holding in his hand onto the counter and it clatters across the granite.

"What *my* problem is? What's *your* problem?" My temper is rising, making heat climb across my body. I'm not going to sit here and take this crap—I had one of the worst nights of my life and don't need any reminders about what I've done.

"My problem is that you went to her house last night knowing full well what was most likely going to happen. And when you two hooked up, you freaked out. Dude, you royally screwed up, and what's worse is she forgave you. That girl is so totally crazy for you that she's willing to overlook your past just to be with you."

"Are you kidding me? You think I planned to

have sex with her?" My hands glide through my hair in frustration.

"It's been building for weeks and you know it," Ethan says.

"Whether or not it's been building doesn't matter. I broke my promise to Marley, and in our house. In our old bedroom. Do you have any idea what that makes me?"

"A guy. It makes you a guy who has finally developed feelings for someone other than your dead wife. Jesus, man. She's been gone for five years. Move on. Don't move on. But whatever you do, don't take Stacey with you on your path to self-destruction. She's better than that and deserves to be loved. Not used and then kicked to the curb because you feel guilty for making a promise to yourself to be faithful to a ghost."

"I made that promise to Marley," I say, my voice sharp and loud.

"Oh yeah? When exactly? Before she sliced her wrists with the box cutter? Did she hold that box cutter to her arms and threaten to kill herself if you ever loved someone else?"

"Stop," I say, barely holding it together.

"No, Ace. When did you promise her? Tell me, because I'd really like to know. Was it when she was lying in your arms bleeding all over the place? Because I'm pretty sure she was already gone at that point."

"Stop!" We're both shouting, tears falling from our eyes as we relive the memories and pain.

"You made that promise to yourself because you felt guilty. Marley was sick, Ace. You couldn't have saved her. She chose to end her suffering the only way she knew how. It sucks, man. I know she was your wife, but she was my sister and I miss her every day." Ethan wipes the tears from his eyes with the backs of his hands and I wipe mine with my shirt. "I'm sorry she killed herself. I'm just plain sorry."

He returns to the eggs, beats them with the fork, and turns on the stove. When breakfast is ready, he fills our plates with eggs, bacon, and toast, leaving a plate for Stacey.

God, Stacey.

"What am I going to do about her?" I ask, unsure of what I'm supposed to do.

"Hell if I know. What do you want to do?" he asks through a mouthful of eggs.

While eating, I try to rationalize my feelings for her. If I can classify them, put them into a box labeled Stacey, then maybe we can see where this thing between us goes. But that would mean also putting Marley's memories into a box and storing it in the far recesses of my mind. I can't store either of my feelings for them in boxes—it's not right, but I can't keep them both close.

"What if I wanted to explore what Stacey and I have? Would that make me an awful person?" I close my eyes, hoping to hide myself from the look of disappointment I'm sure is written across Ethan's face.

"You know I want you to be happy. If Stacey makes you happy, then see where it goes," he says. The squelch of the chair sliding across the floor makes me open my eyes. He's standing beside me and lays his hand on my shoulder. "I know you don't want to hear this, but I'm going to say it anyway. Marley wouldn't be angry about you sleeping with Stacey. She'd want you to be happy and to move on."

He gives my shoulder a quick squeeze then takes his empty plate to the sink. "If you do choose to give it a go, just be good to her. She's worth it, okay?"

I nod, quickly finish my breakfast, then bring my dishes to the sink. As I round the corner heading to my bedroom, I nearly trip over Stacey, who's sitting against the wall with her knees tucked to her chest. Her eyes are red from crying and it guts me knowing I'm the reason for her tears. Squatting down in front of her, I tuck the hair behind her ears and kiss her forehead.

"You okay?" I ask, knowing she's not. The answer is clearly written across her blotchy face. She shakes her head as another tear slips down her flushed cheeks. "I'm so sorry for last night. I panicked and handled it all wrong."

"It's my fault, Ace. I wasn't thinking. I...I didn't know this would be so hard for you. God, I'm so sorry," she says, springing up, wrapping her arms around my neck, and knocking me to the floor. She cries into my shoulder, her tears landing on my t-shirt while I stroke the back of her head.

"It's not your fault, sweetheart. Neither one of us knew what was going to happen or that I would be a wreck afterward."

Stacey lifts her head from my shoulder, sniffs back her sobs, and uses her fingers to wipe away her tears.

"Will you tell me about her? About Marley?" she asks, and that shell around my heart cracks open a little bit more, allowing the ray of hope that is Stacey inside.

Chapter 31

Stacey

Ace won't come over to the house—not since that night. I truly get it now, how hard it is for him to come inside, and I don't blame him. It must be like a form of torture to him.

Since he won't come to me, I've been spending my evenings with him at Ethan's house. We've fallen back into the routine of me cooking dinner and snuggling on the couch. When Ethan grows tired of stolen kisses, he makes his excuses to go to bed and leave us alone. When we're alone, as we are now, it's like without our built-in chaperone, we're afraid of touching each other.

I'm afraid of pushing Ace too far and having to hear those words from him again. I believe he said he wants to see where our relationship goes, but that's not a reason to sleep with someone. I want more. I want it all—love, trust, faith, and passion. Without all four, I can't give myself over to him again. I'm too far gone to have him crush me, and sex would pull me too far down the rabbit hole.

"I'm going to go to bed," Ace says during a commercial break. His hand glides up my side, stopping at the underside of my breast, sending my heart on the downward slide of a rollercoaster. This is usually when I kiss him good night and head back to my house. But tonight there's a charge in the air, like a live wire humming through the room.

I sit upright and feel the heat of Ace's hand sliding down my back to rest on my butt. Heart, meet knees.

"I'm going to go home," I say, yawning. While stretching my arms above my head, I stand and toe on my ballet flats. "I'll see you tomorrow?"

Ace stands, reaches his large hands to my hips, and drags me close. "I don't want you to go," he says, sliding his thumbs through my belt loops. "Come to bed with me."

My stomach does that little flip-flop thing that has me practically melting at his feet. A year ago—heck, six months ago—I would have raced him to his room. But this new Stacey, the one who is going to stand firm, slowly shakes her head side to side, trying to convince herself she's going home. Yep, that's me. Solid as a rock, not going to cave. Not going to follow him to his room. Not going to let him peel my clothes off slowly while he places sweet kisses over my shoulders, up my neck, and then on my lips.

Nope.

Not. Going. To. Happen.

"Come to bed with me," Ace pleads, tipping his head so his forehead rests on mine. The tips of our noses touch, and a sigh of longing floats from my lips. Just a fraction of an inch and our mouths would meet in an explosive kiss. A kiss I could replay over and over on the drive back to my place.

Slowly, I slide my hands up Ace's chest until I reach his thick neck and my fingers cup his strong, bearded jaw. With my hands here, I guide his lips to mine, sealing our mouths together, our tongues battling in a war of who is going to relent first.

Me—staying the night. Or Ace—letting me go home.

When his hands lower over my ass, he lifts me easily and guides my legs around his waist. He turns and carries me down the hall to his room.

Well, damn.

We end up twisted around each other, tangled in his soft sheets, and exhausted from kissing and touching, learning each other's bodies. Yep, apparently my firm foundation wasn't nearly as solid as I gave myself credit for. Note to self: rebuild my resolve.

I leave early in the morning in order to make it back to my place, shower, and get ready for work. Each day is getting easier and I feel happy. I love opening the store every day and feeling truly like an adult. Julia and I talk on the phone at least twice a day, sometimes more when I have a question regarding something specific about the store or an order that came in. And Ellery has proven to be a great employee and friend.

Toward the end of the day, I receive a text from Reggie inviting me over for the weekend and a thrill shoots through me. Even though it was rough when

I first moved up here, our relationship is getting better and almost feels back to normal. Now that Ace and I are…something…she says to bring him too. I laugh while thinking about how well this is going to go over when I ask him to come with me.

***

Overnight bags packed, Ace and I—along with Duke—drive south out of Warner heading to Torrance for what is sure to be an interesting weekend. Surprisingly, when I asked Ace if he'd like to spend the weekend with my crazy friends, he agreed without hesitation. I was fairly certain this was a trip I'd be making alone. Now here we are, holding hands over the center console of his SUV, and all I can think about is the way Ace makes me feel.

In high school, guys came easily. They practically lined up at my door, and being young and stupid, I accepted what they were offering without complaint. I was as easy as they came and enjoyed the rush of something new. After Reggie found out she was pregnant, I did a lot of soul searching and realized she and Jordan had truly been in love. He was her first and, much to my unbelief, only. I never understood why she didn't date or fool around after Micah was born, and maybe that made me a bad friend. Over time, I started wanting that connection to someone; I wanted a real relationship. I wanted to feel loved and adored. With Ace, even though he's still battling his memories every day—every time we're together—I know he's trying. His tender touches, sweet kisses, and even this—holding hands in the car—make me feel special. And I love him for it.

I knew I was in trouble when we were dancing at Reggie's wedding. When I left without saying goodbye, I was hoping to cut any growing feelings toward him because it was pointless to try a long distance relationship. They never work, and it's usually due to both parties being unable to keep their love alive. Knowing now what I do about Ace, it would have been me screwing everything up.

When we finally park outside Reggie and Jordan's house, a smile overtakes my face. Making the decision to move up here was the right one. I'm close to my best friend again and Ace and I are working on us. And for now, that's enough. I'm in love with him, and sometimes the way his eyes soften when he glances at me makes me believe he feels the same.

After dinner, Jordan and Ace head into town to grab a movie while Reggie and I get busy making a quick batch of chocolate chip cookies. Micah is spending the night at a friend's house, which made me a little sad since I won't see him until tomorrow night. But at least I'll get to see the little boy who is as much a nephew to me as any future kids my brother will have.

As I'm spooning the cookie dough onto the baking sheets, Reggie steps up behind me and wraps me in a hug. "Man, I've missed you," she says, planting a kiss on my cheek.

"Ha-ha. Just like Ace, you only like me for my cooking," I tease, and then scoop my finger through the dough and sneakily swipe it across her cheek. She squeals and we burst into laughter. This is what I needed, my friend and some cookie dough fights.

"So, Jordan and I have been trying to get pregnant," Reggie says after the first batch of cookies goes into the oven. Her news sends a sharp pang of jealousy spiking through me that nearly has me buckling over at the waist. I hide it the best I can, but I can see the confusion on her face. A best friend wouldn't be upset. A best friend would jump for joy and give great hugs. So, I force a smile that finally turns into the real thing, and then I wrap my arms around her.

"That's really great, Reggie. Are you?" I glance at her flat stomach, but she shakes her head.

"No, not yet. But hopefully soon." The smile on her face is contagious and soon my jealousy fades and eventually recedes to the back of my mind.

When the guys return, they proudly flaunt the movie and put it in the DVD player. Jordan and Reggie snuggle up together on one couch, and Ace and I take the other. I pull a blanket from the rolled arm and take my spot under his arm. I love the way he tilts his body toward me so his legs create a perfect spot for me to sink into him.

The movie begins and Reggie and I groan simultaneously at their pick. It's a subtitled Japanese martial arts film that has me wanting to take revenge on both guys. I pull the blanket up over my shoulders, drape it across Ace's lap, and snuggle in closer to his side. He drops his hand to my side and holds me close. As much as I love his kisses and gentle touches, if we cuddle like this for the rest of our lives, I'll die a happy woman.

Three cookies, four dead Japanese men, and a bowl of popcorn later, I'm bored out of my mind. Ace is glued to the television and so are Jordan and Reggie. Revenge on Ace is starting now.

I slide down so my head is lying on his thigh, which makes Ace shift on the couch so one leg is stretched out and his foot is propped up beside me and the other foot is on the floor. Poor guy doesn't know what's coming. My hand rests on his thigh under the blanket and slowly moves higher and higher until I feel Ace tense around me. When my palm cups the space between his legs, he coughs and slides an inch or so down the couch.

My man is pretty smart. He places a pillow over his lap and I casually pull it over so my head can lie on it.

He traded his jeans for a pair of black sweat pants before Jordan put the movie on and I silently offer him my thanks for making this so much easier. My hand slides over the growing bulge in his pants and I clench my thighs together. So maybe I didn't quite think this form of torture through all the way.

During a particularly heavy action scene, Ace tilts his head back on the couch and I feel the hum of a low growl in his chest. He reaches under the blanket and pulls my hand off him and jerks his eyes in the direction of our bedroom. Score one for Stacey.

"We're exhausted, guys," I say to Reggie and Jordan. "You kids have a good rest of your night. We'll see you in the morning." I lay the blanket back over the arm of the couch and pull Ace to his feet, making sure to stand in front of him. After Jordan and Reggie say good night, we make our way upstairs to our room.

Chapter 32

Ace

"Shh," Stacey says, pulling me through the bedroom door. "The walls are really thin and the floor creaks." The coy smile on her face makes my heart soar and my fingers itch to touch her all over again. Her fingers tug at the hem of my t-shirt as she guides me to the full-size bed with cream-colored bedding. She sits on the edge and with a look, challenges me to undress in front of her. Slowly lifting my shirt over my head, I watch Stacey as her eyes darken while she gazes across my chest and then turns her focus back on my face. Her tongue quickly darts out, wetting her plump lips, and I'm on her faster than a snake going in for the strike.

The bed groans with our combined weight and creaks with every movement we make. Kissing her isn't enough, touching her is like torture. I need more, all of her. I'm going to claim every inch of her body with a kiss, every freckle with a caress, and every peak will feel the graze of my teeth.

I move over her, one elbow on the mattress while my other hand travels down her body, finding its way under her shirt. She arches her back as my fingers graze her breasts and my lips find hers. Clothing discarded, my lips move over her body, freely pulling quiet sighs from her parted mouth.

"Ace," she pants as my lips claim her once again. I push forward, the bed groans, Stacey's back arches, and I'm hit with the feeling of being home. Every move, every creak, every thrust is like a warm welcome into the arms of the woman you love.

Stacey's legs move up over my hips, wrapping around me, pulling me deeper. Deeper and deeper I fall, and as I collapse on top of her, I realize this is way more than I bargained for. I thought it would get easier, that sleeping with Stacey would be sex and nothing more. But as she lays her head on my shoulder and I pull her close, the feelings of home and of love I'm filled with are dangerous and reckless.

***

Before Stacey wakes up, I slowly slide out of bed, grab a shower, and head outside with Duke, needing to clear my head. When I told her I wouldn't love her, I wasn't lying. Yet, here I am dangerously close to falling for her and having no idea what to do about it.

The lights in the barn are on, and since it's about twenty degrees outside, the barn looks like the place to be. Inside, I find Jordan feeding the horses, talking quietly to them like they're old friends. If you would have told me six months ago I would be hanging out with Jordan Capshaw and watching him turn into a cowboy, I would have laughed in your face. Who knew the rock star had it in him to become a family man and give everything up for the woman he loves?

"Have a good night?" he asks, a shit-eating grin plastered on his face.

"Sorry," I say, knowing Stacey and I couldn't have been quiet no matter what we did.

"Hey, no worries. It just reminds me that I need to buy a new bed for that room. Then again, if Micah ever brings a chick home when he's older, I'll know if they're fooling around." Jordan laughs, tosses me a square section of hay, and points to the stall I'm standing in front of. I feed the horse and help him with the rest.

"So, what's up with you two anyway?" he asks as he puts the wheelbarrow away. "I've known Stacey for a long time and she's different with you."

"Honestly, I don't know what I'm doing. Things are getting out of control with her and I'm sort of freaking out." My hands rake through my hair and I silently curse myself for admitting that out loud. The last thing I need is for Jordan to confide in Reggie what I've just said.

"Stacey used to be the go-to girl in high school, if you know what I mean," Jordan says casually, and it makes my stomach churn into knots. "But over the years she's changed a lot. Reggie tells me that Stacey's happy when she's with you. I don't know what's going on with you or why you'd be freaking out. But I swear, if you do something to hurt her, I'll hurt you. Got it?"

I shake my head, fighting off a nervous laugh. "You do realize you just threatened a police officer, right?"

Jordan shrugs, slaps my shoulder, and walks toward the house. "You coming? Breakfast will be ready and my boy will be home soon."

The four of us sit down to eat just as Jordan and Reggie's son comes through the front door. His wide, easy smile for his parents fills me with guilt and longing. I could have had that. I could have had everything if I would have been able to save Marley. The rest of the day, the five of us sit around talking, snacking, and hanging out like old friends. By the time Stacey and I have our bags packed, I feel like I've crawled into a dark cave, retreating into hibernation. I don't want to be around these people wishing for a life I can't have. A life I don't deserve.

"You've been really quiet," Stacey says when we pull away from Reggie's house. "Is everything okay?"

My jaw clenches as I lie to her and nod, still walking into the darkness. I'm familiar with the dark, comfortable with being alone, and don't want company. Duke whines from the back of the SUV, most likely sensing my bad mood. I ignore him, ignore Stacey's pleading eyes, and focus on driving her home. When I finally pull into her driveway, I move to get out of the SUV, but she shakes her head, opens her door, and climbs out. She grabs her bag from the backseat, shuts the door, and turns her back to me. I watch her walk to the front door, pull out the keys, and step inside the house that started it all.

Twenty minutes later, I'm stepping inside Ethan's house with Duke at my heels. I take him outside, let him do his business, then put him in his crate. Right now, everything feels so heavy, it's pushing on me, dragging me down, and I need to punch my way through it. Quickly changing into some basketball shorts and tearing off my shirt, I take the basement steps two at a time until I'm face to face with the small punching bag hanging from the ceiling.

Over and over and over I punch at it, gritting my teeth, hissing as the skin on my knuckles crack, not caring about the pain I'll feel tomorrow. This is a pain I can handle, a pain I crave because I don't have to feel the damn fissure in my chest where the hurt I've caused someone else is breaking me even more than I already am.

I. Don't. *Punch.* Want. *Punch.* Any. Of. *Punch.* This. *Punch.*

This hurt and this pain. And this freaking beating heart that is betraying everything I've shut down for so long. I just want some peace and to be free of the guilt that's burning me at both ends.

"Ace!" Ethan steps around me, grabs the punching bag, and stares at me like I've lost my mind. Maybe I have. Maybe I'm just as crazy and depressed as Marley was. God. What if I'm just like her?

"What the hell are you doing?" he asks, grabbing

my wrists and holding up my hands. *My bloody, swollen hands.* I glance from my hands to the bag with shock. There's blood all over the bag and splattered on the wall. It looks like a crime scene.

"I need to blow off some steam," I say, yanking my wrists from Ethan's grip. "I also want to get drunk. You in?" Ethan shakes his head and follows me up the stairs. "I'm going to go clean up and then you and I are going out."

Thirty minutes later, I've showered and cleaned up my hands the best I can and wrapped them in sterile gauze and tape. So punching the bag without wrapping up my hands first wasn't the smartest idea. But I feel a little better, so there's that.

"Ready?"

Ethan's sitting on the couch, still in sweats and a t-shirt. He turns to look at me, shakes his head again, and puffs out a breath.

"You're not going out and getting drunk. You can go do that next week like you do every year. But tonight, you're going to sit here and get your head on straight. Because right now, I'm pretty damn worried about you."

"I'm fine," I say, lying again as I sit on the couch with a sigh.

"You're about as fine as a dog with two legs. What the hell is the matter with you?" Ethan crosses his arms over his chest and waits for me to spill everything.

"Look," I say with a shrug. "I slept with Stacey and it was a mistake. It's messing with my head and it was stupid of me to get mixed up with her." My bottom lip trembles as I admit yet another truth.

"Why was it a mistake? Jesus, Ace." Ethan groans, runs his hands through his hair, and glares at me. "The only thing messing with your head is your own damn mind. I see how you look at her, I know you don't really believe being with her was a mistake."

"Yes, it was. She makes me feel things I don't want to feel. Things I shouldn't feel. I don't deserve any of this with her."

"So you're just going to screw her and then tell her sorry for making the biggest mistake of your life? Is that your plan?" Ethan stands up, strides into the kitchen, and opens the fridge. He pulls out a bottle of whiskey and a beer and returns to the couch.

"You know what?" He hands me the bottle of Jack Daniels and continues. "Screw you. I'm done trying to get you to see how good this girl is for you. If you can't see it, then you don't freaking deserve her. Hell, you can even drown your ass in alcohol for all I care. The bottle's all yours."

Ethan twists the cap off his beer bottle and drinks until it's gone. I stare at the bottle of whiskey, trying to figure out how I'm going to forget about Stacey and the way she makes my heart beat like it's only beating for her.

Chapter 33

Stacey

I refused to cry when I got home. If I cried, another piece of my heart would break, and I'm afraid I don't have enough pieces left to believe love exists. Or that I'm capable of being loved by someone else. God, I've tried. I let myself foolishly believe Ace could love me, but maybe he was telling me the truth.

But where does that leave me?

Where does that leave Ace?

It's stupid of me to hope for something different, because if he's proven anything, it's that he can't handle a relationship. And I can't handle being only friends.

Work drags on each day and when I go home, sleep eludes me. After sending two texts to him, both of which have been unanswered, I want to curl up in bed and never leave. What I need instead is someone to talk some sense into me. I need my best friend, and a phone call will have to do for now.

I dial her number, and when she answers, I nearly break down.

"Hey, Stace, what's up?" she asks, her voice chipper and carefree.

I sigh into the line, blink away the tears stinging my eyes, and fall into my pillow. "I'm not doing so good, Reggie." It hurts to admit it, to say out loud that something is wrong.

"What's wrong? Are you okay?"

"It's nothing like that, I'm fine. My heart just hurts."

"Oh, Stacey. What happened? You guys seemed really good when you were here."

Unloading what I know of Ace's history as well as our rocky time together never felt so good. Tears are shed as I recall the good he told me about his wife and how they were high school sweethearts. I know he loved her, he still loves her, and losing her like he did must have been awful. His hurt still feels raw and tender even though it's been five years. Add me into the mix and he probably feels like he's flopping around like a fish out of water.

"What do I do, Reggie? I love him but I don't know if it's enough." My tears are slowly stopping as I listen to Reggie sigh on the other end of the phone.

"Give him some time, Stacey. Given all you've told me, he's dealing with some pretty heavy stuff, things he obviously hasn't dealt with yet," she says, her advice helping to calm my nerves. "He has feelings for you—that much was clear while you were here."

"What if I don't hear from him again? He hasn't

answered my texts." My chin begins to tremble as the tears threaten to release again. I wipe them away with my fingers and hold my chin with my hand.

"You need to understand what he's going through. Put yourself in his shoes and realize he may not come around. You need to stay strong and be able to move on. You're an amazing person, Stacey. Don't become that girl who shuts down or changes because of a man." Truth, it's all I ever get from my best friend. As much as I love her for it, sometimes I want the *everything's going to be okay* speech. Right now, that's what I want to hear.

"Thanks, Reggie," I say, trying to hide the disappointment causing my voice to waver. We talk a while longer before she tells me Jordan, Micah, and she are flying back to Phoenix for a week to visit Jeremy and Emily. They've just had their baby and invited them to visit. When we hang up, I find a bottle of wine in the fridge and pour myself a glass. One glass, and then my little pity party will be over.

On my way to work, I grab a caramel macchiato from my favorite drive-thru coffee shop and head into the center of the city to the bookstore. As I park in the designated lot, the first light flurries of snow begin to fall and I stand with my face pointed toward the sky as I absorb the sight. The skies are hazy and gray, the clouds are dense, and the falling flakes are small and perfect. Several land on my coat and I study their intricate designs and laugh to myself as I realize that it's true—no two snowflakes are identical.

Throughout the day, the snow continues to fall, the flakes growing larger and coating the streets and sidewalks. I've been to Flagstaff a few times back in Arizona to go sledding in the snow, but never have I watched the first snowfall of the year. It's magical and beautiful.

"You want me to sweep the sidewalk?" Ellery asks, holding a large push broom.

"No, thanks. I'd like to do it." She smiles, hands me the broom, and grabs my coat from the back for me. I shrug on the heavy jacket, put on a wool beanie cap, and walk outside into the brisk air. I think I've just fallen in love with Warner, Washington. The blinking stop lights, the falling snow, and the chilly air all remind me of what Christmas should feel like. I happen to love Christmas and can't wait to actually have a white one this year.

Thirty minutes later, I've swept away the snow from my portion of the sidewalk, along with the neighboring stores' portions. Several people across the street are doing the same thing, but their faces are twisted up into scowls. I want to shout to them to smile, but I'm pretty sure they'd throw a snowball at me.

At the end of the day, after Ellery has left, I close up the store and head to my car. A two-inch layer of snow covers my car, making me smile. It looks like I slathered on a layer of vanilla frosting. Once inside, my hands are shaking from the cold, and when I turn my key in the ignition, nothing happens. No groan, no rumble of the engine starting, nothing. The lights still come on inside so I know it's not the battery. What the hell? I quickly get out of the car, lock it up, and head back inside the store where it's warm. I have two options—call Triple A or call Ace. I opt for option two. It's after six, Ace should be home or on his way. Hopefully he answers my call.

Four rings and voice mail picks up. I leave a brief message then shoot him off a text letting him know I'm stranded at work. The good news is there's a fairly comfortable couch in the back room I can sleep on if worse comes to worst. Fifteen minutes later, there's a knock on the door. Please let it be Ace and not some weirdo.

I flip on the main lights and am relieved to see Ace in a bright red ski jacket with a black beanie cap over his head. When he sees me, his face holds no emotion. It's like he's meeting a stranger.

Unlocking the door, I let him inside and lock it behind him. He glances around the store, blows warm air into his hands, and finally turns to me.

"Let's go get your car started," he says plainly.

"Okay, I'll go grab my coat. Thanks for coming." He nods his head then stands by the door as I retrieve my coat and shrug it on. We walk outside to the parking lot where Ace's SUV is parked next to my snow-covered car.

"In the back is an ice scraper," he says, pointing to the back of his car. He unlocks it and I retrieve the ice scraper slash broom thingy and hold it out to him. His fingers brush mine as he grabs it from me, sending a shock through me. He quickly brushes off my car, and then tells me to put it in my car so I'll have one for next time. "You probably need some antifreeze. There's a jug of it in the back of my car as well. Can you grab it?"

"Sure," I say as I move around to the back of his SUV again. Inside is a gallon jug with blue liquid in it. Ace has the hood of my car up and pours the jug into some place in my engine. They don't teach you about this stuff back home in Arizona.

"Go ahead and try to start her up," he says, closing the cap and wiping his hands on his jeans. I try to turn the engine twice and then on the third attempt, it starts up. Relief floods through me knowing my old car isn't dead yet.

I turn the heater on full blast, jump out of the car, and walk up to Ace. My arms wrap around his chest as I hug him. His entire body tenses under me, making me drop my arms. I take a step back only to see his eyes look as gray as the sky was earlier today. His jaw tenses before he opens his mouth to say something, and then closes it quickly.

"Thanks…I guess," I say before returning to my car. It's too much to see the distance he's forcing between us. With my hand on the car door to close it, Ace steps next to me.

"Stacey," he says, his voice low and trembling.

I raise my hand, place it on his, and stop him from saying the words that are ripping me apart.

"It's okay, Ace. You don't need to say anything. Thank you for your help." I close the car door, turn the radio as loud as I can stand, and then slowly pull out of the parking lot. In the rearview mirror, I see Ace's hands grip the back of his neck as he bends over at the waist and squats down in the parking lot. I'm pretty sure I left my heart lying on the snow-covered pavement next to him because my chest hurts so freaking bad, there is no way a heart could still be in there.

.

Chapter 34

Ace

I let her go. I let her drive away from me and it's ripping me apart piece by bitter piece. Those words she said, the pained expression in her eyes...it knocked the wind from my lungs and has me gasping for air. I've destroyed the one thing with the potential to put me back together, to make me whole again. What have I done?

Following her back to her place would only lead to me falling apart even more, yet squatting here in the snow isn't helping either. I can't text her while she's driving in this snow...shit! Does she even know *how* to drive in weather like this? Taking a deep breath, I stand, climb inside the SUV, and drive the route I would take if I were going to the house. Please let her get there safely. When I drive past the house, her car is parked in the driveway and the porch light is on. A sigh of relief passes through my lips as I drive myself home.

The snow keeps falling over the next few days,

and each day I make sure Stacey's car is parked safely at work or at home. I need to make sure she's safe and not lying in some hospital from a car accident.

And now here I am…November 19th and it's a miserable, gray, slushy day. I don't even bother with a shower or calling in to the station. They know what today is and know I won't be in for two days. Ethan has a bottle of Wild Turkey sitting on the counter along with two shot glasses. He's made breakfast and joins me in a toast.

"To Marley," we both say, and then take a shot. The liquid burns as it goes down, choking the air in my lungs, much like the way I felt the day I let Stacey drive away from me. By the time breakfast is eaten, we've both had several shots and I'm feeling pretty good. By lunch, we've called a taxi, and when it pulls up, it honks, letting us know our ride has arrived. It's the same every year since Marley died. Ethan drinks with me and when he's had enough, he sticks with me until I'm too far gone to know my own name. It's better for me this way. At least the pain is gone shortly after breakfast.

We make it to Ned's bar across town where the food's good and cheap and the shots keep coming. Ned's knows I have no limit on this day. Lunch consumed along with at least a half dozen shots later, I'm throwing darts like a pro and having trouble standing up straight. Ethan helps me to a table where he orders a water for himself and a rum and Coke for me.

"You doing okay?" he asks.

When I turn my attention to him, I can't

determine which Ethan I should be speaking to. A smile washes over my face and my whole body feels warm.

"I really need to take a piss," I mumble, and then stand abruptly, making my chair squelch across the wood floor. Ethan walks with me to the bathroom, and after I've washed my hands, he guides me back to the table.

"You ready to end this?" Ethan sits back in his chair and drinks from his water glass. My eyelids feel like weights have been attached to them and it's making it pretty damn difficult to keep them open.

"Dude, no! I'm not nearly drunk enough. I'm still thinking about Stacey. And Marley." I laugh as I start merging their names together. "Starley and Marcey. I'm so confused. Which one am I supposed to love because I can't have both?"

Ethan's jaw clenches—well, at least it looks that way from where I'm sitting.

"I'm serious, Ethan. I love your sister and she's…dead. She freaking killed herself because she was pregnant and lost the baby." Ethan closes his eyes and brings his hand to his forehead. "Maybe you didn't know that. It was one year from the last miscarriage she had. All she wanted was to be a mom and every damn time she got pregnant, she lost the baby. So, you see…it *was* my fault she killed herself."

"Ace, stop," Ethan says rather loudly. He sits up in his chair, takes the drink from my hand, and slams it on the table. "You didn't kill her, you arrogant ass. It wasn't your fault she lost the baby or…babies, whatever. There was nothing you could do to help her because you didn't know how bad it was. No one did."

"What about Stacey? She loves me, you know? I can see it every time she looks at me. I told her not to. I told her I would never love her. Why does she have to love me?" I lay my head on the table, enjoying the cool surface.

Once again, I stand up and then pull out the phone from my pocket. I call a cab and arrange to be picked up.

"Where are you going?" Ethan asks, standing next to me.

"Home. I'm going to my house to finish getting drunk and I'm going to tell Stacey I don't want her to love me."

"The hell you are," Ethan says, trying to push me back into the chair.

"Get your hands off me, Ethan. I'm going to do this. I need to end it before it's too late." I shrug out of his grasp and stumble through the door to an awaiting cab. I give him her address and sit back while he drives through the streets of Warner.

Finally at her house, I pull out the keys and unlock the front door. The house is quiet, and when I call up the stairs, no one answers. I check the window and see her car isn't parked in the driveway. I guess she's still at work. Inside the fridge is a bottle of wine. I pull it out, sit on her couch, and drink straight from the bottle.

A slamming door makes me jump off the couch and drop the bottle of...I glance down...wine, spilling the foamy liquid on the carpet. I turn around only to find the room spinning and at least three

Staceys standing with their hands on their hips staring at me.

"What are you doing here?" they all ask, their voices pinging around in my head.

I stand on wobbly legs, walk around the couch, and watch as she backs up until she's up against the door. I move closer, breathe in her scent of peaches and lilies, and damn near lose it. I scrub my hands across my face then move them to my hair and tug so hard I see red.

"Ace, why are you in my house?" Her voice is as soft as a whisper, her eyes wide as she takes in my disheveled appearance. I glance down to see the pair of gray sweats I threw on this morning is wet from the spilled wine and my sweatshirt has a ketchup stain on it. I don't remember spilling ketchup.

I step closer, leaving no room for air to pass between us. Stacey gasps as I place one hand on the door behind her head. Closing my eyes, I rest my forehead on hers.

"I told you not to fall in love with me," I say, still gripping my hair with my free hand.

"Ace, I—"

"I'm not done," I say, cutting her off. My other hand moves from my hair to the braid falling over Stacey's shoulder. Her hair slips like silk through my fingers and when my hand trails over her breast and down to her waist, she closes her eyes and squeezes out a tear. "Every time I'm with you, I think of her." More tears fall down her cheeks and her bottom lip is quivering, shaking like a leaf in the wind.

If I make it through the night, it will be a Goddamn miracle.

"Ace, please don't. You're drunk and don't know what you're saying," she cries, still unable to look at me.

"I know exactly what I'm doing," I say, slowly turning her head to look at me. I need her to see the pain I feel when the memories invade. The memories steal the happiness I feel when I'm with her and she needs to understand.

"You think I want these memories? The memories of holding my wife's head in my lap while she bled out from her wrists. I saw the life drain from her eyes as the blood soaked through my clothes and pooled on the floor. Those are memories you wish you could wipe away, could forget as easily as you seem to have forgotten I told you not to love me. I won't love again, it's not worth the pain." I know I hurt her, but to what extent, I'm not sure. If there is any ounce of love for me left after what I just did, I hope she can find it within herself to let it grow into something beautiful. Something amazing. But not for me.

I drop her chin, claim her mouth with mine one last time before I pull open the door and walk away. This time for good. From behind the door, I hear her slide down to the floor and burst into sobs, breaking the rest of my heart. I didn't have much left to begin with, but there's nothing left after that.

How could there be?

Chapter 35

Stacey

When Reggie said that someday my ability to pick up random strangers was going to hurt me, I don't quite think she meant they would rip my heart out. But that's what he's done. He's pulled it from me, stomped on it, and then put it in a blender and handed it back to me like somehow I would be able to reassemble it. I can't stay here a minute longer knowing not only does he not want me, but there's no hope for him to have feelings for me.

How could I be so stupid in thinking we shared something? I thought I saw it in his eyes, I really did. Apparently, I'm really bad at reading people and was wrong from the start.

A phone call to Reggie is all it took for me to pack up a few things and stay at her place. Risking running into each other at the house isn't worth it. It's too hard on my heart and this needs to be a clean break, like I'm quitting him cold turkey. It's the only way I know how to survive this.

Once settled into the room Ace and I shared, Reggie joins me on the bed and wraps her arms around me.

"You're going to be okay," she says, squeezing me tight. "I love you and want you to know you can stay here as long as you need."

"Thanks," I say, sniffing back the tears staining my cheeks. I told myself I would give this one last good cry and then I'd be done. No more wallowing, no more tears. Moving on is my focus. Over the next couple days, we settle into a routine. I'm up at the crack of dawn, eat a quick breakfast, then drive the sixty-five miles to work, making sure I leave early enough to account for snow and ice-covered roads. Had I really thought about this part of the situation, I may have stayed in the house.

I close the bookstore early the Wednesday before Thanksgiving and do some shopping at a fancy grocery store in Warner. The little store in Torrance is pretty small and doesn't have a few of the ingredients I need for the stuffing I make. Walking toward the checkout counter, I stop moving when I see Ethan and a pretty blond with her arm draped over his. Seeing him with someone makes me happy, but confused since I've never seen him date. Or mention a girl…ever. I almost thought maybe he was gay.

Taking a deep breath, I step up to them and say hi. "Hey, Ethan." He turns around and his eyes dart to the blond he's with and his cheeks flame red.

"Stacey…hey! Um, how are you?" he asks, casually moving his arm from the blond's touch.

"I've been better," I say, tucking the hair behind

my ears. Ethan glances between the blond and me and then his shoulders sag.

"Stacey, this is Katie, my girlfriend."

It's Katie's turn to blush as she smiles. "Nice to meet you," she says. Her voice is quiet and soft, making an image of Tinkerbell pop into my head. Come to think of it, she is quite petite and the way her hair is pulled up into a messy bun...well, let's just say the resemblance is uncanny.

"Stacey and Ace...I mean, they..." He looks to me for direction but I have no clue what to tell him. We weren't ever officially a couple and I don't even know if you could consider us dating.

"Ace and I were friends. I rent his house." Fresh wounds open up as I speak about him and me in the past tense. "How's he doing?" I shouldn't ask, but something inside me needs to know.

Ethan shrugs and moves ahead in the line. "He's miserable," he admits. Katie takes the basket of food from his elbow and places their items on the conveyor belt. "I'm really sorry he's an idiot. He's really confused and hurting and doesn't know what to do with everything he's feeling."

"Well, he made it pretty clear how he feels about me," I say, blinking rapidly to dry my eyes.

"Again, he's an idiot, Stacey. He's going to wake up one of these days and realize just what he's done by pushing you away."

"It's too late, Ethan. My heart can't handle any more breaks."

"I'm really sorry to hear that," he says as his arms wrap me in a hug. He holds me tightly while rebellious tears slip down my cheeks. "I wish you wouldn't give up on him," he whispers in my ear. "He'll wake up soon and be ready to tell you everything."

"Thanks, Ethan. Tell him I said hi, will ya?"

He nods, and then turns to pay for his groceries. He and Katie walk away, waving, and his words cut me even deeper. Could I wait for him to wake up like Ethan says? Should I?

The entire drive back to Reggie's I play the conversation with Ethan in my head over and over. It's easy for me to read into what he said and turn it into something I want to hear. But what if he was trying to tell me what I so desperately want to hear?

What if Ace does have feelings for me and he's scared of what it means?

Would it make a difference?

***

Thanksgiving morning, Reggie and I meet in the kitchen and start preparing all the food for the day. I really do love to cook, and when she and I get in the kitchen together, magic usually happens. What would normally be a regular turkey turns into an herby masterpiece and the potatoes are the perfect consistency. She and I should really consider opening up a restaurant or a catering business.

Thanksgiving guests start to arrive and I'm suddenly feeling homesick. I miss my parents and my brother. Maybe I should have flown back to Phoenix to be with them since their plans changed a month ago and they were all unable to fly up here. Before we sit to eat, I excuse myself to call them, knowing they'll be watching the game and snacking on turkey and all the trimmings.

"Stacey, honey. Happy Thanksgiving," Mom says when she answers the phone. Her voice alone pulls a sob from me. "Honey, what's wrong?"

Doing my best to hide my sadness, I force a laugh. "I just miss you all and wish I would have flown home to be with you for the holiday."

"We miss you too," she says, sounding just like the worried mother she used to be when I would go crying to her. She always made me feel better, even when I was in trouble.

"How is everyone?" As the words leave my mouth, Reggie's doorbell rings. "I should probably get going, Mom. I just needed to hear your voice."

I leave my bedroom and head downstairs, only to be greeted by the best sight I could have asked for. I drop my phone into the pocket of my apron, squeal, and leap down the stairs and into the arms of my parents.

"What are you guys doing here?" I say, holding them both tight.

"We missed you too, honey," Mom says, kissing my cheek. My brother walks inside next and I couldn't have been given a greater gift right now.

"James! You guys, I've missed you all so much." James joins our family hug and everything is good. Right now, I have what I need most and it's perfect.

Chapter 36

Ace

Every year it's the same, Thanksgiving with Ethan and Marley's parents where we all sit around their table and pretend everything is okay. I don't remember the first Thanksgiving after Marley died, I was passed out drunk somewhere. The next Thanksgiving, her mother cried while Ethan, their dad, and I watched the game. By the third Thanksgiving we all acted like life was moving forward and so were we.

This is the sixth Thanksgiving and everyone is smiling because Ethan brought his girlfriend to dinner. When the hell did he get a girlfriend? Seeing him and Katie together drills a hole through my chest. She fits in perfectly with his family, and here I sit staring at the food on the table wondering what I'm doing here. Why do I spend every holiday with my dead wife's family and not my own? I can't remember the last time I visited my own parents, let alone spent Thanksgiving or Christmas with them.

Paul, Ethan's dad, offers a prayer over the food and we all begin helping ourselves to the turkey, potatoes, stuffing, and everything else.

"My son tells me you've been seeing someone. Stacey, is it?" LeAnn, Ethan's mother asks. My fork full of turkey stalls halfway to my mouth.

"Mom!" Ethan says, his tone sharp. LeAnn is one of the nicest people you'll ever meet, but with her salt and pepper hair pulled back into a fierce bun, she looks like she could take a bite out of you before you even knew she was there.

"What?" she asks, glancing from Ethan, to me, and then to her husband. Paul sits in about the same position as me, his fork halfway to his mouth. "I think it's great you're finally seeing someone."

"Not a good time, Mom," Ethan says, shooting her a warning glare. Katie places her hand over Ethan's and kisses his cheek.

"Maybe it's good for him to talk about her," Katie says, turning her attention to me. She's a good-looking woman, shiny blond hair that falls in waves past her shoulders, deep blue eyes, a pinched nose, and full lips. She's not typically the kind of girl Ethan dates.

"What is it you said you do for work, Katie?" I ask, clearing my throat. Something's not sitting right with me. Ethan never hides who he's dating.

Katie sits upright and her full lips turn up at the corners into a smug smile. "I'm the resident psychiatrist at the hospital where Ethan works."

"Is that why you didn't tell me about her?" My question is directed toward Ethan. His eyes close as his jaw tightens. "You decide to bring your little shrink girlfriend to Thanksgiving dinner to get inside my head? Well, I've got news for you, buddy. I don't need anyone diving inside my head to tell me how screwed up I am."

"Ace, that's not—" Ethan says, but I cut him off when the palm of my hand slams on the table. It stings like hell, but I'm too far gone to care about it.

"Every damn day I live with the guilt and the pain of losing my wife. I should have helped her. We should have stopped trying to get pregnant." My hands fly to my hair and I tug on it. I tug so hard I want to scream. "Jesus. Then I go and meet Stacey and she turns everything I know, everything I believe, upside down. She makes me feel like everything is okay, that it's normal to fall in love and move on. And dammit, I want to move on, but it kills me thinking I'm betraying my wife."

I scrub my hands over my face, drying the tears I can't control.

"I don't deserve a second chance, and I sure as hell don't deserve a woman like Stacey." Pushing back from the table, I stand up and storm into the kitchen. My chest is heaving as I gasp for breath. My heart is racing and the room is spinning—just what I need, a panic attack. I stand at the back door and slip down to the floor, bringing my knees up to my chest, and rest my head between them.

A warm hand falls to my shoulder, squeezes, and then wraps over my back. "I know my son has said it many times, but I think you need to hear it from me as well." LeAnn pulls me closer and rests her head on my shoulder.

"Marley always was a bit dramatic growing up,

you know that. We always thought it was because she was a girl and she was wired differently than her brother. Before the two of you started dating, she changed even more. So much so, we took her to see a doctor. One minute she was happy, but to the extreme. The next minute, she'd crash and hide in bed and refuse to leave her room." LeAnn sighs and my chest constricts as she relives these memories. Things about Marley I never knew.

"The doctor diagnosed her as manic depressive. To be honest, I was in denial about it all. I kept wondering what I did wrong when I was pregnant with her. When the medications made her more like her old self, it was then I realized she really was unwell."

"Why are you telling me this?" I ask, not sure I want to hear any more about her past.

"Because you need to release yourself of this guilt you carry around," LeAnn says, squeezing my shoulders again. "After you two got married, Marley thought she had her depression under control. The thing about her was when she was doing good and she was stable on the medication, she thought she could go off it. When she told me you guys were trying to start a family, she quit the meds cold turkey. I could see her struggling to maintain her control on normal, but she slipped almost every day."

"Why didn't you or she ever tell me this? Hell, Ethan didn't even know she was on medication." I rake my hands through my hair, close my eyes as I take in every word LeAnn is telling me. Everything she's telling me opens a new wound and a part of me feels lied to—almost tricked.

"Marley didn't want Ethan to know. She felt embarrassed and ashamed that she needed medication to maintain what society thinks is normal. So we respected her wishes and didn't tell him. The thing is, it was Marley's choice to stop the medication. She knew the risks, knew the way her moods would swing for no reason. She wanted a child, and to her it was worth the cost."

"We both wanted children," I say, turning to LeAnn. Her eyes are glossy and red-rimmed. Tears have cut through the makeup on her cheeks. She pats my shoulder and rests her head on me once again.

"I know, honey. I should have told you about her condition. To be honest, I assumed she had told you. She should have told you so you two could have made a more educated decision about your future. Ace…I need you to listen to me very carefully. She loved you very much. I love you like a son, I always have. But it's time for you to move on. Paul and I want you to fall in love and make a family with someone else. If it's this Stacey girl, then make it happen. You do deserve to be happy and loved. You will always be a son in our eyes and nothing you could do will ever disappoint us."

I laugh to hide how freeing her words feel. It's like the sun is shining on my chest, wrapping me in warmth and light, releasing me from the guilt I've been holding on to all these years. I know I'll still feel it every once in a while, but to know that Paul and LeAnn give me their blessing to move on…it's…ahhh.

Like peace.
Freeing.
Calm.
And I know what I need to do.

Chapter 37

Stacey

Commuting seriously sucks. My hour drive in the summer in now an hour and thirty minutes or more if the roads are bad. I can't bring myself to go back to the house I'm renting from Ace because I don't want to be surrounded by things that make me think of him.

After Mom, Dad, and James flew back home the Sunday after Thanksgiving, I decided life needed to go on. Ace never called over the holiday, not that I necessarily thought he would. But I did hope he would realize he had feelings for me. Obviously, I was wrong, and Ethan was wrong, and even Reggie was wrong. I hate to say it, but Ace should be a poker player, because no one can seem to read him. He'd take everyone's money before they knew what hit them.

That's exactly what he did with my heart.

During my lunch break, I head to an apartment leasing company in Warner to speak with someone about finding a place to rent. I need to move out of Ace's house if I'm going to move on with my life. When I step inside the brick building with the all-glass window front, a woman about my mother's age greets me with a warm smile.

"Hi there, I'm Peggy. How can I help you?" She stands from the desk, straightens her black pencil skirt, and extends her hand to me. Her black hair is tied back in a fashionable ponytail and her navy blue eyes are soft and friendly.

"Hi, Peggy," I say, and then I suddenly have a case of verbal diarrhea and spill out the last five months of my life. By the time I'm through talking, Peggy wraps me in a hug and guides me to her desk.

"Honey, you've had a tough run. I'm more than happy to help you find a new place to live. Let's go through the details you're looking for and we'll take a look at some over the next few days. How does that sound?"

"That sounds great," I say, wiping the tears away and silently cursing them for falling. "Sorry for unloading all of that on you." We laugh and I spend the next thirty minutes either filling out forms or looking at her computer screen while she searches for rentals in my budget. We make an appointment to go see two tomorrow and two the next day before I return to the bookstore.

While I'm unloading the most recent shipment of books and trinkets, I stumble upon a couple of cookbooks and a book on starting a business from scratch. Adrenaline surges through me as I stare at them and wonder how these totally different books could be packaged together and shipped here. It's like something higher up is telling me something. And I'm hearing it loud and clear.

I love Julia for trusting me with her store and I've enjoyed my time working here. But what I casually mentioned to Reggie before Thanksgiving has really stuck with me. I want to start up a catering business. I love cooking and making people happy with my food. It's still a creative outlet because I can make up my own recipes and make the food as fancy as I want.

Using my employee discount, I purchase the business book and a couple beautiful cookbooks and start planning my future.

***

"So...what do you think?" Peggy asks after we've walked through both apartments. The first one was a bit small and the kitchen was miniscule. Considering I'm working on starting my own catering business, that one will never do. The second one, while the kitchen is larger, is still not enough.

"I'm sorry, Peggy. Neither one will work for me. We still have two more to see tomorrow, right?"

Peggy nods, purses her lips, and locks the apartment. "Yesterday you seemed fine with these places. Has something changed? Do we need to change your search criteria?"

"Actually, yes. I've decided to start a catering business, so I'm going to need a kitchen large enough to handle large quantities of food."

Peggy stops midstride, turns around, and cocks

her head. Her eyes narrow as she quirks her lips to one side, studying me.

"I'm not sure your budget can afford a place with a large kitchen," she says, her voice holding a twinge of disappointment. "But I'll see what I can find back at the office and maybe you'll get lucky."

"Thanks, Peggy," I say as we part ways at my car. I drive back to the bookstore, finish out my day, and then take a look at the state of the roads. It started snowing just after lunch and it hasn't let up yet. The roads from Warner to Torrance are going to be a nightmare. Instead of heading to Reggie's, I decide the best course of action is to stay in the house here in Warner. I shoot Reggie a quick text letting her know not to expect me, then I slowly make my way across the snow-covered streets of Warner.

When I step inside the house, a foul odor assaults my nose. Damn. I totally left garbage in my trashcan and food in the fridge. I'm not looking forward to what it smells like in that thing. After braving the blizzard-like weather to dump my trash in the outside bin, I return to face the fridge. Twenty minutes later, it's cleaned out, and I realize there is no food in the house. Pizza delivery it is.

Quickly dialing the nearest pizza joint, I place an order and settle on the couch to watch some television. Forty minutes later, a knock on the door makes me jump, scaring me so badly my heart is pounding like a hammer in my chest. I grab my wallet and open the door only to find Lucy standing on the porch huddled in the largest coat I've ever seen. Her cheeks are rosy and the hood covering her head is lined with soft, white fur.

"Oh my gosh, how are you?" I ask, pulling her in for a hug. "I feel like I haven't seen you in forever." I usher her inside and close the door, only to open it thirty seconds later to pay for the pizza.

"Hungry?" I ask, bringing the two large pizzas into the kitchen.

"Were you planning on company?" she asks, removing her coat like she's shedding a layer of skin.

"No. Just planning on leftovers." We sit at the table, devour almost an entire pizza, and catch up.

"So you're really going to move out?" Lucy asks, dabbing a paper towel at the corners of her lips. Always so prim and proper. Sometimes I wonder if that's really who she is or if her mother has molded her into the person she believes Lucy should be.

I nod, combine the last slice of pepperoni pizza with the other uneaten one, and place the box in the fridge.

"I can't stay here, it feels weird, and I don't want to feel Ace's reach anymore. I need to get away from him so I can move past my feelings."

"Are you sure he doesn't feel the same way?" Lucy's eyes light up like the thought of love is magical. "He looks at you like he wants to devour you and protect you all at the same time."

"He made it pretty clear he doesn't love me and never will. I can't be around him knowing this." I sigh, remembering the feel of his lips on mine, and how they trailed down my body. A shiver works its way down my back, making the hairs on my arms stand on end. I shake my entire upper body and stand up.

"Sometimes I swear Ace's wife haunts this house," I say, walking toward the living room. "Let's watch a movie so I can stop thinking about him."

Lucy and I stay up past midnight watching movies and make a plan to meet up over the weekend to hang out again. We both bundle up, her in her massive winter coat, and me in the heaviest jacket I own, and we plod through the snow to her house.

"I'm really glad you and I are friends," I say, hugging her quickly. "But I'm freezing my ass off so I'm going to run home." We both laugh and I do exactly what I said because I'd rather not die of frostbite tonight.

Chapter 38

Ace

"Ready?" Ethan asks as he shrugs into his winter coat. I glance at him and his girlfriend from across the room and mutter a curse under my breath. I don't know why I let them talk me into going out with them. I do not make a very good third wheel.

"You and Katie should go without me," I say, unzipping my jacket. Katie jogs over to me and pulls my hands off the zipper.

"You are coming with us, so quit your moping and let's get going." Katie shimmies over to Ethan and plants a kiss on his cheek. "This girl needs to get her drink on."

Groaning, I follow them out the door to the waiting cab where the three of us somehow fit in the backseat. The drive across town to the club is torture, as I have to listen to Ethan and his girl whisper to each other and steal kisses at every freaking red light. Before the cab driver pulls to a complete stop outside the club, I have the door open and one foot on the curb.

"Dude, you in a hurry to get inside or something?" Ethan says, laughing while helping Katie out of the cab.

"Needed some freaking space, man. You two were all over each other."

Ethan softly punches my shoulder then drapes his arm over me. "Feels good, dude. It seriously feels good and you would know if you'd remove your head from your ass."

I shrug Ethan's arm off my shoulder and pay the man at the door, leaving the two lovebirds in the dust. First stop: bar for a stiff drink. Two rum and Cokes later, my eyes catch sight of fiery red hair hanging in waves against a pale, bare back. Everything in my body reacts to the sight and my hands grip the edge of the counter to keep myself steady. Before I know it, I'm on my feet walking in her direction. I need to see her, need to inhale the scent of her—peaches and lilies—and need to touch her. As I approach, the blond she's with stops talking and gapes at me. Her eyes dart from me to Stacey, then back again.

And she turns around.

My heart takes off in a sprint.

Her eyes grow as large as saucers.

My hands move on their own as they reach for her.

She backs away, her eyes growing glossy and her cheeks turning red.

"Can we get out of here?" she asks her friend...Liz...Lisa...*Lucy!*

Lucy nods and they walk toward the door. I

swallow the lump in my throat from the surprise of seeing her here. God, she looks so good, and if I thought for a minute what I feel for her is wrong, then I truly am an idiot. She broke through my walls, loved me tenderly, and never pushed. I see that now and can no longer stand back and push her away.

I love her...so damn much, and I'm not afraid anymore.

Quickly making my way through the crowd and out the door, I shout out her name just as a cab pulls up to whisk her and Lucy away. She glances over her shoulder, and the glow from the streetlamp overhead casts a golden hue over her, making her look like an angel.

My angel with fiery red hair and the spirit to match.

"Please don't leave," I say when I'm standing in front of her. Her eyelids close slowly as though she's warring with herself. "Can we talk, maybe grab some dinner?"

Stacey turns to Lucy, who is already seated in the cab. Lucy shrugs and Stacey's gaze returns to me. Her shoulders sag as she releases a sigh.

"I can't do this, Ace," she finally says, quiet as a whisper. "I've been meaning to tell you, but I've found another place to rent and I'm moving out of your house next week. You can keep the deposit if you want to since I'm breaking the lease early."

I jerk back like she slapped me. She's moving...what the hell?

"I don't want your deposit," I say, reaching for her hand, hoping she'll come with me to dinner. "I don't want you to move out."

"You've made it clear how you feel about me. I'm moving next weekend. Please don't make this harder than it already is." Stacey quickly turns and slides into the backseat of the cab and closes the door. The thud echoes in my chest, matching the heaviness of my heart. I think I just lost her. This is not an acceptable solution. Before I keep her from leaving me forever, I have a stop I need to make and it's long overdue.

Hailing a taxi, one quickly pulls up and I climb inside. I give the cross streets of where I need to go and silently thank myself for wearing a warm coat. It's fifteen degrees outside and I'm not sure how long this is going to take.

The driver stops outside the locked gates and I mutter a string of curses. I never considered the cemetery would be closed at night. Regardless, I ask the driver to wait and I step outside into the bitter cold. Using my phone as a flashlight, I climb over the iron fencing and jog down the road until I reach the section where Marley is buried. Carefully and reverently walking across the snow-covered ground, I find her headstone and kneel down in front and read the inscription carved into the marble.

Marley Annabelle Steele
Beloved daughter, sister, and wife
Taken too soon

I trace the image of a rose and then rest both hands on top of the headstone. Closing my eyes, I draw up her image in my mind until I can see her as clearly as if she were standing right in front of me. Her shoulder-length brown hair is shiny and hanging sleek and straight. She's smiling, her blush-colored lips are parted as though she is recovering from a good, hearty laugh. Her dark brown eyes look at me, filling me an overwhelming sense of peace.

"I miss you, Marley," I say like she's next to me. A warmth settles over me, like a blanket sheltering me from the chill of the night. "I love you and will always love you…but I need to tell you something." I suck in a shaky breath, clamp my eyes tighter, and wait for the image of her in my mind to change into a picture of hurt and disappointment. But it never comes. Instead, her face only brightens like she's happy.

"I've met someone. Her name is Stacey and she's amazing." God, this is harder than I thought. A rogue tear slides down my cheek, followed by another and another. "I wasn't looking for love, in fact, I did my best to stay away from it. I tried so hard to love only you, but I couldn't help it. I fell in love with Stacey, and as hard as I fought it…I want so much to be happy. To love her the way she deserves and to be loved by her."

My hand swipes the tears from my face and still the image in my head of Marley hasn't morphed into anger. I know she's not here, that I'm only seeing what I want to see, but this feels right. I know now she wants me to be happy, and with Stacey I will be.

"I wanted you to know, because you were first. Everyone keeps telling me to move on and I am.

But I don't think of it as moving on…it's more like moving forward. I want to spend the rest of my life making Stacey happy, showing her how much I love her. But you need to know I will also love you too."

I stand, feeling the weight of guilt and sadness slip off me. When I'm on my feet, I open my eyes to see a shroud of fog surrounding me, as though I'm in a protective bubble, immune to the mist.

"I love you, Marley. Thank you for loving me and being first."

Once I leave her gravesite, the fog engulfs me, sending pinpricks of damp, chilled air through my clothes. By the time I'm seated in the cab, I'm shivering like a leaf on a blustery fall day. I release a few tears of relief at the lightness I feel. Never did I recognize how weighed down I felt by carrying the dark feelings for so long. As we pull up to Ethan's house, deep down, I know everything is going to be okay.

I'm going to be okay, and even though she's no longer with me, Marley knows I will always love her, but it's time for me to move forward and show Stacey how I feel.

I won't give up on us.

I will love her until she tells me to quit.

Chapter 39

Stacey

Running into Ace at the club last night was unexpected and I nearly caved when he asked me to go to dinner with him so we could talk. What more is there to talk about? How I gave him my heart and he ripped it away from me, stomped on it, and handed it back to me expecting me to be able to recover? No. I was right to get away from him last night, even if I did spend the rest of the night lying on my bed unable to sleep.

Something in his eyes has changed, they're no longer filled with such sadness. Instead, the cool blue that has held me captive since July has a look of peace and hope. I think I love those eyes even more.

I spend Saturday and Sunday with Lucy shopping and getting pedicures. The apartment Peggy found for me won't be ready until the middle of December, leaving me just over two weeks to pack. The kitchen isn't great, in fact, it's downright small, but it was the largest of all the kitchens we looked at, so it will have to do. I plan on keeping my job at the bookstore until I become too busy catering, then I'll help Julia find someone to replace me.

Monday morning, the sun is shining, making the snow sparkle like glistening diamonds. The roads are clear, making my drive easy and uneventful. With my morning coffee in hand, I open up the bookstore and take a look around, inhaling the crisp scent of paper. Ellery won't be in for a couple more hours so I wander around the store straightening displays and helping customers when they come in. There's something peaceful about being in a quiet bookstore.

"Hey, chica," Ellery says as she strides through the door wearing a massive grin and sporting a new haircut and color. Her normal sable brown hair is now streaked with a gorgeous plum color and cut just below her chin. She looks incredible.

"You look amazing!" I say as she unloads her coat and belongings in the back room.

"Thanks," she gushes, fluffing her shorter locks with the palm of her hand. "I was in need of change."

"You and me both." I sigh as we fall into our daily routine.

Around noon, a pair of good-looking college-aged guys walk in and start immediately flirting with Ellery. She gobbles it up and inside I'm feeling the claws of jealousy digging into my stomach. Maybe it's time for a change for me as well. I know I'm not twenty-two anymore, but I look good for twenty-seven—almost twenty-eight.

Crap! My birthday is only two days away and I haven't made any plans. Come to think of it, Reggie hasn't even made any plans. I pick up my phone and send her a text.

Me: My bday is in 2 days. GAH! I'm getting old :(

Lately all I've been doing is wallowing and it's gone on far too long—it's seriously time to get out of this funk.

Reggie: Take the day off work and the next day too so we can celebrate properly!

Me: Can't. I can leave early and come in late though. Come up here and hang with me. I need some Reggie time.

Reggie: You got it! YAY! I'm so excited!

Me: You think you can use any more exclamation points?

Reggie: YES!

I laugh at my friend and slide my phone back into my pocket. The rest of the day passes quickly as I use the computer at the front desk to plan my birthday night. Okay, not the best use of the company computer, but the afternoon has been slow and I'm excited for a night out with my BFF.

***

"See you at Giovanni's later?" I ask Ellery as I prepare to leave the bookstore. She smiles and nods eagerly, then waves me out the door. The rest of the afternoon I have plans with Reggie at a spa where I'm getting a massage, facial, pedicure, and my hair done. It's my birthday and I'm treating myself to the ultimate afternoon of relaxation. When I pull up to the house, Reggie's already there sitting in her car with the heater on and a smile overtakes my face. I jump out of my car, squealing, and run to her and pound on the driver's window. She jumps and screams, holding her hand over her heart.

"You're here, you're here, *you're here*!" I squeal again as she climbs out of the car. We wrap each other in tight hugs and head inside the house. I quickly give her the tour and try to hide how sad I am about leaving this house and moving into a small apartment. Reggie makes herself comfortable in the guest room and I grab the outfit I plan to change into later. Once we have all our things collected, we jog downstairs just as the doorbell rings. I glance at Reggie and we both shrug our shoulders.

I open the door to see a man holding a vase of gorgeous flowers in an array of pinks, plums, and deep purples.

The man glances at the paper in his hand. "Stacey Goodwin?" he asks. I nod, unable to contain the smile on my face. "These are for you." He hands me the vase and turns to leave. I close the door, rush them into the kitchen, and pull the card from the plastic holder.

Stacey,

I wanted to help you celebrate your birthday so please accept these flowers as my gift and apology. I miss you...always.

Yours,

Ace

Reggie reads over my shoulder and sags against me. "Oh, Stacey. He does love you," she says, squeezing around my waist in a hug. A tear slips down my cheek but I swipe it away before one can turn into two.

"You're wrong," I argue. "Let's get out of here." I lay the card on the counter, steal one last glance at the beautiful flowers, and wonder for the millionth time if I'm the one who is wrong.

After four hours at the spa, I'm relaxed, thoroughly massaged, and ready to celebrate my birthday with renewed vigor. Taking a cue from Ellery, I had my stylist add some streaks of plum to my hair, giving it a rich, glossy sheen. I love it, and when I shimmy into my birthday dress, I feel amazing.

Take that, Ace Steele. Look what you are missing out on.

Reggie and I meet up with Lucy and Ellery at Giovanni's and eat an amazing dinner of pastas and salads. Our waiter brings out a decadent slice of chocolate cake for my birthday and the four of us moan our way through the giant piece. Our cab arrives and takes us to the club where we dance and drink girly drinks until we're all seeing double.

"This is the best birthday ever," I say, hugging my three friends. I'm having the best time and haven't thought of Ace since leaving the spa. Shit, except now I'm thinking about Ace. And his lips. On mine. Heat spreads through my body as the memories of his touch flood my mind. Shaking my head to clear my thoughts, the girls and I get another drink and hit the dance floor again. Two hours later, I'm sliding into a cab with Reggie, who is holding my head in her lap. I'm a sappy drunk and tonight is no exception. I keep telling her how much I love her and miss hanging out with her. She runs her fingers through my hair, letting me vent.

"I miss Ace, even being friends with him is better than nothing. But I love him and he doesn't love me. He won't ever love me and I hate being that girl who gets depressed over a guy. I don't like myself like this."

"Have you given him a chance to talk with you? Maybe he's changed his mind," Reggie says, patting my shoulder. "He sent you flowers for your birthday and said he was sorry."

"Sorry for what, though? For leading me on? Breaking my heart? Sleeping with me?" The cab starts to spin and I make myself sit up before I lose my dinner. My phone buzzes in my purse, indicating a text. I pull out my phone and try to focus on the blurry words.

"It's from Ace," I say, feeling my heart plummet to my feet. "But I can't read it. Will you read it for me?"

Reggie opens the text and gasps, but tries to hide it.

"What does it say? Is it bad?" I ask, biting the inside of my cheek.

"He's selling the house and needs you out as soon as possible." Reggie moves to return my phone but I shake my head. "You want me to reply?" I nod and tell her what to type.

Me: Okay. How long do I have?

Ace: A week.

"A week?" I say, groaning while laying my head against the back of the seat. "Where am I going to go? What am I going to do with all my stuff?"

"You can stay with us until your apartment is ready," Reggie offers. I know I'm welcome, but after making the drive from her house to work for those days I did, I don't want to do it again.

I shake my head and have her send my reply to Ace. If he wants me out in a week, I'll be out. If I have to stay in a hotel for a week and a half, then so be it. He's officially kicking me to the curb and it burns like the end of a red-hot poker being shoved through my chest.

Chapter 40

Ace

I'm a first-class jerk asking her to move out of the house so quickly, but I have ulterior motives. And I'm not sure I've ever been more nervous in my entire life. The butterflies in my stomach have butterflies and they're performing a circus act.

What if she won't talk to me?

What if I've hurt her too much and am too late?

No. I refuse to let her slip away from me, not after my head finally caught up to my heart. I need Stacey like the air I breathe. She's the light in the darkness pulling me from self-destruction. She tore down my walls only to rebuild them with her inside, keeping me safe and showing me love.

And now I'm going to work my ass off to be worthy of her love, hopefully for the rest of our lives.

Knowing Stacey loves Thai food, I stop by the best place in Warner and order food to go. As I drive back toward the bookstore, my hands are sweating on the steering wheel and my heart is pounding heavily in my chest. It feels like each beat is followed by a bowling ball slamming against my ribs. I'm no longer afraid of my feelings for her, in fact, since visiting the cemetery, everything has become clearer, as if the fog has lifted and the sun now shines around me. I've lived in misery, guilt, and denial for so long that I now feel amazing and free.

In the parking lot beside the bookstore, I take a few deep breaths, will my heart to slow down, and my palms to stop sweating.

"It's now or never," I say to myself, gathering the to-go bag, and step out of the SUV into the brisk winter air. I called earlier to make sure Stacey was coming in since yesterday was her birthday and I had dropped the bomb on her about selling the house. I can only imagine how pissed she's going to be when I show up out of the blue.

I blow out the breath I held from the SUV to the door and push it open. The jingling bell above the door alerts Stacey and the other girl working here of my arrival. Both heads turn my way and Stacey's eyes widen in shock and her jaw drops, though it closes quickly. She steps around the counter, crossing to me quickly. Her steps are hurried and her arms are folded tightly across her chest.

A smile works its way over my face as I take in the sight of her. She's wearing the outfit I first saw her in when we met in July—a simple pair of worn jeans with holes in the thighs revealing her creamy white skin and a white, relaxed peasant top. She's added some deep purple streaks to her hair, adding even more edge to her already feisty self.

"You look…damn, you look good," I say as she stands in front of me, peaches and lilies surrounding me like an embrace.

"What are you doing here, Ace?" she asks, cocking her leg in irritation.

I hold up the bag containing the Thai food. "I brought you lunch. I was hoping we could talk while we eat." She glances at the to-go bag and then turns her focus back on me. "It's Thai…your favorite."

A flush washes over her cheeks, sparking a longing within me. Please let her still love me, because if she's moved on, it's going to crush me.

"I'm only agreeing to this because I have a hangover from hell and I'm starving," she says, dragging me toward the rear of the building. She opens a door to reveal a small table and four chairs, a sink, and an ancient coffeemaker sitting on the small counter. "Did you come to ask me to be out sooner? Because I think a week is pushing it. You realize you're forcing me to get a hotel room and put my things in storage for twelve days, right?"

Stacey sits on one of the metal folding chairs and points to the one across the table, the one farthest from her. Ignoring her request, I take the seat right next to her and begin to pull out each container and the utensil packs.

"It's time for me to sell the house and put the past behind me," I say, handing her a fork. She takes it from me, careful to keep our fingers from touching. This distance between us is worse than actual miles because if she'd let me, I would brush the hair off her shoulder, trace the line of her jaw with my fingertips, and cover her lips with mine.

"What caused the sudden change of heart?" she asks, opening the container of beef panang. The rich scents of peanuts and coconut milk hover between us like an invisible wall I need to find a way to break through. Do I lead with the complete truth or will it scare her away? Hell, I'm all in and she needs to know.

"You did," I say, my eyes never leaving hers. She doesn't react in any way except to dump some sticky white rice into the panang and take a bite. Her eyes fall to the food and then close as she moans her appreciation of the meal.

"I needed this so much," she says, and then takes another bite. I don't know if she's taking her time to consider my words or if she's gearing up to let me have it. Either way, my stomach is knotted so tight there is no way I can eat anything.

"You wanted to talk, Ace. So talk. What more could you possibly have to say?" And there's the fire I've come to love in her.

"I need you to listen," I say, scooting my chair closer to hers. My knees connect with her thighs just like they did back on the airplane all those months ago. The connection I felt toward her then is still present now, however it's magnified tenfold. I know what it's like now to have her love, to touch her and to kiss her, and I don't ever want another day to pass without being near her.

"Fine, I'll listen." She opens another container to find the order of chicken pad thai topped with extra crushed peanuts—just the way she likes it. "Why did you get all of my favorite foods?" She glances at my fork sitting on the table and the lack of food in front of me. "And why aren't you eating?"

"Doesn't matter," I say, shrugging my shoulders. "What matters is that after five…no, six years, someone has finally broken through the shell I created around my heart. She found her way through the shield, loved me despite all my flaws and the guilt I was harboring. I can honestly say that this woman makes me a better man, and I don't want to spend another day without her."

Stacey hasn't moved, not even a muscle. Her eyes are misty and wide, and her chin is trembling as though she's on the verge of tears.

"Why are you here, Ace? I don't want to know these things about you," she says, taking her eyes off me. "About *her*," she whispers as twin tears slip down her cheeks.

I slide off the chair and kneel in front of her, take her hands in mine, and press my lips to her forehead. "I love *you*, Stacey Goodwin. I was afraid of the feelings I had for you, and when I told you I wouldn't love you…I lied. I already loved you but was ashamed and felt like I was betraying Marley." She lifts her chin, pulls her bottom lip between her teeth, and closes her eyes, letting more tears glide across her smooth skin. I release her hands and brush the tears away with the pads of my thumbs, cupping her face in my hands.

"Can you forgive me for being an idiot? I am serious when I say I don't want to go another day…another second without being near you."

"You were also a bit of an ass," she says as a

laugh tumbles from her soft lips.

I nod, agreeing with her wholeheartedly. "I was an ass," I say, moving closer. "Do you forgive me?"

Stacey nods, moves to her knees in front of me, and wraps her arms around me in the warmest hug I've ever had. In her arms, the world falls away, my troubles...*poof!* are gone. The only thing I see, I feel, is Stacey and the way my heart is piecing itself back together one shattered fragment at a time.

"I love you, Stacey, and I really want to kiss you right now," I say, pulling away from our hug. Her brown eyes darken as they find mine and when she leans in, covering my lips with hers, I find the release my soul has been searching for since the day Stacey waltzed into my life.

She's mine and I plan on spending every day memorizing the landscape of her body, the depths of her eyes, and the expanse of her soul. She pieced a broken man back together and made me understand how deeply I love and how to let it heal the pain of my past.

Stacey is my everything and I'll love her until she asks me to stop.

Epilogue

10 Months Later

Stacey

The house Ace and I bought has a massive kitchen. It was the first and only requirement I had when he asked me to go house hunting with him the day he told me he loved me. He sold the house he and Marley had lived in and the week after we moved into our new house, he asked me to marry him. Coincidentally, it was also the week Reggie told me that she was pregnant. I was over the moon excited for her because I knew how much she and Jordan wanted more kids.

Now here Ace and I sit in the hospital waiting room. His ring is on my left hand and I've never been happier. Our wedding day was beautiful, warm, and perfect. It was on Memorial weekend and in Reggie's backyard. White lights were strung through the trees, looking like magical stars. And during our first dance as husband and wife, I fell even more in love with this man who was no longer filled with sadness. Each day, his love for me grows, and dancing with him was like dancing on a cloud.

Vic and a very pregnant Jemma, along with their two-year-old daughter, return with ear to ear grins on their faces.

"She's beautiful," Jemma says, rubbing her own swollen belly. Subconsciously, my hand moves over my flat stomach and my heart begins to race. "You can go on back now. She's waiting for you." I hug Jemma, who squeezes me tightly. Even though I don't see her on a regular basis, we've become good friends.

"Thanks," I say, pulling back, leaving my hands on her shoulders. "Not much longer for you either." We laugh as she glances down at her belly.

"I am ready to send out an eviction notice to this little girl," she says. Vic moves behind her, places a soft kiss on the side of her neck, and shakes Ace's hand.

"This next one had better be a boy," Vic says with a laugh. "If not, then you are cut off, permanently." Jemma slaps his shoulder and we all say our goodbyes. My stomach churns as we walk toward Reggie's room. From outside, I can hear Micah gushing over his new baby sister and it warms my heart.

After Ace and I bought the house and moved in together, he told me all about Marley and her miscarriages, which ultimately caused her depression to spike, which ended in her taking her own life. We haven't talked about having children, but I'm hoping he wants them as much as I do.

I knock quietly on the light oak door of Reggie's room and open it when I hear her tell us to come in. Jordan is sitting in the chair next to her bed, wearing a proud smile while holding his daughter. Tears spring to my eyes at the sight. I was the one with her when she had Micah all those years ago, and to see her and Jordan now married, and him holding their second child, is one of the best things I've ever seen.

"She's amazing, Reggie," I say, wiping the tears from my eyes as I move to stand beside her. "You look beautiful."

"Thank you," she says, and I lean down to hug her. "Jordan, can you let Stacey hold Annie?" Jordan stands and walks over to me, handing me his tiny daughter. Her little hands flail when he lays Annie in my arms, but she settles into my arms with no fuss. She has a full head of dark black hair, the cutest button nose, and full pink lips.

"Oh, Reggie, she's perfect." After a while I ask Ace if he wants to hold her. His eyes widen and he glances at Reggie, who smiles and nods, giving him permission. I transfer Annie into his arms and he holds her like she's the most precious thing he's ever seen. My heart swells at the sight and the nerves in my stomach begin to settle.

It's going to be fine, we're going to be fine.

Annie wakes up and cries for her momma, wanting to be fed. I hand her back to Reggie, give her a quick kiss on the forehead, and then hug Jordan. Ace and I say our goodbyes and then walk through the hospital hand in hand, out to the car. He opens the door for me, presses his lips against mine, and when my mouth parts to release a sigh, his tongue tangles with mine.

"Let's make some of those," he says against my lips. His hand travels from my shoulder, down over my breasts, and stops at my waist. Every ounce of fear, every worry, and every last nerve floats away on the breeze. My hands pull his face back to mine and I kiss him again, because kissing Ace is like igniting a fire. A small spark quickly turns into a raging inferno. I rest my head on his chest, look up into his pale blue eyes, and smile.

"We already did," I say, feeling my heart grow with love for this man and for the life growing inside me.

The End

Acknowledgements

When I set out to write *Raining Down Rules*, I truly didn't know there would be three books written in this series—let alone that Raining Down would grow into a series. When I completed *Raining Down Redemption*, I felt that Stacey needed a story of her own, and when Ace presented himself, I knew they would help each other and eventually fall in love. Which leads me to my first set of important thank yous.

Thank you, Chris Stapleton, for *Fire Away*. Thank you for the touching music video and showing a side of depression that not many people ever experience. Ace was born from your video and my need to help him recover from losing his wife. I do hope the character in your video would be proud of the story I wrote and that he could someday again experience a love like Ace and Stacey share.

I would also like to thank my beta readers, Michelle and Kaitlyn. As always, your feedback and advice is priceless!

To my parents, thank you for continuing to encourage me to write and share my stories. I promise, you will get to see your favorite book of mine in print one day soon—if I can ever stop editing it.

To Bonnie and Jamie, thank you for being the best friends a girl can ever have.

Thank you, Colleen Hoover for writing *Maybe Someday*, because it's amazing and everyone should read it—even the Aces of this world.

Thank you to Jennifer and Jessica at Limitless

Publishing for saying *Yes!* to Ace and Stacey. It's been a great year with you and I can't wait to do this again.

To Gillian, my editor at Limitless, thank you for your magic. You just keep making this series better and better.

Finally, visit www.ChangeDirection.org to help change the culture of mental health in America so that all of those in need receive the care and support they deserve. The Campaign encourages all Americans to pay attention to their emotional well-being—and it reminds us that our emotional well-being is just as important as our physical well-being.

About the Author

BK Rivers grew up riding through rolling fields of grain on horseback, driving hay trucks and catching frogs in a silver creek. She traded country life for the big city and now lives in the Phoenix suburbs with her three children. When she's not writing, she can be found baking anything sweet, in fact it's been said her brownies are so good they save marriages.

The inspiration for her novels comes in many forms, but mostly from her Gotye channel on Pandora. She writes young adult and new adult novels to the beat of Gotye, Snow Patrol and many others.

Facebook:
http://www.facebook.com/BKRivers.Author

Twitter:
https://twitter.com/WriterRivers

Website:
http://www.bkrivers.com/

Sign up for my newsletter to stay up to date on new releases:
http://eepurl.combq525r/